BLOOD DOMINATION

BLOOD DESTINY SERIES

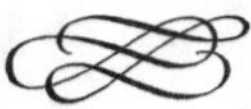

CONNIE SUTTLE

Print Second Edition (2018)
Print ISBN: 1-63478-057-4
Print ISBN-13: 978-1-63478-046-9
ISBN: 1-939759-17-X
ISBN-13: 978-1-939759-17-7

Published by:
SubtleDemon Publishing, LLC
PO Box 95696
Oklahoma City, OK 73143

Cover art by Renee Barratt @ The Cover Counts

To Walter, Joe, Larry, Lee, Dianne, Sarah and Mark.
Thank you.

ACKNOWLEDGMENTS

As always, this book is the result of collaboration. If it weren't for the support of my editor, my cover artist and my beta readers, it would be less than it is. All mistakes, as usual, are mine and no other's.

About the Author:
Connie Suttle lives in Oklahoma with her husband and a conglomerate of cats. They have finally banded together to make their demands, which has proven disconcerting to all humans involved.

You may find Connie in the following ways:
Facebook: Connie Suttle Author
Twitter: @subtledemon
Website and Blog: subtledemon.com

ALSO BY CONNIE SUTTLE

Blood Destiny Series:

Blood Wager

Blood Passage

Blood Sense

Blood Domination

Blood Royal

Blood Queen

Blood Rebellion

Blood War

Blood Redemption

Blood Reunion

Blood Destiny Series Boxed Set (Books 1-10)

Blood Recall

Blood Alliance*

Legend of the Ir'Indicti Series:

Bumble

Shadowed

Target

Vendetta

Destroyer

Legend of the Ir'Inditi Boxed Set

~

R-D Series:
Cloud Dust
Cloud Invasion
Cloud Rebel

~

Latter Day Demons Series:
Hot Demon in the City
A Demon's Work is Never Done
A Demon's Due

~

Seattle Elementals Series:
Your Money's Worth
Worth Your While*

~

BlackWing Pirates Series
MindSighted
MindMage
MindRogue
MindMaster*

~

Black Rose Sorceress Series
The Rose Mark

Rose and Thorn

Black Rose Queen

Queen of Thorns and Roses

Future Wars Series

Buffer Zone

Black Zone*

Other Titles from SubtleDemon Publishing:

Malefactor

Transgressor

Underhanded*

by Joe Scholes

*Forthcoming

CHAPTER 1

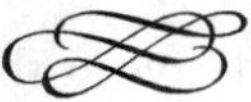

*J*ovana was beautiful.

Xenides hated her.

If not for a command given by his now-deceased sire, Xenides would have killed her long ago. Instead, Saxom had instructed his eldest to keep Jovana alive and hidden, as she might be useful in Xenides' war against the Vampire Council.

"You should do this for me—in our sire's memory and with no compensation," Xenides growled. Xenides sat on a Louis XVI sofa in Jovana's private quarters. Jovana's Paris apartment was tastefully decorated in antiques, many of which Saxom had given her. He'd collected many things throughout his lengthy life and now Jovana had enough to keep her into the next century. She wasn't satisfied with that, however. She had expensive tastes and only wore the best in designer clothing. Therefore, she often agreed to the odd assignment for Xenides. For a healthy fee, of course.

"Our sire is dead and compulsion is merely a joke to me," Jovana murmured, rising to gaze out a window. Evenings in Paris appealed to her and were the deciding factor in her choice of living quarters.

Lucius had taken her for his lover long ago, and he'd never informed anyone that Jovana wasn't susceptible to compulsion.

Saxom had known it anyway, and together he and Jovana had killed Lucius before Saxom made her vampire. She'd agreed willingly to the turn—after all, her beauty was fading away and she worried that Lucius would leave her behind. She'd risen a Queen Vampire, just as Saxom knew she would, and she'd created havoc at Saxom's bidding for more than two hundred years.

"Jovana, our sire left me in charge of his wealth for a reason," Xenides pointed out maliciously.

"So you could keep me under your thumb," Jovana snorted, turning back to her vampire sibling. "He knew I would walk away from you and your foolishness if he didn't."

"You could sell what you own and keep yourself for a very long time," Xenides snapped.

"Of course I will not sell my things. This is mine," Jovana swept out a hand. "And I deserved a fair share of our sire's wealth when he died. You refused to give it to me."

"I will pay for your services as always, Jovana," Xenides sighed. "How much this time for your assistance in capturing the little princess?"

"You should be glad I have no feelings for you, Xenides," Jovana huffed. "Else I would be quite jealous. You talk of her too often."

"You have no reason to be jealous. I only wish to utilize her talents, as you are so reluctant to do so."

"Of course I am reluctant. You fail to see the ignorance in this quest. You should allow me to kill the little bitch and be done with it."

"You will not kill her, and avenging our sire's death is not ignorance," Xenides hissed, his eyes turning so deep a red they were nearly black.

"No need to be angry, Xenides. I will do this for you." Jovana inspected a well-manicured hand. "Six million will suffice until the next assignment."

"Then I suggest you don't spend it in one place, Jovana. As soon as I have the little female under compulsion, you and I will part ways."

"Where and when?" Jovana ignored Xenides' threat.

"Don't worry; I'll lure her to you. You won't have to leave your precious city behind."

"What about the Council?" Jovana didn't bother to hide the contempt in her voice. After all, Wlodek always treated her coldly and ignored her advances.

"I have my own plans where they're concerned," Xenides replied. "I intend to kill Wlodek and then watch the others scatter like the frightened vermin they are. I will only contact you again if the situation becomes dire. You are dead weight to me, Jovana, and without your particular talents, you would be completely worthless."

"Please, see yourself out," Jovana snarled, turning her back on Xenides. "I shall expect the transfer of funds in two days."

Xenides didn't bother with a farewell; he merely slammed the door so hard on his way out the wood split. Jovana cursed at his retreating back.

～

"She hasn't looked at that."

Griffin glanced at Merrill, who leaned back in his chair. Griffin studied the Medal of Freedom lying in his hand, his fingers tracing the contours of enameled metal. Lissa received it from the President of the United States and hadn't bothered to look at it or to read the enclosed letter the President had written. The commendation remained sealed inside an envelope and lay on a corner of Merrill's desk.

"I don't know that I blame her," Griffin sighed, settling the medal inside its case.

"She's down to half a pint of blood a day. Gavin almost refused to leave on assignment due to Lissa's depression, which angered Wlodek, of course. Wlodek is threatening to come here himself and place compulsion if she doesn't straighten up. Those are his words, not mine." Merrill picked up his new letter opener and examined it. Lissa had given it to him; it was a replica of a Roman sword and he had no idea if she'd known what an appropriate gift it was when she purchased it for him.

"Tell Wlodek he doesn't have to come," Griffin closed the velvet case and returned it to Merrill's desk with a sigh. "Let's go wake her."

I have no explanation for Griffin, or why he shows up when he does. He was there, Merrill standing right behind him, when I woke one evening. It was five weeks after I discovered that Tony had taken my blood to use in experiments, consequently giving six men a fatal disease. He'd used me as a weapon. It was like stealing a gun and going out to commit a terrible crime. Only in this instance, my blood was killing innocent people. That bothered me more than I can say and lowered me into an energy-sucking depression.

"Do you know that it's Sunday, June twenty-seventh?" Griffin smiled down at me and lifted a stray lock of hair off my forehead. That was the only thing that was going right at the moment. My hair was now more than three inches in length. If I'd been myself, I might have asked Merrill if I could go to a salon and get it cut and styled. It probably looked a bit shaggy.

Griffin's words depressed me even more. Those poor men that Tony and his research biologist experimented on had seven weeks to live. I had no idea how ill they might become before death arrived to claim them. How could Tony approve these experiments on humans so quickly? It made no sense to me.

Now, six men lay in a hospital somewhere, fighting a disease they'd contracted with an administration of my blood. I knew they were suffering and that made me feel worse. Tony had only given a first name for the research biologist behind this debacle; he'd called him Larry. I thought of him as Larry the lizard, but that was giving lizards everywhere a bad name.

"Little girl, none of this is your fault. You need to stop thinking about that." Griffin's fingers touched my cheek. His hands were so warm against my skin. I'd felt cold—very, very cold—for the past five weeks. Griffin's talent for reading my thoughts hadn't diminished or gone away, either. Normally, that would arouse my curiosity and I might turn my attention to discovering how he did that. Not now.

"We're going to fix that," Griffin smiled gently as light formed around the fingers touching my cheek.

~

"Franklin and Greg are coming; I've made arrangements for Greg to receive his chemotherapy treatments at a nearby clinic," Merrill informed me. Griffin had done something and hadn't tried to hide it from me, either. He explained carefully that he couldn't bear to watch me waste away when there wasn't any need for it.

I felt better and I didn't know whether I wanted to thank Griffin or curse him for that. Merrill handed a bag of blood to me afterward and they'd both watched me drink. Griffin never blinked as I consumed my normal two-thirds of a pint.

He left shortly afterward and Merrill wrote a note for Lena, asking her to pick up an electric mattress pad for me in London the following week. Griffin knew I felt cold and passed that information to Merrill.

"Lissa, sweetheart, Charles will come tomorrow evening and drive you into London so you can get your hair done," Merrill touched fingers lightly to my strawberry-blonde curls. If my hair is shorter, it curls. It only straightens out if I keep it longer and it had been long—past my shoulders long—before I'd attempted to kill myself in the sun last February.

"That sounds like so much fun for him," I grumped. There wasn't any way, though, that Merrill or any of the others would let me out of their sight without an escort.

"He finds it quite enjoyable; he has asked every other day if he could take you for an outing."

"Poor Charles. He needs to get a life," I said.

"Have you ever wanted a brother, sweetheart? Charles wants that role, I think." I blinked up at Merrill as he spoke those words.

"Really?" I'd never had anything like that. My face fell immediately. A brother was someone who would keep your secrets. I would never have that luxury with Charles.

"Lissa, most things you could tell Charles. He does not carry everything he hears directly to Wlodek, you know. Charles has an insatiable curiosity, but he also knows how to keep secrets."

He knew I wouldn't consider confiding in Charles from my expression. "My poor baby." Merrill gently touched my cheek. "Franklin and Greg will arrive on Wednesday. When you go to London, please purchase welcoming gifts from both of us." Merrill smiled and removed his hand.

I still had my ID and credit card, plus a little cash, but Merrill had my cell phone and laptop again. I realized he didn't want any communication between Tony and me. Well, I didn't want any communication between Tony and me.

What I did want, however, was communication with the Grand Master, Weldon Harper. I wanted to check in with him, thank him again for getting Paul the werewolf policeman to help with the child kidnapping case and see how his grandchild was doing. Daryl Harper, Jr. was cute as a button.

I also needed to contact my Packmaster, Thomas Williams, in Sacramento just to let him know I was still around. Merrill must have been on my wavelength, just as Griffin had been. "Buy yourself a new cell phone and computer, Lissa. Charles can help you with those things. He's technologically inclined."

I nodded. Merrill and I were in the kitchen; that seemed to be the best place to have conversations for some reason. He and I were the only ones in the house—Lena had already left before I'd gotten out of bed for the evening.

She was still doing housekeeping chores, but since Franklin had been out of the country, she didn't eat dinner at Merrill's manor. Lena went home instead to her family in a nearby town, between Luddesdown and London. The drive to London nearly every day had gotten to be too much, so a move was made at Merrill's suggestion.

"May I borrow your computer?" I asked. I wanted to go online and get some shopping ideas for Greg and Franklin.

"As long as you don't attempt to contact Mr. Hancock." That brought a loud and indignant gasp from me. "I should know better," Merrill said and smiled.

~

I still had the gift cards to the bookstore that I'd gotten for Greg and Franklin. I hadn't had an opportunity to give them away and Charles and I were now browsing through an electronics store for a new cell phone and computer after I'd gotten my haircut.

The stylist had trimmed and shaped; consequently, my hair looked much better. Charles and I were currently examining laptops; Charles was completely happy doing this, I could tell. He and the sales geek were having an intense conversation over things that sailed right past me regarding the laptops on display.

"You'll like this one," Charles pointed out the laptop he'd been discussing with the sales kid—he looked like a kid to me, anyway. The laptop wasn't huge, was another Mac, (that was my stipulation) and cost around three thousand pounds.

In my human life, that would have been out of the question. Now, money just flew out of my hand, or Merrill's bank account, as it were. The cell phone was next; it was a replacement iPhone, and then we bought several computer games and a tablet that either Greg or Franklin could hold in their hands or set on the kitchen counter and play games and check e-mail.

I also bought a program for Franklin's laptop that would keep recipes on file and categorized so he could get to them easily, plus a shopping list option where Frank could put his grocery lists. I hoped he liked it.

Charles picked out a word processing program and a couple other things for my computer; we got the cell phone set up and the clerk got my new programs loaded into the laptop before we ever left the store.

Charles and I went to a bar for our usual glass of wine afterward and Charles called Bryan Riley on the way, asking if he wanted to meet us. Bryan walked into the bar shortly after Charles and I arrived.

"Bryan!" I was both surprised and pleased to see him. He took a chance and gave me a hug, then sat down next to me in the booth.

"I heard something, Charles, as I was leaving the studio tonight," Bryan said, before turning to tell the waitress what he wanted.

"What's that?" Charles ran a finger around the rim of his wineglass.

"It should hit the news tomorrow, but all the manufacturers of the flu vaccine are destroying what they've made up this year and are being forced to start over at the last minute. This will create a panic, as you might imagine. In addition to that, we couldn't get a verifiable reason for the vaccine dump from our sources. We have feelers out for estimated deaths due to a vaccine shortage."

"I wish they could keep that quiet," I muttered.

Xenides, along with his best buddy terrorist, Rahim Alif, had succeeded in introducing vampire DNA into the flu vaccine, just as I said. Now, I hoped the people most vulnerable would be able to get vaccinated with untainted drugs.

I shivered, thinking about what might happen if they didn't. Health organizations across the globe were predicting a serious flu epidemic come the fall season.

"What do you know about that?" Bryan turned sharply to stare at me.

"Bryan, I wish I could tell you, but I can't," I sighed. "How many deaths worldwide do you think might be attributed to an insufficient amount of flu vaccine?"

"There's no way to tell for certain; flu season won't come for another two months," he shrugged. "September is the month recommended to get the vaccine. I've heard some serious numbers tossed about, but they're only guessing at this point. And we don't know how much of the vaccine the manufacturers will be able to replace between now and then." Bryan thanked the waitress when she set a wine glass down in front of him.

"Crap," I said, rubbing my forehead. I was wishing at that moment that the wine I was drinking would have an effect on me. If so, I'd order an entire bottle of the stuff and get blitzed.

"Lissa, this is out of our control," Charles reached for my hand across the table. I hesitated for a few seconds and then placed my fingers inside his. He offered an encouraging smile. "Just repeat after me: I can't do anything about this, so I shouldn't worry," he said.

"That's easy for you to say," I informed him tartly.

"It is easy for me to say," he grinned. "Just watch my lips." He repeated his statement.

"Why are you worrying over this?" Bryan studied my face carefully —he was in the news business, after all. He sensed a story; I just couldn't give it to him.

"Lissa thinks the world's troubles are hers," Charles replied for me, squeezing my fingers gently before letting them go.

"Not all of them," I said, sipping my wine. "I can't do anything about flying saucers or cockroaches. Or even flying saucers driven by cockroaches."

"Seen large alien cockroaches, have you?" Bryan was smiling, now.

"I've seen some pretty big ones. I saw some in Georgia that were filing complaints with the FCC. They were upset because their antennae couldn't get television reception after everything went digital. I hear lawyers are filing class action suits on their behalf." I hadn't felt like teasing anyone in a long time.

"Is that what they use their antennae for?" Bryan chuckled.

"That—and communicating with the mother ship," I said. We talked and laughed a little longer, until I recalled something Bryan said when I'd first met him.

"Bryan, you mentioned the Aristocracy when I met you before," I said. "Can you explain that to me?"

"I can explain it," Charles offered. He looked around, just to make sure we wouldn't be overheard. "More than six hundred years ago, five hundred of the oldest and most powerful vampires decided to form the Council and hammer out the laws," his voice was hushed.

"The wolves were reproducing faster than we ever could, and that was part of the reason we formed our own government. The wolves were already organized under a Grand Master and back then, they were based in Europe. The race war was disorganized, at least on our part. The five hundred agreed that we would be annihilated if we kept up our habit of isolation. The Council was formed and the oldest known vampire became its Head. The original five hundred were known as the Aristocracy after that. Of course, some of the original members are dead, so the Council chooses vampires to take the vacancies when they occur. Gavin is one of the original five hundred."

It didn't surprise me a bit that Gavin was one of the five hundred. He was older than dirt, after all. And, as Wlodek and Merrill were older than Gavin, they'd probably seen the Earth cool. "Does Wlodek have an official title?" I asked. "It's just so hard to say Head of the Council all the time."

"His Latin title is a little easier," Charles muttered. "Sanguis Rex." I hadn't been far off when I'd called him King of the Vampires. I knew what Rex meant.

"Blood King?" I made a guess. Charles nodded. "Geez Louise," I muttered to myself. "Does anybody call him that, nowadays?"

"Nope." Charles signaled for the waitress to bring our check. Well, I sure as hell wasn't about to call Wlodek that.

"Lissa, you should e-mail me," Bryan coaxed as we said our goodbyes. I said I'd try before following Charles to his car.

"I wasn't getting you in trouble, was I, when I asked about Wlodek and the Aristocracy?" I watched Charles's face as he drove me home.

"No," he turned and gave me a nice smile. "I was just happy to be able to give you information that sires normally pass on. Merrill would have told you, if you'd asked him."

"Sometimes I don't know what's acceptable to ask and what isn't," I said uncomfortably, gazing out the windshield again. Or windscreen, as Charles calls it. He was doing his usual—driving like a maniac. "Does the Aristocracy have special privileges, or anything?"

"You've already had first-hand experience with them," Charles snorted. "The annual meeting, where they put you on display like the prize heifer."

"I would have said ewe, but you're pretty much correct," my voice held a bit of sarcasm. That's how I'd ended up engaged to Gavin. There were others offering with Wlodek's blessing, and Gavin was the one who frightened me the least. That didn't mean he didn't frighten me. He did and still does, for the most part. I'd said that aloud, before I even realized it.

"Lissa, I know that," Charles reached over and patted my arm. "Although I don't think he'd intentionally hurt you."

Maybe someday, Charles and I would have a talk about trust; something Gavin was forced to earn slowly. He'd placed me under compulsion and dragged me in front of the Council in the beginning, so they could decide whether I lived or died.

My turning had been the result of a wager, and my sire had never intended to take responsibility for me. That meant I was a rogue (according to the Council), right from the start. Gavin was sent to kill me and was subsequently ordered to stay awhile since I'd been working for William Winkler.

Winkler was a werewolf security mogul, working at developing software that would recognize criminals. The vampires were terrified the software might be used to hunt them down, so Gavin was instructed to keep an eye on me and watch Winkler at the same time.

Then, when Winkler made the public announcement that the software didn't work and secretly sold it to the NSA, Gavin snatched me up and hauled me off to the Council, expecting them to sentence me to death. Gavin would have performed the execution, too, if he'd been instructed to do so. It was lovely to think about, especially since I was engaged to him. I fingered his ring while these thoughts ran through my mind.

"Lissa, you can't think about that," Charles admonished. Everybody else was reading my thoughts today, why not Charles?

"Why isn't Merrill on the Council?" That was another question I wanted answered. I had my doubts that it would be.

"He has refused several times. Any time there's a vacancy, they ask him. He turns them down every time."

"Do you know why?"

"Nobody does." Charles turned off the highway; we'd be driving over narrower roads as we made our way to Merrill's manor. I always liked this part of the trip—Charles drove slower and I was able to see the fields and small villages.

"Wlodek gets investment advice from Merrill, too, although I'm not supposed to know that," Charles grinned. "If Merrill tells you to invest in something, that information is pure gold. And, since I handle most of Wlodek's financials, I call his brokers to set things up. Then I make the same investments myself. I'm in really good shape, now."

"Cool," I said.

"You'll be a member of the Aristocracy, too, when you marry Gavin." Charles had gone back to a previous subject. "None of the human companions are allowed membership—it's against vampire law. They're not allowed inside the Council Chambers, either. If a male or female companion is questioned, only three Council members need to be present and it's usually done at a neutral site."

"That's not scary for them, I'm sure." My words made Charles clear his throat. He wasn't a member of the Council but it was a good bet he'd be at any questioning in order to take notes.

"Human companions are placed under compulsion," Charles admitted. "And they're instructed to tell the truth and not be afraid."

I wasn't sure how I felt about that. "Why are they brought in?" I asked.

"Various reasons," he replied. "The worst ones are when their vampire has broken the law, or is suspected of breaking the law. The Enforcers go after the companion. They employ human investigators at times to capture the companion during the day. The human investigators turn those companions over to the Enforcers at night, just so testimony can be taken."

"So, even if the human loves the vampire and wouldn't normally testify against them, they have to?" I had mixed feelings about that information.

"Lissa, if there's nothing the vampire is guilty of, that comes out. The companion is released and sent back to their lover."

"What happens to the companion if the vampire is guilty?"

"The vampire is declared rogue and the companion is asked if they are involved with the crime or crimes, in any way. If they are, then they are executed, just as the vampire will be." Charles downshifted to turn a corner. He really liked driving his car, I could tell.

"So only vampires are allowed inside the Council Chambers?" It was a rhetorical question. At least I thought it was.

"There are other races," Charles said. If I'd been driving, that would have caused me to slam on the brakes. Charles was driving, however, so our trip was uninterrupted. My brain merely ceased to process information for a moment.

"What other races?" I asked breathlessly. "Werewolves?"

"Oh, a werewolf has never been inside the cave, either," Charles said. "I can't really talk about the others; some of them, it's impossible to talk about."

"Charles, I want to smack you for bringing this up," I said. "Now it'll bother me."

"What I can tell you is this—the last time someone of a different race was allowed inside the Council Chamber was four years ago." Charles smiled at the memory.

"Did they get out again? In one piece?" That worried me.

"Yeah," he replied. "They did."

~

"What did we buy for Franklin and Greg?" Merrill asked after Charles helped me unload everything and drove away.

"Look at this." I showed him the tablet, all the games I'd gotten, plus the recipe software. "I already had gift certificates to the bookstore, so they can buy what they want to read and I know that Greg and Franklin like to play scrabble," I showed Merrill the computer scrabble game. "And they talked about going to Las Vegas when I saw them in New York. They can use the video poker, blackjack and other stuff to sharpen their skills."

"This looks good," Merrill nodded at the pile of gifts.

"I'm going to leave it on the kitchen counter unless you want to do this some other way," I said.

"No, this is perfectly fine," Merrill smiled. "Your hair looks nice."

"Oh, thanks," I said, patting my hair a little. I'd nearly forgotten about the haircut.

❧

"Keep both pairs," Greg was saying over Franklin's shoulder as I made my way into the kitchen the following evening. Both were leaning over the tablet. Well, somebody had downloaded a poker app, looked like.

"Little girl, I blame you for this," Franklin said, looking up at me and smiling.

"I'm innocent, as usual," I said, putting on my best, innocent-looking expression before getting a hug from him.

"Your hair looks good," Greg gave me a hug and a kiss.

"Yours, too," I patted his head. Thankfully, he hadn't lost anything to the chemo yet.

"Have you seen the news today?" Franklin hugged me hard before turning serious for a moment.

"No, honey." Bryan's remarks from the evening before came to mind and now I was worried, too.

"They're trashing all the flu vaccine and rushing to make more, but that could take four to six months," Greg said. "Merrill suggests we stay away from the general population during flu season since we may not be able to get vaccinated."

"I know that sounds confining, but it'll only be for a little while, I hope." I was wondering if Merrill told them the real reason the vaccine was being destroyed. "What are they saying caused all this?"

"Some sort of taint in the eggs used," Greg told me. "But Merrill gave us the real reason. He also told us who figured it out." Greg put his arm around me. "While many people might die of the flu, many more might have died otherwise."

"It may turn out to be six of one, half a dozen of the other," I grumbled. "Either way, the bad guys win."

"Where do you think the bad guys are right now?" Franklin asked, pulling me away from Greg. I stood next to him; he was sitting on a barstool at the island. I put both arms around him and leaned my head on his shoulder.

"Honey, I don't know. And I have to tell you, I killed four misters while I was in the U.S. Somebody knew what to look for when they were turning vampires."

"That's what Wlodek and I both think," Merrill walked into the kitchen. "We just can't seem to put our finger on what that is."

"The other thing I wonder is if Saxom managed to turn any females," I added.

"That's a frightening thought," Merrill said. "I'm hoping it's unlikely, since they're so difficult to make."

"Our Lissa, one of the few, the proud, the boobed," Greg smiled.

"Like you don't have nipples?" I went after him.

"I don't have to wear a bra unless I want to," Greg huffed, hopping out of my way.

"Those are free range nipples, then," I said, trying to tickle him.

Merrill and Franklin were both laughing while I half-heartedly chased Greg around the kitchen. No way did I want to tire him out.

"Want something to eat?" I asked when things settled down.

"I want pancakes and bacon," Greg said, plopping down onto the barstool next to Frank.

"Coming right up," I said. Greg and Franklin got pancakes with strawberries and whipped cream, along with crispy bacon. While they ate, I went to send a few e-mails on my new computer.

Weldon, I wrote, *how's the baby?* I thanked him for getting Paul to help on the kidnapping case and told him I wouldn't mind meeting Paul someday, if the opportunity came along.

The e-mail to Thomas Williams was just a quick hello to him and his family, letting him know I was fine. As fine as I could be, anyway. At least I wasn't wallowing in self-pity now and my appetite was back.

I have no idea what or how Griffin does what he does, but it works. I even sent an e-mail to Winkler, asking how he was and how things were going. Kellee was five months pregnant now and had to be showing. It probably irked her, since she was pregnant with twins and might be huge before it was all over. When Winkler knocked somebody up, he was serious about it.

The last thing I did was call Gavin.

"Cara, are you feeling better?" I hadn't been doing very well when he left.

"I feel better," I said. "I'm still worried about what's going to happen to all those people, but there's really nothing I can do about it now. I did as much as I could do already."

"Those people would have died," Gavin agreed. "Now, there will be a shortage of vaccine and only the high-risk cases may get it, but it will be better than it might have been."

"I know," I sighed.

"Cara, if you will go to the bedroom where my things are and look in the top dresser drawer, you will find the gift I purchased for you," Gavin went on. "I didn't give it to you before, because you were not in the proper mood."

Proper mood was Gavin's tactful way of saying depressed funk, I guess. "I'll go down there now, while you're on the phone," I said, and trotted down the hall to the bedroom that Merrill had given him. Of course, he only used the closet and the chest now; he spent his days in my bed while he was here.

There was a small box inside the drawer, and I lifted it out. "Is it the little box?" I asked.

"Yes, cara. Open it." I opened it. Nestled on the satin was a beautiful sapphire ring. It wasn't huge and wasn't just for dinner parties or special occasions—this ring I could wear every day. It had small diamonds surrounding the oval sapphire. I pulled it out and slipped it on my right hand.

"I love it," I said. "I can wear this all the time and not just once in a while." I admired the ring for a moment.

"That is what I wanted when I purchased it," Gavin said. "Now, I have a question for you. I did not mention this earlier, since you were not in a good place."

"What is it, darlin'?" I asked.

"Did they mix up my money clip with someone else's, when you bought it? These are not my initials, although the clip is very nice."

I nearly slapped my forehead; I'd just handed the box over to him and hadn't explained anything. "Honey, that's your money clip," I said. "Those are the initials I asked the jewelry store to engrave. LLM, right?"

"That is what is engraved on it," Gavin acknowledged.

"It means Lissa Loves Me," I said. "In case you forget."

Gavin didn't say anything for a moment. I figured I'd offended him or done something truly dumb. Finally, he chuckled. "Cara, I would never have figured that out," he said. "But now, it will be a reminder."

"Do you like it, otherwise?" I asked.

"Very much. My old one was asking for retirement." We talked for a while longer, and he told me he loved me. I told him I loved him, too, and missed him. He likes to hear that, I think.

"I cannot have him killed—for obvious reasons," Wlodek paced behind his desk. Merrill sat in one of Wlodek's guest chairs. Wlodek's Monet was back on the wall after a lengthy and expensive repair job.

"He has done everything in his power, in an attempt to bring her back," Merrill said, holding Lissa's old iPhone in his hand. It contained voice mails and e-mails that Anthony Hancock had sent. Her old computer had also been in Merrill's possession and he'd destroyed the thing himself.

"Kenneth White has informed me that each of the six subjects was infected not only with her blood, but with the ash of two others. A dead vampire cannot perform a turn, as you know," Wlodek growled. "And a full turn is the only way to save any of them now. If it had only been Lissa's blood introduced into their systems, I might have looked into their backgrounds and made a decision on an individual basis, even if it is unorthodox. As it is, with another vampire's DNA in their systems, it is impossible. They are doomed. Lissa cannot successfully turn any of them."

"That's not the only reason Hancock wants her back," Merrill said.

"He claims he loves her."

"We have enough trouble with her attempts to trust Gavin, after what they have been through. This is too much. I fear for her emotional stability."

"She is stronger than you think, in that respect. She became depressed when she discovered that six innocent men had been sentenced to death, using her blood as a weapon." Merrill watched his sire pace.

Wlodek had no idea what Merrill would become when he chose to make the turn, or that Merrill would never be susceptible to his or any other vampire's compulsion. A true Vampire King had that ability; along with the power to place or remove compulsion on any human or vampire, except a Queen.

Wlodek had discovered he'd turned a King Vampire, however, shortly after Merrill woke. From the beginning, Merrill had such a strong sense of right and wrong, along with the capacity to see justice done without letting his emotions play a part that Wlodek had no trouble allowing him to live.

A Queen, on the other hand, was notoriously emotional. That was why they were good together; two halves of a whole, to protect the vampire race. In the history of the vampires upon the Earth, there had only been two pairings, a King and a Queen, living at the same time.

"You're thinking of Sarita," Wlodek stopped pacing and faced his vampire child.

"Sarita loved you," Merrill said. "She was never mine, as you know."

"And you did not want her, as I recall. Nevertheless, you did work well together."

"We did work well together," Merrill agreed.

"And I did love her, just as she loved me," Wlodek sat down in his chair. "That did not prevent her from giving herself to the sun."

"She was three hundred years old," Merrill said. "Not old at all, for one of our kind."

"She always wanted children," Wlodek toyed with his gold pen. "She would never have taken a human child to turn it, but she watched so many children over the years. I think that's what eventually destroyed her. Perhaps she was turned too young, Merrill. She was barely twenty-three when we found she wasn't susceptible to compulsion. It was either the turn or death for her."

"She lived for three hundred years," Merrill reiterated.

"Old and young, at one and the same time."

"As you say." Merrill inclined his head.

"I worry—not so much about Hancock, he is easily dealt with," Wlodek changed the subject. Sarita was a sore topic for him and he didn't speak of her often. Many times Wlodek wished he'd been the one to turn Sarita, instead of his eldest child. Things might have turned out differently if he had.

"What I do worry about is the information I am receiving from my Enforcers and Assassins," Wlodek forced his thoughts away from his last lover. "Radomir questioned Liam before beheading him in Barcelona. Liam could not reveal the name of his sire, but he did tell Radomir that Xenides and others are actively searching for Lissa. Our suspicions are correct; he desires to use her as a weapon."

"If we had been given information by the Grand Master, Xenides might not be completely aware of her talents—and her weaknesses," Merrill agreed. "I understand that Weldon Harper allowed the young werewolf to travel with them in order to keep an eye on him and to follow his contacts, but I would have killed him immediately. This has placed Lissa in much danger. It is fortuitous that she managed to escape the one sent after her in New Mexico."

"Agreed," Wlodek sighed. "Had they captured her, we would now be facing a terrible crisis. Not only can Lissa slip inside any home or building, no matter how well protected, but she can also take others with her. World leaders would die easily and unsuspecting. Others could be captured and turned to add to Xenides' army. This is more frightening than anything I have ever seen."

"Do we need to hide our girl, now, to protect her?" Merrill asked.

"I am afraid this must be so. I cannot have her and Charles followed discreetly every time they go out. We need our Enforcers and spies elsewhere. Everyone I have is out tracking Xenides and his contacts."

"I have a proposition to make in that respect," Merrill said.

"And that would be?" Wlodek asked, a rare bit of curiosity in his voice.

"Griffin is asking for her help."

Wlodek held his breath for several seconds. He knew about Griffin, as well as what he was. "I heard he was retired."

"He is. He wants her to help one of the others, now. There is something of a crisis going on elsewhere, and her talents might be utilized for that."

Wlodek watched his vampire child's face. Griffin was as close as any brother to Merrill, and their friendship had spanned more than fifteen hundred years. Merrill provided assistance to Griffin when they'd first met and now, as a favored friend, Merrill reaped benefits from that friendship. Wlodek only suspected what some of those benefits might be and had never questioned Merrill about any of it. He didn't need to know everything, after all.

"How long?" Wlodek asked. "And will he guarantee her safety?"

""I don't believe he would deliberately place her in danger, and you know time and distance have no meaning to him or his kind. He says he can have her back in a week, our time, if you want."

"Make it a month," Wlodek made a counter offer. "We can hope that Hancock will be satisfied with what he has and go forward with that. Perhaps Xenides will be thrown off the trail as well. We will use this time to decide what to do with Lissa when she returns."

"Hancock's lucky we aren't pulling our vampires away from him," Merrill snapped. "If Lissa asked, Weldon Harper would pull his wolves away as well."

"Kenneth White drew that to his attention, I believe," Wlodek almost smiled. "I'm thinking about asking Dalroy and Rhett to offer their services. They are my hidden Enforcers inside the U.S., you know."

"I suspected as much," Merrill nodded. "Griffin will come and pick up our girl in two days. He will explain as much as he can to her, then. She is curious about him anyway.

CHAPTER 2

"*L*issa, Griffin is coming to see you tomorrow," Merrill informed me the following evening. It was July fourth and Franklin, Greg and I had just had a friendly argument over how tacky it might be to celebrate Independence Day in Great Britain.

"Why is he coming to see me?" I asked. "He's your friend and I'm doing okay, I think."

"He'll explain that when he arrives," Merrill said. "And he's not just my friend. I believe he likes you very much."

Honestly, I had no idea what to do with that information. Griffin seemed like a very nice man in an older, fatherly sort of way. No, he didn't look old; he didn't look any older than Merrill did and Merrill appeared to be in his mid-twenties. There was just something about Griffin that gave off that vibe to me. Not to mention the depth of knowledge and experience in his hazel eyes. I couldn't explain my feelings about him any better than that.

"I've known Griffin all my life," Franklin got in on the conversation. "You can say anything to Griffin. Tell him anything. He'll only have your best interests at heart."

"Fine," I said. "At least I won't toss and turn in my sleep, worrying about why he wants to see me."

"Too bad we can't shoot off fireworks," Greg grumbled, turning back to the holiday. He was missing the celebrations back in the States.

"Want to go flying instead?" I asked. Greg stared at me as if I were crazy for a moment before the light came on.

"You can do that?"

"Are you afraid of heights?"

Greg snorted. "Not at this stage of the game," he said.

"What about you, Frank? I can take you both at the same time."

"I've never done anything like that," he said. "Greg and I kicked around the idea of going skydiving. This will be better, I think."

"Good. We'll go. And, as an added treat, we'll go through the ceiling and out through the roof." Greg looked as if he were worried about that, but I grabbed his arm and then Frank's and we were mist in a blink.

Ignoring Merrill's call to be careful, we did go through the ceiling and then through two more floors plus the attic, coming out over the roof of the house before zooming off toward the coast.

"I'm sorry I never asked you to do this before," Franklin said as he and Greg watched the ocean wash up on a beach covered in pebbles not far from the port city of Dover. We could see the white cliffs down the way, shining under a waning crescent moon. Greg and Franklin had their arms around each other, so I just sat down off to the side and allowed them their moment together. They let me know when they were ready to go home.

"Little girl, I have to ask you to trust me," Griffin said the following evening.

"Frank said I could," I told the tall, brown-haired man. He did have a nice smile, I'll give him that.

"I'm retired, now," he informed me. "But I used to take on some pretty nasty things. That was my job. Others are still doing that job and I need you to help one of them. This is going to involve some major travel. Don't worry, we'll have suitable clothing and such waiting when you get there; you don't need to pack a bag," Griffin held up a hand. "The thing is, I can only get you so far and then someone else will meet us at that point to take you to your destination." I watched Griffin closely; he was excited about this, I could tell. I just didn't know why.

"What about blood and things like that?" I needed a food source, after all.

"That will be provided," Griffin assured me. "I've talked this over with the Liaison, and he's quite excited about it, too."

"To whom are you taking her?" Merrill asked, uncharacteristically curious.

"Dragon," Griffin grinned. I stared at Griffin, my mouth surely open in surprise. Dragon? There was somebody named Dragon? That didn't sound promising. Who named their kid Dragon?

"What sort of help does he need?" Merrill's left eyebrow lifted. Right then I was wondering what Mr. Spock might have looked like with piercing blue eyes. Griffin snickered.

"Hey, get out of my head," I grumped. "Will I be able to phone Gavin? You know he'll want to know where I am."

"Your communication devices will not work where you're going," Griffin informed me. He sounded almost happy about that. "Wlodek will let him know that you will be unavailable for a time."

"You want me to do this?" I turned a puzzled gaze to Merrill.

"I think it will be good for you," Merrill said. Well, I'd heard that before.

"Come with me, little girl. It's time you saw the wider universes." Griffin took my hand before I could protest and just like that, we were gone.

~

Griffin and I were standing in a spacious kitchen, with twenty-foot plate glass windows overlooking a rocky beach far below the house. It was evening wherever we were; a full moon hung low over the water.

Either we'd gone back or forward in time or we weren't on planet Earth any longer.

I was staring at the moon in shock, trying to determine just where the hell I was and how Griffin had managed to get me there when a two-year-old child ran past me, screeching. "Justin, slow down!" A woman's voice shouted and I whirled in a blur to see whom it was, receiving another huge shock.

Griffin placed a hand on my shoulder just to calm me, I think. Here was the woman in Merrill's photograph, alive and in the flesh, with long, pale blonde hair and blue eyes. She was drop-dead beautiful on top of that.

I'd thought she looked gorgeous in the photograph on Merrill's bedside table, but the reality was so much better. No wonder he was head over heels for her. No way could anyone else compete with that. No way.

The sad thing, though? Her husband was standing right behind her. She had a ring on and so did he. Poor Merrill. Griffin squeezed my shoulder again. The child was now standing before me, staring at me curiously with gray eyes. His father's eyes. I saw that right away.

"Hello, young man," I knelt down to his level. He reached out and patted my face.

"Carry me," he demanded.

"You get your way a lot, do you?" I asked, smiling and tapping his nose. He laughed so I lifted him up. He seemed happy to sit on my hip and was now toying with my hair. Griffin was about to make introductions when a giant appeared next to us, scaring the bejeezus out of me. Reflexively, I misted at least twenty feet away in the blink of an eye, the child still in my arms.

"Holy shit," the blonde's husband swore.

"Lissa, it's all right, this is Pheligar, the Liaison," Griffin was trying to reassure me. Nobody else seemed to be having a cow and the kid, Justin was his name, I guess, loved the fact that we'd just gone across the room in no time flat.

I put Justin down carefully and sized up the Liaison. Not only was he around eight and a half feet tall, but he had blue skin, blue eyes and close-cropped, wheat colored hair. He wore loosely woven clothing—a tunic over shapeless pants—plus sandals. He looked like a huge, blue hippie. The skin and eyes were what amazed me, however.

"Is he safe?" I glanced at Griffin.

"He is," Griffin assured me. I walked over to the Liaison and stood before him, looking up at his face. He looked down at me. We stood like that for several seconds.

"Honey," I finally said, "I don't want to offend you or anything, since I don't know what your customs and culture are like. But I have to tell you, your skin is like a summer sky. Your eyes put all that to shame, though. They're like the bluest northern sky, the blue that you almost can't believe on the days you actually get to see it." I hadn't seen daylight in a long time and I missed it. And this guy? He was like a walking sky to me.

Who knows whether I offended him or not? He reached down and lifted me up so I'd be on a level with his face, frightening me so much I nearly misted out of his arms. Something held me back, though, and it wasn't any of my doing.

"I am doing this," he said in perfect, unaccented English. "I have not received a compliment of this magnitude before. I appreciate your words."

"Uh, you're welcome." My words were almost a squeak. How many people can say that they, as grown adults, were picked up by someone that was nearly twice their height?

"Lissa, this is Pheligar, the Liaison between the Powers That Be and the Saa Thalarr." Griffin now stood beside the blue giant. I was officially in a science fiction movie. Powers That Be? Who were they? And the other words—Saa Thalarr? What language was that? I definitely needed to take language lessons.

"Neaborian is not available on any language discs or in any books that exist in this time frame," Pheligar informed me, picking the thoughts right out of my head.

"Pheligar, if you'll set her down, we can introduce ourselves," the blonde said, sounding a bit snippy.

"You smell like sunlight," I said to Pheligar as he settled my feet on the floor. That brought a slight smile to his lips. "Larentii feed on sunlight," he said as he let me go.

"Then you are truly lucky," I said. "I wish I could see sunlight. Nowadays it just fries my skin."

"We know you're vampire," the blonde's husband remarked as they led Griffin and me toward a sitting area behind the kitchen.

"If you'll lower your shields, Lissa might tell you something of yourself," Griffin observed dryly. I had the idea that he wanted to laugh with glee, but was holding it back for some reason. Pheligar came along behind us; he'd picked up Justin and was allowing the child to pound him on the chest.

The blonde looked at her husband, who shrugged and then lowered his shields. The scent almost overwhelmed me when it came. Power. That's what I smelled. Along with the tiniest bit of vampire. I knew that as surely as I knew anything. He wasn't that old, however. Not for a vampire, anyway. Less than three hundred would be my guess. Now I knew whose apartment it was that we'd borrowed in London.

"Merrill said the apartment belonged to a friend," I said. "It has your scent all over it. I smell power. A lot of it. You were vampire; I still smell a bit of it around you. Less than three hundred years old, I think."

"Holy fuck." The blonde woman was staring at me now, as was her husband.

"This is Adam Chessman," Griffin said, patting my hand. We'd sat on a comfortable sofa across from the blonde and the former vampire Chief of Enforcers, Adam Chessman. I'd heard his name, here and there. Someone told me he'd disappeared. Here he was—alive, well, and now something other than vampire.

What I also knew was that whatever he was, his smell was very similar to the extra scent that Merrill carried. Don't get me wrong, Merrill was still mostly vampire, but the other part of him was something wondrous. The first time I'd smelled Merrill, it reminded me of a fresh breeze blowing through a field in springtime.

"You've heard of me?" Adam asked. He was a handsome man, no

doubt about it, with gray eyes and nearly black hair. Merrill might be more handsome, but Adam was the one married to the blonde.

"The vampires talk about you, sometimes. Said you took Saxom down and then disappeared," I answered.

"I did destroy Saxom," Adam nodded and put his shield back in place. It made me wonder about the shield around the woman and the ones around Griffin and Pheligar.

"I am Kiarra, First among the Saa Thalarr," the woman introduced herself. Her name rhymed with tiara, the way she pronounced it. "You know about Saxom?"

"I know next to nothing about Saxom," I answered honestly. "I'm getting to know his turns very well, however. I've killed several of them so far, and most of them have been misters. If the Vampire King and his court would turn me loose, I'd take out the rest of them."

Kiarra was standing now and staring at me, a hand over her mouth. "Enough about Saxom," Griffin whispered next to my ear. I nodded. The topic was obviously upsetting Kiarra.

"Have you always been able to turn to mist that quickly?" Adam asked, covering the ensuing silence.

"Not always. The first time I did it, it took five minutes, I think. My time improved after that, until it's instantaneous." Kiarra sat down again as I explained my misting talents. Adam rubbed her back solicitously. Something about Saxom, even the mention of his name, sure upset her in a hurry.

"You've seen her take Justin with her," Griffin said. "Lissa can transport just about anything or anyone," he added.

"I was never able to turn that swiftly, until Kiarra offered her blood," Adam said. "And I could only transport myself. This is more than interesting."

"She can mindspeak, too," Griffin went on. "She's perfect for this assignment."

I turned to stare at Griffin. He was going to have to explain things to me, some day. Adam mentioned getting Kiarra's blood and then being able to turn to mist faster. I wondered what else her blood had done for him. At least one of those things was present—he'd fathered Justin. The boy looked exactly like him.

"Pheligar, do you wish to place the implant or would you like me to do it?" Kiarra asked, turning back to business.

"I will do this," Pheligar stood and handed Justin off to his mother.

"Implant?" I squeaked. All the alien stories were about to come to life for me. The tales about experimentation on board spaceships crowded my mind; I was just about to panic and go to mist.

"Lissa," Griffin turned to me and took my face in his hands, "it is alien technology, but it's a shield that an advanced race created. It will allow you to stand in full sunlight without being burned. You'll be sluggish if you wake, that's just your nature, but you won't burn, I promise."

"How long will it last?" I asked. I sure as heck didn't want to be tossed into sunlight, only to discover the batteries had run down.

"It has a normal lifespan of a hundred years," Griffin replied. Well, somebody was way more efficient than we Earthlings.

"Is this going to hurt?"

"See for yourself," Pheligar knelt before me, holding a small, flat disc in his hand. His hand was so large it made the disc appear microscopic. "It goes here," he placed the disc on the tip of a finger and pressed it against the back of my neck. When he pulled his finger away, the disc was gone. "It has been placed," he said. "Did you feel pain?"

"Uh, no," I said, surprise in my voice. He could do that without causing pain? That was exceptional. "Where were you when I got bitten by werewolves?" I blurted.

"Possibly on the Larentii homeworld; I would have to check the timeline just to make sure," Pheligar replied. Well, nothing got past him—I could see that right away. "I am giving you the required communication skills as well," Pheligar tapped my forehead with a large, blue finger. I stared at him in shock after my eyes refocused from the bright flash he'd created. Communication skills? What did that mean?

"Pheligar will take you to Refizan," Griffin stood.

"Wait, aren't you going to explain this a little more?" I asked. "Where is this Refizan place? What am I supposed to do there? Who's going to take me home when this is over? Where are you going?" I was panicking—this was happening much too quickly.

I should have saved my breath; Griffin disappeared and Pheligar had me out of there in a blink, landing me in a smaller apartment with fewer windows and not nearly so nice a view.

Two men were there, waiting for me. One was around six-three and wider across the shoulders than Gavin. He had Asian features, wore a scowl on his face and had long black hair, braided down his back. His arms were also folded across his massive chest, as if he disapproved of me right off the bat. I was going to have to take lessons from Wlodek and get that non-expression thing going. I needed it more and more often, nowadays.

The other man was around six feet tall with light-brown hair, hazel eyes and was mostly human looking but didn't have much of an expression going, either. If I expected Pheligar to make introductions, I was very wrong. "Here is the girl," he said and promptly disappeared.

"Fuck," I muttered. I wanted to shout it, but didn't know how much trouble I'd be in if I did. This was their plan—just to dump me somewhere and leave me to my own affairs?

"They sent a vampire," the brown-haired man declared. Well, it was nice to meet him, too. He was dressed in something that looked like surgery scrubs—in blue. The Asian man was barefoot and wore dark, loose pants with a long-sleeved white shirt. He might have been handsome—I mean really handsome—if he'd get rid of the scowl plastered on his face. It didn't look as if that might happen any time soon.

"They told me I'd have clothing and blood supplied," I said, since neither of them seemed willing to speak after the vampire comment. At least brown-haired guy hadn't called me a fucking vampire.

"Down the hall, second bedroom on the right," the brown-haired man said, jerking his head in that direction. Okay, maybe I wasn't supposed to know their names.

"You will not be biting either of us, if you wish to keep your life," the Asian-looking man finally said something.

All righty, then.

"Honey," I said, "as hard as you are, I'd probably break a fang." I stalked away from both of them, going to the designated second bedroom on the right. The Asian-looking guy had to be Dragon, I thought, as I checked out my bedroom.

At least Griffin had been correct about the supplies—there was a full-size refrigerator contraption, with cold blood in the bottom half, frozen blood in the top. Clothes were in the closet—the styles differed from Earth; I saw that right away. Loose trousers, loose tunics; Pheligar was dressed better for this place than I was. The shoes were fabric, with rope soles on most of them. A couple pairs had hard rubber soles and there was a pair of rubber rain boots. I'd need those if it were wet out.

Pheligar hadn't lied about communication—there was a stack of newspapers lying on the bed that I could easily read, with plenty of articles about a religion imported from another star system (yeah, I said star system) that was attempting to take over.

I sat down to read, and the more I read, the angrier I became. The rogue religion was attempting to take over the entire planet, looked like. Journalists were being killed, along with politicians and public servants, or just about anybody who disagreed with these guys or stood in their way.

The priests for this religion were so sneaky and slick that nobody could pin the crimes on them or their church. Tales had spread that the religion had most of the law enforcement either too frightened to arrest them or paid off in some way. These were only rumors at this point, which served to unsettle the population and terrify everybody.

The religion called itself Solar Red, whatever that meant. Maybe my translation was too literal. The other thing that drew my attention in this particular newspaper was that these Solar Red priests were rumored to practice human sacrifice. Why didn't somebody go and shut them down? I grabbed a newspaper and stalked out to the living area. Nobody was there, so I walked into the kitchen.

"Is all this true? About these Solar Red assholes?" I shook the newspaper I held at the brown-haired man. "Are they really killing people?"

"Yes," he shrugged indifferently, scrubbing a mug. He had his shirt sleeves rolled up and was washing dishes.

"How much night do I have left?" I watched as he rinsed the mug and placed it on a draining mat.

"Around six Earth hours," he grumbled.

"Good. Where's the nearest Solar Red temple?"

"About two miles that way," he pointed to his left, not really looking at me.

"Good. See ya before dawn," I said, dropping the newspaper on the kitchen table and turning to mist right in front of him. I then went straight through the wall.

The city I flew over that night was as large as many Earth cities, and was lit half as brightly. I'd already discovered that Refizan was solar powered. Like any city I was used to, it had its share of tall, rectangular buildings. A few Refizani had gone wild and built something circular or in a pyramid shape. I guess geometry is the same, no matter where you are.

The brown-haired guy was right; I found the temple about two miles away. The guards posted outside had guns and looked to be serious about shooting trespassers, but my mist didn't set off any warning bells.

I misted inside and found a gathering of priests, all dressed in formal, dark red robes. They smelled evil, and the fact that they were taking bites out of a human heart before passing it on to the next guy didn't improve my opinion of them.

Well, I'd misted over a river on my way to the temple. Too bad nobody was there to see what I did next. I had sixteen heads lopped off sixteen priests in about thirty seconds. Then I hauled them as mist to the river; it was flowing swiftly as I hovered above its surface. Sixteen bodies were dropped into the dark waters with a quiet splash. My clothes were bloodied afterward, but at least the job was done.

I made one more trip to the temple, found the Refizani equivalent of a garden hose, dragged it in and washed down the marble floor. Then, taking the hose with me, I shredded it before dropping it into the river. I could smell the ocean five miles away and hoped that the priests would end up there or in a shark's belly before it was over.

~

"Where the hell have you been?" Dragon guy demanded when I showed up at the apartment again, my clothes covered in blood.

"I did a little worshiping at the Solar Red temple," I said, brushing past him and heading toward my bedroom, second door on the right.

~

As messages go, mine was received loud and clear; the news program I heard when I walked into the living area the following evening was abuzz with it. I was the only one in the apartment, so I drank my dinner as I watched the news on a flat, built-in screen on the wall.

"And to worsen the insult, the perpetrators washed the floor of the inner temple before leaving, without alerting any of the others to their presence. There are no leads or explanations as to what happened to these priests," the reporter said.

He sounded almost gleeful, to be honest. "The remaining six hundred priests in the temple on Red Street are threatening retaliation of course, but that has been their stance for months now."

I waited an hour, but Dragon dude and no-name didn't show so I went out to the street after dressing in my local, non-sexy, shapeless duds. I could go back to the temple, I suppose, but they'd be on their guard now and I didn't know anyone that I might trust to yank a bullet out of my body if I were shot. I roamed the streets instead. I heard whispers of where retaliations might take place. The consensus seemed to be the poor side of town, wherever that might be.

"Where is that, what you're talking about?" I asked one man, who didn't seem to worry whether he was overheard or not.

"The pity streets?"

"Yeah." I guess I gave him the Refizani equivalent of an Earth "yeah."

"If you go to the southeastern edge of the city, you'll find them," he replied. "Are you a journalist?"

"Yeah. That's exactly what I am," I lied. I went to find a deserted alley. That super dude had his phone booths; I had alleys. Not a bit of glamour in my less than super-hero changing place. I went to mist and flew over rooftops, going right through tall buildings instead of leaping them if they were in my way. I found the pity streets. Strange lingo these Refizani had. Very strange.

Normally, I think children might have been playing in those narrow, brick-lined streets. This was a very old portion of the city, with crumbling facades lining the uneven walks out front. I smelled fear throughout the place. Misting overhead, I passed over buildings that had scraps of laundry drying on lines hanging across rooftops. Somewhere, perhaps a mile away, bells rang out to mark the hours.

Refizani days were divided into twenty-eight hours. Around second bell, I heard the noise; a car was coming down one of the narrow lanes. So far, I hadn't seen one of the solar powered cars anywhere in these neighborhoods. I misted toward the sound, eventually flying over the thing. It looked like a van of some sort.

It pulled up outside a house and three men, dressed in the red uniforms of Solar Red guards and armed with rifles, stepped out silently. They didn't smell pure to me and were certainly up to no good. "Grab them," one whispered to the others. "If the man fights, kill him. We'll dump the body elsewhere." I didn't like where this was going one bit. Those fuckers didn't get a chance to knock on the apartment door; I knew by scent that a man, a woman and five children slept inside. No way was I going to take chances with babies' lives. Or their parents, for that matter.

Hauling three frightened, gun-toting men across town was no picnic let me tell you, and the farther I hauled them the more frightened they became. What I did learn, though, was that they couldn't fly. I dropped them from about a hundred feet up, right over the street that ran in front of the temple. Then I went back for their van.

"You mean she figured everything out this quickly?" Kiarra stared at Pheligar of the Larentii as he reported the latest events on Refizan.

"The first night, after reading the newspapers Dragon left on her bed," Pheligar replied. He seldom smiled, but a corner of his mouth quirked slightly, surprising Kiarra. "We took a chance, hoping she would take the initiative without our interference," he added.

"Dragon and Karzac are there for our enemy. They can't go against Solar Red without violating the rules," Kiarra nodded. "Remind me to thank Merrill and find an appropriate gift for allowing this," she added.

"I fail to understand how the Reth Alliance allows Solar Red to remain in operation," Pheligar offered a rare opinion. Larentii seldom expressed their judgment or condemnation on anything.

"I agree—somebody should get rid of them. Some days I hate that no interference rule," Kiarra grumbled, patting Pheligar's back absently. He blinked at the unexpected contact before his slight smile widened.

"The van appears to have been dropped from a great height, although that in itself is impossible," the journalist declared. I was watching the news again while I had my usual for dinner.

Footage was shown of the van in question; it was crumpled up in the same street where I'd dropped three armed men. There wasn't any word on those guys, though. Maybe the temple didn't report it when their hit men came up missing. I went to shower and dress.

"May I buy you a drink?" The man seemed nice enough and didn't smell evil, but I wasn't interested in a date and nobody had bothered to give me any money so I could reciprocate. Hell, I didn't even know where in the universe I was, for Pete's sake.

If nobody came to retrieve me eventually, I could be stuck here forever. I'd just have to hope that didn't happen. I'd been hanging out near the bar, expecting to get a little more information, but these Refizani were tight-lipped tonight.

"No, but thank you for the offer," I was as polite as I could be before moving down the street. The street reminded me of one I'd seen in Paris in what might have been a lifetime ago. Merrill, Franklin, Greg and I had gone there to find a dress for me to wear to the annual vampire meeting. Cafés and restaurants lined both sides of the street and plenty of people were wandering toward a nearby wharf; we weren't far from a particularly scenic loop in the river.

"I heard they were bringing them downriver," someone said quietly. My ears immediately perked up.

"If you can't find locals to sacrifice, you pull some in from elsewhere," his companion observed. "An entire family disappeared last night. The local authorities claim they're searching for them." The man snorted as if that was the last thing he might believe. The two men were sitting at a tiny table outside a café, drinking something that smelled like tea, only a kind I'd never scented before. I trotted away as quickly as I could.

Where do you go if there are people coming down the river to be sacrificed? There weren't any flashing neon signs anywhere, proclaiming where that spot might be. Surely, there were landings somewhere. I'd seen ships and boats on the first night but they'd been far away when I'd dumped my dead priests into the water. I misted toward the river.

There was a huge landing area about three miles past the spot where I'd dumped my priests and about a half-mile from the temple, thanks to a bend in the river itself. There were priests and more gun-toters waiting in a van at one of the slips.

Another good-sized ship was tied to a dock nearby and sailors were unloading crates and glaring at the priests while they did it. I had an idea. I'd already carried one van as mist. Why not one loaded down with priests and thugs?

I heard the sailors calling out and shouting as the van simply disappeared before their eyes. These Solar Red guys got a trip to the ocean that night; I dropped the van from high enough that I had time to mist inside the van, kill all six inside it and then mist out again before it ever hit the water.

When a boat pulled up later at the same dock, seven priests and four guard thugs came off the boat searching for their escort. They turned this way and that, surprised that nobody was there to meet them. Except me, that is. The sailors and the other boat had left already, so there weren't any witnesses this time. The priests died; I then dumped them in the river half a mile away. Rushing back afterward, I went looking for the prisoners they'd brought with them.

A man, his wife, and their four and six-year-old children. Why were they attacking families? Was it to make everybody afraid? To tell the population that no one was safe, no life sacred? What kind of religion was this?

"I don't know where to take you," I told them as I cut the ropes that bound them and took the gags from their mouths. They'd even gagged the kids. If I'd known that before, I might have shredded their kidnappers instead of decapitating them as I had.

"We have family here," the man said softly.

"Do you know where they are?" I didn't know one street from another—or the city's name. I also hadn't seen Dragon in two days, or the no-name guy. I didn't even know if they were still alive.

"We can find our way," the man said. "I don't know how you did this, but we thank you."

"Well, honey, I can't have you remembering me." I placed compulsion on all four of them to forget me. I told them that they'd been abandoned by the priests and gotten loose by themselves.

Dragon and no-name were both waiting on me when I returned to the apartment two hours before dawn. They stood at the hallway entrance, blocking the way to my bedroom.

I started to shoulder my way past them; I wanted a shower and a little more blood before going to bed. Hauling a van five miles to the ocean, even as mist, is harder than it sounds.

"Wait," Dragon dude said, reaching out a hand to stop me.

"What?" I didn't sound very friendly, honestly, but then they'd been less than receptive when Pheligar dumped me in the apartment and just took off. The only nice thing I could say about them is that at least they hadn't called me leech, bloodsucker or fucking vampire.

"I am Dragon," he held out his hand. He was introducing himself? That was a shock.

"You'll stoop to shake hands with a vampire?" I asked sarcastically.

"I deserve that," he said, still holding out his hand.

"Lissa," I said, and grasped his fingers with mine.

"Karzac," the other man held out his hand. "I am Dragon's healer and this is my home planet."

"Honey," I said, shaking Karzac's hand, "your planet has gone to the dogs. I've dumped a bunch priests and several of their thugs into the river, after they had their heads removed, of course. Another three were dropped in the street in front of the temple. Too bad they didn't know how to fly; they might have gotten away. Two vans are in the river and a third was dumped in front of the temple. If I had longer nights, I might be able to get more of them."

"You've done more damage than that; they're frightened and they have no idea who could do this sort of thing without our enemy feeling the power signature," Dragon almost smiled, his dark eyes lighting up a little.

"I'm just a force of nature, I guess," I said. "You say they can feel a power signature?"

"Our enemy, who is not Solar Red, can. That's why Karzac and I are so tightly shielded—to prevent him from locating us. He is allied with Solar Red, but we are not allowed to attack them. Our power to combat the enemy was given to us—it is not natural. Yours on the other hand, is. Attempting to detect you would be like searching for a single blade of grass among other blades of grass. We had no idea what Pheligar was doing when he dropped you in our apartment. Any other vampire would have been easily seen by Solar Red and would certainly be unable to do these things."

"I'm special," I grumbled.

"You don't sound pleased about it." Karzac examined me carefully. His eyes were a green-gold. He had nice eyes.

"Right now I'm pooped," I told him. "I'd really just like a bath and a little more blood before I pass out."

"Are your supplies adequate?" Dragon asked, standing aside and giving me a clear path to my bedroom.

"There's enough in there for two more vampires, I think," I said. "I'm glad I don't have to hunt for my dinner."

"If you have need of more, let me know. I will send mindspeech to Pheligar," Dragon offered.

"He can hear mindspeech? Wow. Maybe I'll send him mindspeech myself and let him know that as instructions go, his are non-existent. Goodnight." I started down the hall toward my bedroom.

"You have mindspeech?" Dragon was surprised again.

What do you think? I sent to him.

I think your voice comes through quite clearly, he replied. *Pleasant dreams.*

Would that it were possible, I returned, shutting the door of my bedroom behind me.

CHAPTER 3

I might have to ask Dragon and Karzac where they go while I'm asleep. They were never there when I woke. Not that I minded—it allowed me to drink my dinner while I watched the evening news before going out.

Journalists were reporting that Solar Red was threatening the local police after their priests and thugs disappeared from the boat slip. The temple sent out a press release, saying the local authorities weren't doing their jobs, and then made an offer to the government of Refizan to provide their own security to the population.

If that wasn't an offer from the fox to watch over the hen house, then I was still human and just about anybody would tell you I wasn't. It wasn't the local population that was in danger from attacks—except attacks from Solar Red, that is. The ones in the most danger were the priests of Solar Red and I was about to go out and put even more of them in danger.

Tonight was the night I decided to go back to the temple. Even though the doors were heavily guarded all around, that wouldn't keep me out. The temple was a tall octagonal building, nearly three stories high with eight wide, double doors. Four of those doors were on the southern half going into the main temple itself; the other four on the north side opened into the priests' quarters, the refectory and the administrative offices.

That would have made me snort if I still had lungs and breath to do it. What did they do or discuss inside those offices? Killings and sacrifices? I'd bet it wasn't prayer and feeding the hungry. No time like the present to slip inside and see if I could find out. Just to be on the safe side I slipped through a crack beneath one of the northern doors. I knew it wasn't the refectory—there would be a smell of food behind that door.

What I found was a warren of rooms and offices. Had they promoted everybody? I didn't see any spaces for the common herd. Nobody was getting a corner office, that much I knew since the temple was almost round.

The sound of voices chanting drew me down a long narrow hall and then down more stone steps into inky blackness. Beneath the temple, I found spaces for the common herd—there were multiple levels with mazes of sleeping cells and rooms on each level, many of them holding sleeping priests.

I discovered that night that there were more priests there than the local authorities or media suspected. The darkness throughout the lower cells and cubicles might have discouraged anyone else, but I could see just fine, no flashlights or torches needed, thanks.

I found the torches eventually, along with the chanting priests; there were burning torches placed at all four corners of an altar. A man was chained naked to its stained marble surface. It stank of blood, both old and fresh.

This was a regular occurrence, I could tell. There was no mercy or clemency for this poor soul; he'd already been tortured. Burns and slices that oozed blood covered his chest and arms, while something had been branded across his face right over the eyes, rendering him sightless.

Some schmuck was drawing out a lengthy, sharp knife as six of his best buddies, all dressed in the red robes of the priesthood, recited an ignorant litany that the sacrifice would feed the god. As of now, that god was on my shit list.

Schmuck with the knife was the first to go; he didn't have time to squeak before his head, along with a lot of his blood, was splattered against the stone wall that surrounded the circular chamber.

The six remaining priests all tried to flee through the door at the same time, making it ridiculously easy to pick them off. They still hadn't seen their enemy and that was fine with me. They were all relieved of their heads; it was obvious they weren't using them to think with, anyway.

After using my claws to slice through the chains that held the prisoner, I turned him to mist and got the hell out of there. I felt his fear and pain as I misted away faster than I'd ever gone anywhere before.

I had no idea where the nearest hospital was and that made me want to weep. The man was probably dying but I wanted to give him as much of a chance as I could. *Dragon!* I sent out a shouted message. *Where's the nearest hospital from the temple?*

Two miles, south and east, came the swift reply. I misted in that direction as quickly as I could. The building was taller than those surrounding it; I dived down and right through the sliding doors into the Refizani version of an emergency room.

Someone waited there for me and it surprised me greatly. Karzac, dressed in physician's blue, stood fierce and steady, anticipating my arrival. He knew I was there somehow, although I was still mist.

Follow me, he instructed, his mindspeech terse. He strode down a hallway as quickly as he could, turning into a room on the right.

I'm in, I sent as I zipped past Karzac. He closed and locked the door behind him. There was an examination table inside the room so I rematerialized, laying the tortured man as carefully as I could across the surface.

Karzac can multitask—he was cursing and examining the man at the same time. "Young woman, please make yourself invisible or leave. I must call for assistance. This is the Vice-Governor of the realm." Karzac was a doctor, all right. He was used to giving orders.

I went immediately to mist while Karzac lifted a small communicator and shouted into it, calling for additional personnel and medical supplies. He unlocked the door, too, so they could all come inside.

Karzac was elbow deep in treating the man when I left. Misting back to the temple, I found it angrier than a kicked anthill. Three vans pulled out of a nearby rectangular building; it was a garage, I discovered. I followed the vans, thinking along the way that if the god had been hungry, I'd left him plenty to snack on.

The vans traveled northward outside the city, following a road that ran alongside the river much of the time. The last of the houses and warehouses were left behind after an hour and we traveled another hour beyond that before coming into wide farmland. Four priests stepped out of each van after pulling to a stop, and together they all walked toward an open field.

"We beg the god to come to us," one of the priests lifted his arms in prayer. He and the other eleven went to their knees in the pasture, waiting for something to come. I hovered as mist, waiting to see who (or what) the priests were waiting for. Ten minutes went by, with all the priests remaining on their knees before anything happened.

Eight men showed up. Right out of nowhere, just as I'd seen Pheligar do and what Griffin could do as well. One walked ahead of the other seven. Was that the god? I misted closer for a better look.

"You have disappointed me," that one said. He was tall—nearly as tall as Gavin, with dark hair and pale, yellow eyes. The scent that washed off him was one I'd never forget, either. If somebody else could smell more evil than that, I didn't want to meet them. "You were to bring me the one I requested, yet here you are empty-handed while he receives treatment for his wounds. Explain this!" he shouted.

"We cannot." The one who'd invoked the god spoke, his head still bowed. "Something invisible crept past our guards."

"That is a lie. My enemy would give away his presence if he were to do such a thing," the man snarled. "Tell me and I will consider sparing your lives."

"We speak the truth." The man was terrified. He was speaking the truth. I knew that. This wasn't much of a god if he didn't know the truth from a lie.

"You will return to the others and inform them that they must perform better or your life and theirs will be forfeit. You will leave me now but the others must remain." The god stared speculatively at the other eleven priests.

"Of course, lord," the priest rose, bowed several times and took off swiftly across the field toward one of the vans. He was inside it and backing up when the god lost his façade of humanity. I might have shrieked if I could have, when he became a monster.

A gleaming, copper-scaled serpent he became, nearly fifty feet in length and at least three feet thick, with spikes surrounding a crest on his head, more spikes at the end of his lengthy tail, and teeth—they were many and each was long and sharp. He had two priests gulped down his thick throat before they could even contemplate running. Another two followed the first two, but they'd gotten up and tried to get away by that time.

Four was the giant snake's limit, I guess, because he slithered back, allowing his seven apprentices to come forward. They changed, too, just not into giant serpents. These turned into something ugly, their human-like skin splitting while the ugly thing emerged, like a butterfly's chrysalis bursting open to reveal a monster.

They kept their humanoid shape but were a muddy brown in color, were completely hairless and had fangs wide-spaced in large mouths. They fell on the seven remaining priests, ripping and tearing into them. They weren't as neat in their table manners as the serpent had been, either. The monsters clawed the priests apart before eating them, and it was difficult listening to the screams before they died.

Is this what was hanging over the priests' heads if they didn't perform, or were the priests apt pupils who were rewarded or punished according to their performance? My money was on the latter. They didn't have to torture the poor schmuck I'd hauled to the hospital. He could have been handed over whole, but he wouldn't have been.

When the priests were consumed, leaving bloody and torn clothing scattered across the field, the serpent regained his human shape. His seven apprentices all stayed the same, however.

"Go and feed upon the population, turning them into others such as yourselves when you sate your hunger," the god instructed before disappearing. The seven ugly creatures started walking toward the city. Well, god or no god, I was about to see if I could kill these things.

They didn't turn to fight until I'd already taken three heads. They can move in a blur if they're threatened though. I found that out as they rushed me. They also can't fight what they can't see—I learned that, too, going to mist when they all attacked at once. One got a lengthy claw into my left arm when I materialized to take his head, but he died just like the others.

Vampires turn to ash when they die. Humans and werewolves just drop where they're killed. These things, whatever they were, blasted out in some sort of heavy sand or particles when they died. It was as if they wanted a last chance at doing harm, but their particles weren't large enough to do much damage.

By the time I was done, I stood there in that wide, empty field, holding my arm (which was bleeding sluggishly) and wondering just what it was that I'd killed. I was also feeling extremely thankful that vampires didn't explode when they died.

Still pondering my current list of ambiguities, I misted to the apartment and found Dragon sitting at the kitchen table having a cup of strong tea. "What happened?" he asked, eyeing my wound as I materialized inside the kitchen. Going to the sink, I turned on the tap, preparing to wash out my gash.

"You're not going to believe this," I said. "I followed twelve priests out to farmland north of here, and they stood out in a field, calling for their god. A man and seven others just appeared out of nowhere. The one who thought he was a god threatened one of the priests and sent him back to the temple. He then changed to this awful snake thing that had to be at least fifty feet long and ate four of the priests."

Dragon pulled a first aid kit from under the sink and had gauze in his hand when he drew in a breath and stared at me.

"You didn't get this from him, did you?" He had my arm in his hands quickly.

"No," I said. "His seven dwarves turned into something ugly and they ate the other priests after tearing them apart. The serpent guy changed back to his human-looking self, told the others to eat people in the city and turn some of them, then took off. I killed the dwarves, but one of them gave me this." I nodded toward my arm, which Dragon still held in his hands. He blinked at me; I noticed how dark his eyes were—they were nearly black. Dragon has nice eyes, when he isn't scowling.

"Those things are demons," Dragon informed me calmly while he took over scrubbing my wound. It hurt, but then it hurt when I was doing it, too. "I imagine you witnessed the dusting when you killed them?" He focused on removing a bit of debris lodged in the wound.

"Dusting? Is that what that was—when their bodies turned into sand particles and blasted toward me?"

"Yes. All of them do it and the older they are, the larger the particles and more dangerous and deadly they are. It is a final effort to destroy an enemy." Dragon poured more soap into my wound and kept working. Well, I'd been right on that account, at least, and was thankful these demons were relatively new.

"Where do the demons come from?" I asked. "Can they really turn people into what they are?"

"Yes. It happens quickly," Dragon answered my second question first. "All a demon has to do is bite a humanoid and within thirty seconds the humanoid's life is no longer his own. The demon's seed is in their saliva and is nearly impossible to eradicate, once it is introduced into the bloodstream. The serpent that you saw tonight is the enemy I hunt. He is a member of the race known as the Ra'Ak, and the demons are Ra'Ak young. If this Ra'Ak had sensed your presence, he would be hunting you, now. If you managed to escape, that is."

"That's comforting," I grumbled.

"I wish I had been there; I could have challenged him then," Dragon mumbled, rinsing my wound under the faucet.

"Is that why you're here? To kill that thing?" I studied Dragon's head; he was still bent over my arm. His hair was the blackest I'd ever seen, hanging in a thick braid down to his waist.

"That is my purpose, as it is for every Saa Thalarr. We were created to challenge the Ra'Ak. They are a great evil and were never intended to be among the Worlds of Light. They destroyed the Dark Worlds, long ago. All but one, that is. The High Demons' world is still intact."

"High Demons? Are they like those things I saw earlier?"

"No," Dragon gave a quick shake of his head as he dried off my arm. "Will this heal during your sleep?" he asked, lifting his dark eyes to my face.

"Yes, but it might be a good idea to wrap it up, so the edges will close properly."

Dragon wrapped my arm. "High Demons might be indistinguishable from most humanoids," he explained as he wound gauze around my gash. "Until they become angry or turn for some reason. Then they are very dangerous. The Ra'Ak have no hold over them and cannot defeat them, unless there are many Ra'Ak to only one High Demon. That is why their world survives."

"Sounds as though the High Demons should have kicked Ra'Ak ass and kept them away from the things they didn't need to get into," I huffed.

"The High Demon agenda is known only to the High Demons," Dragon muttered softly. "We do not attempt to explain their doings."

"If I see Mr. Long, Coppery and Snaky again, what should I do?" I asked.

"Stay away," Dragon said. "Every part of his body is poisonous—teeth, claws and spikes. Each scale, even, is tipped with deadly poison. Those priests would have died anyway if the Ra'Ak had merely brushed against them."

"Good information to have," I drew a shaky breath. I had the fucker's scent, now. I'd know him from half a mile away, in fact. There'd be plenty of time to get out of his way.

"Call me with mindspeech if you see him again," Dragon instructed. "I warn you, I will have to come within his presence by conventional means. If I employ my power, he will sense this and destroy the planet using the power and abilities that he has at his disposal. Any Ra'Ak has the strength to destroy worlds, but that is not their true goal. They survive upon the flesh and blood of humanoids.

They seek a food source, first and foremost. It is the work of my kind to see that the Ra'Ak do not devour the universes."

"Holy crap," I muttered. "You live this dangerously all the time?"

"Quite a bit of the time, yes," Dragon smiled and tied off the gauze. "Karzac is working late tonight."

"My fault," I said. "I hauled a torture victim to him at the hospital. He may still be working on that guy."

"That's why you wanted the information."

"Yeah."

Karzac wandered in half an hour before dawn, looking as if he'd been in a fight. I made a cup of tea for him before going to bed. Dragon had already gone to sleep; I could hear his soft snore as I passed his bedroom.

～

"Sorry, didn't realize anybody would be here." I'd strolled into the living area to get my news fix, carrying a bag of blood. Dragon and Karzac were both up watching the news so I turned to go back to the bedroom.

"You will not upset us by having a meal in our presence," Karzac scooted over on the sofa; Dragon had the easy chair taken up. Seriously, that man was all muscle and had his shirt off tonight. No surprise where he gets his name; he had dragons tattooed everywhere, including one huge one on his chest and another large dragon on his back, with smaller dragons flying up and down his arms.

I sat on the end of the sofa; Karzac now had the other side. We watched the news together while I sipped my blood—it was a partial bag and just enough for my meal.

"The Vice-Governor of the realm is in critical condition at a local hospital," a journalist announced. "Authorities claim he was tortured by Solar Red. The temple is denying the allegations, asking instead for proof of their involvement. No arrests have been made."

"Fuckers," I muttered, rising to dump the empty blood bag inside the canister in my bedroom. I'd figured out what it was for, finally. It was kept cool; plugged into a socket so the bags wouldn't smell because of residual blood left within.

"Are you off today?" I asked when I came back and sat down.

"This is off-day; everyone is off on this day," Karzac explained. "You may go to the streets this evening and there will be people sharing food and drink—no one will be working except journalists, medical personnel and law enforcement. Those employees switch and have every other off-day."

"That's nice," I said. "Now, tell me how Solar Red came to be here in the first place."

"The Ra'Ak brought them in," Karzac muttered, sounding angry and frustrated. "This is a legitimate if brutal religion from another star system," he added, turning to face me. "We have space travel, as you might imagine, and these priests were shipped in by the hundreds. At first, they convinced the populace to listen to them because Refizan was experiencing a dramatic rise in crime—killings and thefts, among other things—that began shortly before Solar Red arrived. All carefully orchestrated by the Ra'Ak, as you may have guessed. The Solar Red priests promised order and safety, wriggling their way into acceptance in this way. The crime rate dropped sharply after they came, but now it is rising again. The Ra'Ak are behind this; they are attempting to take the planet and the darker and more evil it is, the easier it will be for them. Refizan is peaceful and has no standing army—hasn't needed one for a very long while. We are protected by Alliance troops if we are attacked, but a renegade religion is not considered an attack."

"I am going out tonight; there are demons in the east side of the city," Dragon said. Only then did I notice he had two swords lying on the small table beside his chair; they were sheathed. He lifted them up, along with a shirt.

"Is that how you take their heads?" I asked, nodding toward his blades.

"Yes. I have a lengthy bus ride ahead of me to get to them," he sighed.

"I can get you there in no time," I offered. Dragon looked at me sharply. "I do it all the time," I said. "Karzac should know; that's how I got the Vice-Governor to the hospital yesterday."

"She did do this," Karzac nodded. "I was so focused on the patient I failed to remark on this feat."

"If you wouldn't mind; I detest riding the bus."

"So the buses don't have drivers?" I asked. Karzac did say everybody was off.

"They run along metal rails in the streets," Karzac replied. "The stops are computerized; everything on Refizan that can be is automated."

"Come on," I urged Dragon. "Just tell me where you want to go and I'll get you there. If there are lots of demons, I'll help." I stood up and offered Dragon a smile.

"What happens when you do this?" Dragon asked as I came to stand beside him.

"You turn to mist, just like I do," I said, and took his arm, causing both of us to disappear. We flew high over the city, searching the area where Dragon indicated the demons were—he'd sent mindspeech as I misted us along. I scented the demons when we were directly overhead, so I dropped Dragon behind them and came back to corporeality. *I see them*; Dragon sent mindspeech with a curt nod. I silently agreed as we crept along the streets behind the monsters.

There were fifteen of them, all walking toward what looked to be a large block party. This would be ideal for them—just wander up to unsuspecting people. These demons hadn't turned into the muddy brown monsters I'd seen the night before; they still appeared human, although their scent told me otherwise.

Get them before we have witnesses, Dragon instructed and drew his blades so quietly I barely heard them leave their sheaths. Dragon wore his swords crossed over his back and kept them nice and sharp, I could tell.

I turned to mist and flew forward. Forming claws only, I removed four demon heads in two seconds or less. The others turned on us then and Dragon and I were fighting among them quickly.

Eerily silent, they rushed us one or two at a time, grimly intent on taking us down. With no thought for their safety, they fought just as silently as they'd done the night before, but I'd been so busy trying to kill them then that I really hadn't noticed how quiet they were.

It was like fighting robots—there didn't seem to be true sentience in any of them. Dragon and I ended up fighting back to back, as the demons attacked us. If they got close, they died. Dragon was death on those things, as was I. They were all dead quickly and piles of sandy particles littered the brick street around us.

"Nicely done," Dragon inclined his head respectfully as he sheathed his blades.

"Are there any more? I'm thinking about paying the priests a visit if there aren't others," I said, flicking a dusting of demon particles off my tunic. The clothing was my biggest beef with the planet—if you didn't count Solar Red, demons and the Ra'Ak, that is.

"None at the moment," Dragon said. "Take me with you as mist; I wish to see the inside of this temple."

I wish we hadn't gone. It wouldn't change anything for those two young girls—who knows from where they'd been abducted; they couldn't have been more than twelve or thirteen and those assholes had raped them first and were now cutting on them.

At least three hundred of those Solar Red fuckers were there, either to participate or watch the sacrifice. I was ready to take out as many as I could but Dragon had some sort of control while I was mist, and he and I fought with each other while those girls died.

Take us home, now! Dragon issued orders when all I wanted to do was curl up somewhere and weep. He was dumped in the living room of the apartment; Karzac was shouting as I did it and I misted into my bedroom and blew the door shut with my mist.

"What happened?" Karzac demanded, examining Dragon for injuries.

"I'm not hurt," Dragon held his healer off. "She was about to take on three hundred priests who were in the main temple; they'd raped and then sacrificed two young girls. She's furious right now, but I don't think there was any way she could have taken all of them on and they would have seen both of us, I think. We couldn't risk it, so I forced her to come back."

Karzac cursed long and well in his native language. Dragon sat down heavily on the sofa—he hadn't liked what he'd seen any better than Lissa had. He wondered if he should send mindspeech to Pheligar and ask him to take her off the planet.

~

"Director, here are the reports and images from all the security cameras." Tony watched as his assistant placed several flash drives and a file of information on the desk. Watts was good at what he did and as discreet as they came. He'd been army intelligence before coming to work for Tony.

"Is there anything on these?" Tony tapped the pile of flash drives.

"There are images of several, but Rahim and Xenides both are on those from the Atlanta facility."

"Get those images extracted and run them through the software," Tony ordered.

"Of course. I'll have that done right away."

Tony opened the file to read through it. "Have there been any other sightings or anything new on those two?"

"A suspected sighting of Xenides in Barcelona, sir, but nothing concrete to go on."

"Do we have figures on the estimated deaths that might occur if there isn't enough flu vaccine?"

"You're not going to like it, sir."

"Give it to me anyway." Tony held his head in his hands.

"While the normal death rate is expected to be a quarter to half a million deaths worldwide each year, they're estimating two to five million this year, if the new strain of the virus is as bad as they think it might be and there isn't enough vaccine to go around."

"That's bad enough, but it could have been worse."

"That is correct, sir. The new vaccine will be late in coming,

51

obviously, but it should help some. That's why the estimate is as low as it is."

Tony shook his head. When had two to five million deaths become a low estimate? "What about the supply to the southern hemisphere?"

"Only a little of the tainted vaccine was shipped; the patients who received it are being watched closely but it is as we feared; they are exhibiting symptoms of the deadly anemia."

"What is the economic impact?" Tony wanted to pound his head against his desk.

"The Pharmaceutical companies are devastated, but the ones that manufacture over-the-counter remedies have experienced a boom."

Tony lifted his head. "See if there have been any major purchases of stock in those companies," he said.

"Of course, Director." Watts took the flash drives and walked out of the Director's office. Tony waited until Watts left before opening the top drawer on the left hand side of his desk and pulling out a framed photograph.

The photo had been taken from a security camera in the Atlanta office. It showed Lissa, holding a magazine. She had no idea her image was recorded and of all the images of her that Tony now had, he liked this one best. She had such a thoughtful look on her face as she stared off into the distance.

He figured she'd been thinking about the missing children in Great Britain; the headline on the magazine cover was about them, after all. Rumors were numerous, claiming Lissa helped bring the culprit down, although she'd been across the ocean at the time. He wished she were with him now and wondered where she was, exactly.

All his information said somewhere in Kent, but he couldn't get anywhere close before running into a brick wall of some sort—as if something were strong enough (and determined enough) to keep him out.

"Lissy, I'm sorry, baby," he apologized to the photograph. He'd even stuffed a personal note inside the envelope that held the President's commendation. Either she hadn't read it or she was still so angry with him that she refused to respond in any way.

He couldn't blame her, but that didn't keep his heart from nearly seizing in his chest every time he thought about how he'd arranged for her unconscious body to be violated. The ensuing results of that violation were far from comforting. Six men—top agents—were dying and there wasn't a thing he could do about it.

Larry Frazier was on a forced leave of absence. The research biologist was having difficulty dealing with it as well. He'd skipped vital steps in his eagerness to see results with human subjects instead of going through normal procedures and waiting to see if there were any dangerous side effects.

Tony toyed with the idea of contacting Weldon Harper but thought better of it; he might be in enough trouble with the Grand Master as it was. The vampires certainly weren't going to talk to him or allow him to contact Lissa. He was lucky Wlodek hadn't forced his vampires to leave the department.

The President was reluctantly advised regarding the status of the Paranormal Division and its potential demise—he'd studied Tony silently, wearing an expression of grim disapproval as he'd listened to the facts regarding the incident. The President was also disturbed over what would happen with the six agents. He hadn't fired Tony—not initially, anyway.

Lissa had kept the President, the First Lady, and the Secretary of State alive; now, due to Tony's foolishness, she was beyond his reach. Perhaps forever. Tony sighed, placed the photograph inside his desk drawer and closed it.

~

"What if I want to meet her?" Amara watched Griffin's face closely. Amara was Griffin's mate and had been for a very long time.

"You can't. Not now, anyway," Griffin said. "Part of the punishment, you know."

"That wasn't interfering. It's nothing compared to what some of the others have done."

"Amara, we both know that." Griffin pulled her against him. Amara was beautiful, with long, dark hair and almond-shaped dark eyes. Griffin had fallen in love with her the moment he'd seen her the first time. Nothing changed for him over the years. He still loved her as much as he ever had and she still loved him. "I haven't heard anything from Dragon or Pheligar and I don't know if I should ask. It might raise suspicions. They don't know I'm being punished."

"Like you'd care if they knew," Amara snorted, burying her head against Griffin's chest. Griffin stroked her hair and kissed the top of her head.

I walked the streets of Refizan's capital city through a moonless night. A part of me knew that Dragon was right; there wasn't any way I could have taken on three hundred priests. Not without being seen, anyway, and I'd had Dragon as a passenger. He was too important to expose to those shitheads.

Dawn was scheduled to come in another two hours of Refizan's twenty-eight hour cycles. Karzac and the other physicians at the hospital had managed to save the Vice-Governor, but the man was blind now; his body brutalized. He would be scarred physically and emotionally. As I might be, after seeing the bodies of those two poor girls.

I hoped they were in a better place. Many were the times I'd heard of some horrible thing done to the innocent and it made me want to take away the pain and fear they'd experienced before they died. For them, death had come as an escape from those things. Death wasn't always the enemy, as many people thought. It was what came before death that we should worry over at times.

I thought again about the disc that Pheligar placed on the back of my neck and found myself wondering how good it was and if I'd still drop over in a rejuvenating sleep when the sun rose. Sunlight wasn't capable of destroying my body, now. At least that's what I'd been told. I had mixed feelings about it, actually. If they left the disc there and it truly did work for a hundred years, the means of taking my life had been effectively removed. Was this a plot Griffin and Merrill hatched between them, so they wouldn't worry about me? I shook my head in confusion.

A dog barked off in the distance; I was now walking into a residential area and I scented the vampire before he reached my side. "What do you want?" I asked unkindly as his footsteps echoed mine on the concrete walkway.

"I haven't seen a female vampire on this planet in a very long time," he replied softly. I hadn't glanced at him at first—my nose told me what was necessary to know. I looked at him now.

He wasn't tall; perhaps five-eight or so, with a thin build and elegant, well-shaped features. Finely dressed, too—he wasn't wearing the usual loosely woven trousers and tunic. He wore a dark suit fashioned of expensive silk cloth; I could smell it. Blond hair was carefully brushed away from his forehead and dark gray eyes held mine for a moment.

"What would you say if I told you I wasn't from around here?"

"I think I would believe you," his eyes crinkled a little when he smiled. He was old—very old. Much older than Wlodek, even.

"Please tell me you're not in league with Solar Red," I said, looking away from him. We'd continued our walk while we talked; he shrewdly checked me out, just as I did him.

"Those criminals," he snorted. "We do what we can, but it is difficult to predict where they will be from one night to the next and we have to ensure we are not seen or suspected, else they will hunt us down during the day."

"Yeah. They're funny that way," I grumbled.

"I assume that is sarcasm, as I do not believe that Solar Red is amusing in any sense of the word."

"You are correct, sir," I said. "I am Lissa and I have only been here a few days."

"Lissa, I am Gabron and it would be remiss of me if I failed to notice that Solar Red's troubles have only begun within the past few days."

"I'm not at liberty to discuss that," I said.

"Do you have a particular destination in mind?" he asked as I walked aimlessly along.

"No," I sighed. "I don't even know where I am. I just saw something horrible earlier and I've been trying to get it out of my mind by walking."

"I also have been walking lately. Mostly I wonder what will be left of our planet if Solar Red has its way."

"Are there temples in other cities?" I halted and turned to Gabron.

"A few, but most are much smaller than the one here. The majority of their priests are concentrated here, in our capital city. They are attempting to get a better hold elsewhere, but they truly do not have a good hold here. They are making an effort to rectify that, and swiftly."

"I know," I nodded, beginning to walk again. Gabron discreetly kept pace with me. "Do you know why the Refizani government is so reluctant to move against this religion?"

"We have not had this sort of problem in thousands of years," he replied. "We are peaceful, have no army and are disinclined to believe that anyone might be capable of such evil. Few are willing to stand before these priests and denounce them as well; that creates a target, as you may have guessed already. What the Governor of the Realm must do is pass a motion to remove them from our planet, and with the legislative body often at odds with the Governor, this is not so simple a task."

"So, nobody can get together and move against them, is that what you're saying?"

"Sadly, that is exactly what I mean," Gabron nodded slightly. "And as you might suspect, there may be a few legislators who are accepting bribes from Solar Red, in order to champion their cause. Or to keep them away from their door—it no longer matters what reasoning they employ. I believe this is why the Vice-Governor was attacked; he spoke openly against these devils and nearly died for his troubles."

"Yeah." I understood that, all right. I'd seen his near-death first hand. "Look, I wish I had more time to talk, but I really should go home, now," I said. Dawn was getting closer. No vampire, no matter where they were, would ever be unaware of the sun's approach.

"If you will tell me where you live, I will walk you there," Gabron offered. I had no idea if he were being polite or if he just wanted to know where I lived so he could keep an eye on me.

"I honestly don't know the address; I just know it when I see it," I said. I didn't add that I knew it from overhead and not from the street.

"I understand your caution, little Queen. However, if you need anything or merely wish to talk, come to this address," he lifted a business card from a pocket and handed it to me. "Anyone there will honor your wishes if you ask to speak with me."

"Thank you," I said, accepting the card.

"Dawn will arrive soon," he reminded me, sniffing the air. "I must go to my own quarters now. I am very pleased to have met you, Lissa." He bowed politely to me and left my side in a blur.

CHAPTER 4

"$\mathcal{L}$ittle girl, are you only now getting back?" Karzac stood in the kitchen, having a cup of tea before going to work. He was already dressed in his Refizani version of blue scrubs.

"Yes." I flopped down at the kitchen table and looked up at him. His light brown hair was carefully combed, but it might look a bit wild when he came home. That's how it had been after he treated the Vice-Governor. "How long have you been a physician?" I asked.

"More than fifteen thousand years," he said, sipping tea.

"Holy crap. Really?" I wanted him to drop his shields sometime, when it was safe. I wanted to see what that scent might be like. "Do you know anything about Blackfan Diamond Anemia?"

"I do," he nodded.

"Is there a cure?"

"Only on a few advanced worlds."

"Dang," I sighed.

"Why do you ask?" Karzac was curious.

"Because an idiot let another idiot take my blood while I was unconscious and it was given to six men. They're dying now."

"They were attempting to recreate your talents in humans."

"Yeah. The schmucks." I was still angry with Tony. Wouldn't mind slapping him into a wall, actually.

"The results are promising for perhaps a month, before the disease makes its presence known," Karzac agreed. "Of course, they should have experimented on lab animals or used computer models before making the attempt on a humanoid."

"They jumped the gun a little," I grumbled.

"I must go to work," Karzac said. "And you must go to bed. I imagine you will not wish to wake in the floor come evening."

"No. It wouldn't be the first time, though." I got up and walked toward my bedroom. Karzac snorted a laugh behind me.

"How is Lissa?" Gavin watched as Merrill dropped his bag on the safe house floor. Merrill didn't often do this sort of thing—it generally wasn't required. Merrill and Wlodek both determined that Merrill should go—after all, they'd never had this kind of problem before. Saxom's vampire children had been in hiding for a very long time and Wlodek and the Council had no idea how many there were.

Gavin was beginning to realize what kind of chaos might come—Saxom had arranged for his vampire children to surface in the event of his death, in order to extract a terrible vengeance. Tampering with the influenza vaccine would have caused worldwide death and devastation had the tainted doses been shipped and administered.

"Lissa is doing well," Merrill sighed. "I heard from someone yesterday that she is performing above expectations." Merrill wasn't about to say that he'd gotten his information from Adam and Kiarra instead of Griffin.

"She always does that," Gavin muttered.

"I watch her, sometimes, and I know it irritates her greatly that she cannot make her own decisions," Merrill observed.

"It may have been different if her turning sire had been there from the beginning, placing proper compulsion for her to accept the five year confinement. Instead, she was free for several months without the benefit of a sire's instruction or supervision." Gavin set aside the folder of information he'd been studying. He and Merrill were in Barcelona; Xenides had been sighted there briefly and they were hoping to pick up his trail.

"I wonder if he placed any compulsion at all while she was turning," Merrill mused. "Do the Council's records reflect if any members asked that question?"

"I haven't seen them," Gavin said. "Perhaps we should look into that, if Wlodek permits. I only read through Lissa's files, not those of Sergio Velenci."

"I also did not look at his or Edward's," Merrill agreed. "And I have asked Charles to contact the appropriate sources in the U.S., to see if he can obtain her medical records when she was a child."

"You wish to delve further into the abuse at the hands of her father?"

"Among other things," Merrill agreed.

"Will you allow me to see what you find?"

"Of course. Perhaps it will help us know her better."

"Mr. Hoffman, you understand that this information is personal and confidential," Jennifer Stanfield informed Charles. She'd worked for Gerald Michaels for thirty years as his legal secretary, but Gerald was getting quite old and would be retiring soon.

Charles offered a tidy sum of money for the records from Gerald Michaels' legal representation of Howard Graham, Lissa's father. Charles told Ms. Stanfield that he was writing a book about Howard Graham as a fictional account.

The fifty thousand he'd offered her, with half paid in advance, helped make up her mind swiftly. The files were copied while she worked late and she'd just put the box in the mail, marked for next day delivery to a post box in London. She felt better that the duplicate files were leaving the country, after all.

"The rest of your fee will be delivered in two days," Charles assured her, hanging up. Charles learned that Gerald Michaels had obtained all of Lissa's and her mother's medical records before Howard Graham's case had gone to trial.

Mr. Michaels didn't obtain all of them legally, either—he'd paid for some of them under the table. This was a big case for Gerald Michaels and it was a major coup for him that Howard Graham had avoided the death penalty. Charles would have the information by the following evening.

∼

"Child, you should come with me, I think," René studied Aubrey's face carefully. "It may not be safe here—after all, I expect Bartholomew to carry my message to Xenides swiftly."

"Father, I don't believe I'm in danger," Aubrey replied. "This is my native country, after all. I'd like to stay for a time, should you permit."

"Of course I permit," René sighed. "I only worry for you." René and Aubrey sat on the wide porch outside René's villa in Spain, watching a sliver of moon rise over the trees. René didn't often visit the villa; he'd bought it a century before so Aubrey could comfortably stay in his country of origin.

Bartholomew had been in Barcelona briefly and René still knew how to contact him. Bartholomew dealt in information—for a fee, of course, and had contacts everywhere. René had no doubt that Xenides would have the information soon—René was claiming Blood Vendetta against Xenides for the death of Aurelius, his and Gavin's sire.

René desired to see Xenides die at his hand. Aurelius had been respected by all vampires. Aurelius, Wlodek, Merrill and a handful of others had laid the groundwork for the current laws governing the race. He'd been a founding member of the Council, but his death had come shortly after its creation.

René wanted to growl every time he thought of his sire's murder, and cursed himself for doing the odd theft for Xenides. All arranged through Bartholomew, of course.

"I leave tomorrow evening, child," René turned back to Aubrey. "Think on this. I will be happy to have you accompany me when I go."

"Father, I want to stay," Aubrey said.

"Very well," René sighed. "I will go back to England alone. I have additional arrangements to make. Others may lead me to Xenides; therefore I must make appropriate contacts."

"The festival of the god will be celebrated by Solar Red in three weeks," the journalist said, using the temple as a backdrop for her newscast. "The High Priest claims that the god himself may come for the ritual. As yet, the ceremony has not been described. We are attempting to obtain information."

"Great," I muttered as I sucked on a unit of blood. "Nothing like holding a ritual and nobody knows what to wear."

I retraced my steps from the night before and started asking for directions—I intended to find Gabron to see if he knew anything about the upcoming Solar Red shindig.

There was no indication as to what the business might be that was listed on Gabron's card, and I admitted to myself that I wanted to see this. After all, I'd never seen a vampire with a business card before. What I got, however, was plenty of stares and a snicker or two as helpful Refizani citizens pointed in what I hoped was the proper direction.

What had Gabron gotten me into? Was this a trick of some sort? The front of the building was tasteful; I couldn't see anything wrong with it and two men were walking inside ahead of me when I stepped through the door.

I learned right away what the snickers and stares were for—naked women wandered through a marble entryway or lounged around in suggestive underwear on chaises. The vestibule was circular, with a narrow doorway opposite the entry that led down a hall. More women, naked and semi-clothed, lazed in doorways spaced evenly down that hall. Well, I'd walked straight into a whorehouse. It made me think of Winkler for a moment.

A vampire sitting behind the reception desk lifted an eyebrow when I walked in, while the two men who'd preceded me struck up a conversation with two of the women. Maybe the men were regulars; how was I to know?

"I'm not sure we can help you here," the vampire was now walking toward me. He only stood a bit taller than I did, with red hair and a dusting of freckles across his nose. His blue eyes were his nicest feature. "The Over-Under House is five blocks away," he informed me, "and you'd more than likely be happier with what they offer, so I'd suggest," and that's as far as he got—he'd come close enough to catch my scent, drawing in a sharp breath. I thought he was going to fall on the floor and gasp like a landed mackerel.

"Briden, what's wrong?" One of the naked females came over and rubbed suggestively against the vampire. I figured she might be a regular blood donor, with some of those gallon pins tucked away in her jewelry box.

"Leska, I need to take this one to Gabron."

"We don't need any new girls," Leska pouted.

"Honey, I won't ever be a new girl. Or an old girl," I said. "If I'd known what this place was before I walked into it, I'd have stayed out." I almost turned and walked out right then.

"No, please, Gabron will be quite upset if he learns you left without speaking with him," Briden reached out to take my arm. I avoided his hand easily.

"Please, follow me." He was begging, now.

"Lead the way," I sighed, reluctance and unhappiness evident in my voice. Leska frowned at me as Briden led me down the hallway.

In addition to the women posing suggestively in doorways, we walked past several rooms with closed doors. With my vampire hearing, there was no doubt as to what was going on behind those doors.

Normally, I didn't have a problem with this sort of thing, as long as the female enjoyed her profession and I know many do. Gabron could have warned me, I think, before handing over a business card. This wasn't a place I felt comfortable walking into.

"Gabron, you have a visitor," Briden said softly after tapping on the last door at the end of the hall.

"Come," Gabron said, so Briden opened the door and ushered me inside. Well, now what? I was hoping to find other vampires, not a building full of hookers.

"Sir," I said, leveling my gaze on Gabron, "I'm actually sorry I came, so I won't take up your time." I turned to go. Briden appeared to be greatly disappointed.

"Don't you want to know about the Blood Council?" Gabron asked softly.

"If it's anything like the Council I'm familiar with, then the answer is no," I said, turning back to give Gabron an assessing stare.

"We are meeting in less than an hour," he said. "You may go as my guest and then we will discuss differences and similarities," he offered, touching fingertips together while he studied me with hooded eyes.

"And if I go to this meeting, do I have assurances that I will get out again?"

"You are distrustful."

"You know it," I said. "So far, I haven't met too many people who have done anything to earn or keep my trust. I'm sorry if that offends you."

"Little Queen, all I ask is that you attend a meeting with me. You may make your own decisions, always."

"You have no idea whether I'm a Queen or not," I said. The idiots back home certainly didn't know it and I wasn't going to disabuse them of that notion. All I needed was for them to declare me rogue again and send Gavin or one of the others after me. Actually, since Gavin shared my bed when he was home, all he'd have to do is flex those claws of his while I was asleep; he went to sleep later and woke earlier than I did.

"Lissa, then. It was not my intention to offend."

"Fine. I'll go to the meeting," I grumped. I was more than a little out of sorts, I think.

"That is all I ask. May we get you anything? Do you require blood? I can send someone in for you."

"No. I've had dinner," I held out a hand, politely refusing Gabron's offer.

"Briden, get someone else to handle the front desk," Gabron ordered. Briden nodded and walked out the door. "Please sit," Gabron offered a chair. I really didn't want to sit or do anything else except get the hell out of there, but I held my temper and my tongue and sat down.

"This is a good front for us," Gabron said, looking over a ledger on his desk and entering amounts on it from slips of paper at the side. "We own several such as this across the city. Brothels are legal here and we adhere to strict health and safety codes. All our employees choose this profession and are not coerced."

"I'm not judging your business; I'm just questioning my motives for being inside it."

"If you want a massage, your mate may give you one, but if you want something done by a trained therapist, you seek one out," he said, writing down more numbers. He wasn't looking at me while he said this.

"Are we talking massages, here?" I lifted an eyebrow.

"No, we are talking sex," he said.

"Just so we're clear," I returned. The corner of his mouth twitched slightly. "And I wasn't looking for sex when I walked through the door. I was looking for you."

"Would that you were looking for both," he sighed. I snorted at his answer.

Briden returned, opening and closing the door softly. "Briden, will you bring Lissa when it is time?" Gabron asked, rising from his seat, lifting a nice jacket off the back of his chair and slipping it over his shoulders.

"Of course," Briden nodded at Gabron. Gabron left the office.

As soon as Gabron was out of hearing, Briden turned to me. "I've never seen a female vampire," he said softly. "Who turned you?" He sat on the chair next to mine.

"He's dead," I said. "And he wasn't from here anyway."

"You didn't kill him, did you?" Briden was nearly aghast at the thought.

"No. I watched while he was executed, though. He didn't take responsibility for me and where I come from, that's a crime."

"Here, too," Briden muttered. "He wouldn't accept responsibility for you? In our culture, any number of experienced sires would have paid him if he agreed to hand you over to them. Any female turned would be a major gift to the race itself. Are females common on your world?"

"No, not common at all," I shook my head.

"Yet he refused to act as your sire?"

"It's a long story," I said.

"I would very much like to hear it, but we should go now," Briden said, rising from the chair beside me. I stood and followed him out the door. Briden unlocked and led me through a door at the end of the hall, then down another, dimly-lit hall toward a dead end.

Jumping lightly as we reached the back wall, (he must have touched a button somewhere) the wall itself slid aside. After we walked through, the wall slid quickly back in place. Not as fast as the doors on some of those sci-fi movies, but I wasn't sure how they did that to begin with.

Steep steps led downward; it would take a vampire to manage those stairs. We were in total darkness the entire way and only a vampire would see the narrow steps or manage the leaps across strategically placed chasms. The place was deep, I knew that, and we reached a cave eventually. Wondering if vampires everywhere had a cave stashed away for meetings, I followed Briden inside it.

This cave blew me away. The Council's cave outside London was good sized, but this could hold a real crowd. It was built like the old Greek theatres, in a bowl-shape with stone seats circling around and chairs and a table on the round stage at the bottom. I imagined that the acoustics were very good, too, so I didn't say anything as Briden led me inside. Heads turned and I heard gasps as he led me downward to one of the lower levels of seats.

Every vampire in the city had to be there, so many were present. I estimated at least a thousand. Were they all invited to the meetings? Our Council would have a conniption if somebody from the outside asked to attend.

We sat in the third row; the stage was still empty when we took our seats. Things quieted after a bit while eleven vampires made their way onto the round, stone stage and took their seats at the table.

Gabron was last and he sat at the table's center. Figures. There were so many vampires around me that I'd have to get closer to the eleven sitting at the table to sort out scents. I already had Gabron's.

Two vampire assistants walked onto the dais and placed communication devices in front of the Council members. One assistant stepped forward and announced the first order of business to the crowd—an application for a vampire to marry a human. I was seeing something much like the companion vote on Earth, except these laws were a bit different. The vampire himself sat on the first row and he rose when asked.

"This is your third human marriage, is it not?" A Council member asked. Gabron seemed content to listen.

"Yes. My other two marriages have been successful; you should have the information there. My last wife died at the age of two hundred fourteen. Her death certificate, listing natural causes, is submitted."

"We see this; this was twenty-seven years ago, is that correct?"

"Yes. I have been in mourning for a while and at first did not think to take another wife."

"Did the last one ever ask you to attempt the turn?"

"No, Eminence. She did not wish it, as she knew what the results were likely to be."

The Council member merely nodded—nobody else asked any questions. "Have the records on the female been reviewed?" Gabron spoke now. The others all said yes. "Very well, the vote will be taken." A large screen lit up over the Council, each member tapped in a vote, and all of their votes were listed, right beside their names.

That was different. They were all in favor, looked like. If Vilmos had been brought before the Council to give testimony on Earth regarding his companion, a lot of things might have been avoided, I think.

There was other business—fines were levied against one of the brothels because two of the girls decided to do a little work outside the walls, as the Council termed it. The girls had been fired and compulsion was laid. The one who'd laid the compulsions stood (he was also on the first row) and testified that the girls would not be releasing secrets.

There were a few Refizani-owned brothels, but I got the idea they weren't nearly as good as the ones the vamps had. I understood, too, what would have happened to the two girls if they hadn't had compulsion laid.

A few other things were on the agenda—mostly things that didn't matter—and then the heavy stuff came. A vampire was led out in cuffs. No chains, just cuffs, and one of his two guards (they were huge) held a thin metal wand.

The prisoner hissed at the Council so the wand was pointed, causing the cuffs to light up. The prisoner dropped to his knees, howling in pain. That made me wonder just what those cuffs might be and how they worked.

The prisoner struggled to his feet afterward when commanded, choosing to stand quietly in a designated spot on the dais. I doubted he wanted more pain from the cuffs he wore. Auburn hair hung in thick ropes down his back while deep-set eyes stared angrily at the Council, his mouth set in a cruel sneer. Not the kind of guy you wanted to approach in a bar, that's for sure.

"Hartolz, you have been brought before us, accused of killing among the population as well as aiding Solar Red. This resulted in the deaths of three priests at our Detector's hands so that our race might be protected—not just from the population but from the temple as well. How do you answer these charges? Remember to speak the truth." Gabron had stood for this one, placing compulsion. It reminded me a bit of what Merrill could do.

"They offered much money," Hartolz growled. "And a place as a priest afterward. They promised me blood and frequent sacrifices."

"Hartolz, I see that your last prison stay did nothing toward your rehabilitation," Gabron said, sitting down. "Does anyone else wish to ask questions? There were no questions from the Council and without realizing, I had my hand in the air.

"We will strike the prisoner's testimony from the record past this point," Gabron said. "Lissa, come forward and ask your questions."

I looked at the seats surrounding me. The aisle was far away and I'd have to walk around and disturb quite a few vampires to get where I wanted to go. Well, what the hell? I misted to the round stage, disappearing from point A and appearing at point B. That caused a few gasps in the crowd.

"What do you know of the ritual that is coming in three weeks?" I asked Hartolz.

Hartolz's eyes widened when he saw me, and then he blinked several times in astonishment. "Answer the question," Gabron commanded, compulsion heavy in his voice.

"Many sacrifices, on public communication," Hartolz replied, "so there will be no doubt as to who is truly lord of Refizan. I was not given information on exactly how it would be done, but the high priest was quite satisfied over the whole thing."

"Will this ritual take place during the day or at night?" I asked.

"In the evening. I was promised at least one of the sacrifices to show the people how great and powerful the priests are."

"Really?" I had nothing but contempt for this guy. I was close enough to smell the taint on him. He'd been hanging out with Solar Red too long. If werewolves could get a taste for killing, the vamps could get it, too. Hartolz had it bad. "How long have you been associated with Solar Red?"

"Six months," Hartolz replied.

"When were you captured?"

"Two days ago. I was sent out to investigate the disappearances of priests sent to pick up sacrifices from down the river. That's how I was apprehended." I wanted to snicker at his words but held it back.

"And did you find any evidence of the missing priests before you were taken?" I schooled my face toward non-expression.

"Some sailors on a nearby boat swore they saw the van with the priests inside it disappear."

"Did they, now?" I crossed arms over my chest. "Did you pass this information to Solar Red?"

"No. I was captured before I could contact them."

"Gee, that's too bad," I muttered sarcastically. "Did you ever get to see the god?"

"No. The high priest said that he did not want to lose my services."

"Yeah. I can understand that," I said. I wondered what vampire would taste like if the god gulped one down.

"I have never seen a female vampire," Hartolz spoke out of turn. He was around three hundred; I got a good whiff of his age.

"It's not likely you'll see another, either," I said. "I have no other questions. Thank you for your indulgence," I dipped my head respectfully to the Council and misted back to my seat.

"Very well," Gabron said, not even blinking at my disappearance. "We will take the vote, now." The votes racked up on the screen—all of them guilty. I wondered how they were going to do this.

I had mixed feelings when a section of the stone floor slid aside before the Council's table. Bright reflections of fire shimmered against rock walls as the circular stone cover rolled back. Cuffs were removed from Hartolz's wrists, compulsion was laid for him not to resist and he was shoved into the hole. The cover slid over the chasm quickly. I could hear a few screams before they were terminated suddenly.

Well, that was different.

"Is there further business to be brought before the Blood Council?" One of the two assistants came forward and addressed the crowd.

"We wish to speak with the Queen." Two vampires stood in the back.

"You must address the Queen yourself, we do not command her," Gabron said. "It is my understanding that she is merely visiting. Do not offend her."

"I want to invite her to my home," one of the two said. They were far enough behind me that I was having difficulty making out their features. Their words brought on a spate of hisses.

"Lissa, do you wish to respond?" Gabron asked. I really didn't—what was this guy planning? Dinner and a movie?

"I am quite busy," I said. "What are your reasons for inviting me?" I squinted, trying to see him better, but he was hidden behind a crowd of other vamps.

"Just to talk," the vampire said. More hisses followed that answer.

"I'm sorry; I really don't have the time. Perhaps we will talk someday." I turned in my seat to face the Council again.

"Briden, will you escort Lissa to the stage?" Gabron was taking charge, now. "The meeting is dismissed."

"I'll get us down there," I said, as vampires started moving all around us.

"How?" Briden's voice was cut off as I misted him to the dais where the Council members now stood.

Gabron and the two vampires who'd escorted the prisoner came to stand next to Briden and me. "We will go out the other way," Gabron said quietly, motioning the two guards to follow behind us. They herded me off the stage and through a side door that closed as soon as we got through it—the rest of the Council were already inside the antechamber.

"Lissa, tell me again that you are not a Queen," Gabron hissed.

"I never said I wasn't, I just said you didn't know that," I reminded him grumpily.

"I have never heard of any vampire doing what you just did," another Council member stared at me. Briden hadn't spoken at all; I think he was still in shock.

"And you probably won't hear of it again," I said. "Are we done?" I studied Gabron's face. Not a muscle twitched.

"I would attempt compulsion, just to keep you here for a while so I might ask questions, but somehow I get the idea that it would have no effect," Gabron replied.

"What questions do you have?" I didn't know if I wanted to hear them or not.

"Please, come this way," one of the assistants was there at my elbow and Gabron was already moving ahead of us, along with the rest of the Council.

~

"This is blood, mixed with wine," A glass was offered to me. We were still far below ground level but in comfortable quarters; it was someone's home and we were inside a spacious library. Shelves lined the cavern's walls, with sofas and chairs placed throughout. Low tables were scattered here and there, generally in front of the sofas.

"Please, sit." Gabron had already been served and was now attempting to get me seated in a chair next to his sofa. Other Council members were sitting here and there nearby, all within easy range to listen in. They all wanted to hear what I had to say. I just wasn't sure what or how much to tell them.

"You don't have to tell me where you're from, or how you arrived," Gabron said. "I only need to know whether you will be able to help us when the time comes."

"Help you with what?" I asked.

"With Solar Red," he replied, sipping his drink. "Please, try this, it is very good." I sniffed my glass, couldn't get any scent off it except blood and wine, so I tasted it. It was good. I'd just have to be careful; I knew what alcohol did to me.

"It depends on what you want to do," I said. "I'm all for getting rid of them and the quicker the better. But I have to tell you, they may be in league with something terrible."

"The god."

"He might be posing as a god, but he's about as far from that as anything I've ever seen." I sipped more of my wine-flavored blood.

"You have seen this?" Gabron's eyes bored into mine.

"I saw him eat four priests because they didn't do what he wanted," I said. "And then turned his henchmen onto seven other priests. They didn't last long, either. I have it on good authority that he's not something you want to come anywhere near. We should concentrate our efforts on Solar Red and leave that thing to someone else."

"If we work on the priests a little at a time, when the night of the ritual arrives they will perhaps call their priests in from the other temples. I wish for every one of these criminals to be present for the event, allowing us to go against all of them at once."

"How many do you want out of the way?" I asked.

"I imagine it will only require a few deaths," Gabron ventured. "I believe they are worried already, and will seek to pull together if just a few more die under unexplainable circumstances."

"I can handle that, no problem," I nodded. "How many priests do you think are in other cities?"

"My informants in other cities give me a number roughly equal to four hundreds," Gabron drained his glass and held it up. One of the assistants came and poured more for him, dipping his head in a slight bow afterward. Well, Gabron was Wlodek's equivalent on Refizan. I wondered what his official title was.

"So, you think we need to get rid of a few priests discreetly, so the others will be brought in?" Gabron wasn't bad looking, I decided. I wondered what he was like when he fought.

"Yes. I have heard rumblings through my spies. That discussion is already taking place within the temple. Many highly placed priests want to bring the others in now, but that suggestion has been tabled temporarily. With merely a few more deaths among them, that proposal will be raised again and enacted. These assassinations must be accomplished within the next two weeks so priests from other temples will have time to arrive and fit in as reinforcements."

"I see," I said.

"Of course, Solar Red will be searching already for those responsible in the disappearances of their missing priests, and those efforts will be increased, once more of them begin to vanish."

"Of course they will," I muttered. "Do you have any idea what form these searches might take?"

"Every citizen of Refizan is expected to have gainful employment unless they are physically or mentally incapable. Do you have such employment, Lissa?"

"Nothing, other than priest removal," I said. "What will they do, start checking IDs or something?"

"In a manner of speaking. Solar Red is exerting their influence on purchased legislators. This law has not been strictly enforced, nor have the authorities instigated a search for many years, but it will be implemented soon, according to my sources. And citizens are required to report anyone they see who does not appear to be employed or have the proper implant on their wrist." He tapped the underside of his own wrist; it held what looked to be a square of raised skin on it.

"Crap," I said. I didn't have one of those and wondered if Dragon or Karzac knew of a way to get one for me.

"I can arrange this for you, if you wish," Gabron offered, a corner of his mouth twitching in an almost-smile.

"Give me a little time," I said. "I may be able to do this myself. I'll let you know."

"Do it soon," Gabron told me. His gray eyes now held a warning. "And work must be arranged for you. I can place you on the payroll for our house upstairs."

"That might be the last place I'd want to work," I said.

"I would merely place you on the payroll, not expect you to participate," he offered dryly.

"If you knew my fiancé, even that's too much," I said.

"You are betrothed." He made it a statement.

"Yes. He's insanely jealous and I'm not about to lie to him," I said. "I really need to go. Do you have any other questions?"

"None, other than to ask you to meet me in my office in two days," he said.

"I'll do what I can," I said.

"Briden will see you out," Gabron nodded.

"How far underground are we?" I asked.

"Approximately seventy ticks," he replied. A Refizani tick was roughly equivalent to three feet. I could get through that easily.

"Briden doesn't need to see me out," I said, turning to mist right in front of Gabron and going straight through the ceiling of his library. The city looked so pretty and peaceful from high above as I made my way slowly toward the apartment.

Too bad Solar Red and the Ra'Ak had the planet in their grip. I didn't have time to do any sightseeing; I needed to get one of those ID chips and a job, I guess. If Dragon didn't have any ideas, I'd have to go back to Gabron and I sure wasn't looking forward to that.

Even taking things slowly so I could think, the trip back to Dragon's apartment only took ten minutes. When I became solid inside the kitchen, I found Dragon, Karzac and Pheligar waiting on me.

~

"Do our records reflect anything such as that?" Elidek asked Gabron.

"No," Gabron shook his head. He'd only seen one Queen during his lifetime and her qualifications were that she wasn't susceptible to compulsion and was a decent fighter. "I have only seen one other vampire who could turn to mist and two who had mindspeech. I wonder if she has that gift."

"You are the only one I know who now has that talent; sadly, there is no other with whom to share it," Elidek sighed.

"The Elemaiya do not come often to this planet," Gabron observed. "It takes their blood in some small measure, at least, to produce a vampire with those talents. My mother was a quarter, making me an eighth. I received mindspeech, along with strong compulsion. It is my understanding that the greater the amount of Elemaiyan blood, the greater the gifts. Our little Queen must have a great deal of that heritage and be of the Bright Elemaiya, just as I am. The Dark race creates criminals with the same talents at times."

"Why do they not come here? The Elemaiya, I mean."

"They are Travelers as you know, and they prefer those worlds less technologically advanced. We have had space travel for a very long time. They tend to stay away from those worlds. They are more in danger of discovery in those places. At least that is what my mother always said. If a child is half Elemaiya, they may choose with which race they wish to live. Should they be less than half-blood, the race will not claim them. If any of those become vampire, they make the finest turns."

"As you have proven, Prominence." Gabron shrugged at the compliment.

CHAPTER 5

"What's going on?" I asked, trying for nonchalance, even though I was shivering.

"There is no need to fear, little one; I am merely here to give you an ID chip and Dragon will provide you with employment at his business," Pheligar replied, already reaching for my right arm.

He had the tiny ID chip on a finger and just as he'd placed the disc on the back of my neck, he had the chip under my skin in no time flat and with absolutely no pain. Of course, I couldn't help staring at his blue skin while he did this. The only thing his skin didn't have was fluffy white clouds floating through it.

"What's the job?" I turned my gaze to Dragon after Pheligar released my arm.

"I run a self-defense studio," he said. "Which has seen increased enrollment lately. Mostly due to Solar Red, the disappearances, and other violence that the Ra'Ak have brought to this world. Unfortunately, you will be cleaning the studio after the classes."

"I don't mind; I clean pretty well," I said. "I've cooked for werewolves; was even a Packmaster for about thirty seconds not long ago," I added. "I'm a great bodyguard, too, if anybody needs it."

"I can see that you might be," Dragon almost smiled.

"I will go, unless you need additional supplies?" Pheligar asked.

"I have plenty of blood," I said.

"I have shielded your bedroom," Pheligar informed me. "If anyone comes to search the home, the entrance will not be evident."

"You can do that?" I was admiring this guy more and more, I think.

"Little one, your flattery is much appreciated, because it is honest," he said, smiling slightly before he disappeared.

"I will come to Lissa any time I wish to ask Pheligar for something," Karzac said, staring at the space previously occupied by the Larentii. "Your ID chip can be used to pay for anything you need," he added, tapping the raised spot on my wrist.

"When should I start my job?" I asked.

"Tomorrow evening; Pheligar has arranged the records, making it appear as if you've done the job for the past three months. Since I've owned the business, in fact," Dragon said. "I will come here on my break and take you to the dojo with me." He handed a chip key over. "In case you need to get in or to lock up and I am not there."

"Damn, why don't they wear jeans, here?" I asked, patting my loose-fitting clothing. I didn't have any pockets in my trousers.

"I have a chain; you can hang it around your neck," Karzac offered, heading toward his bedroom to get it. I hooked the chain through a slot on the chip key and then fastened it around my neck.

"I've been seeing priests at the restaurant near the hospital," Karzac informed me. "I think they are hoping to get word of the Vice-Governor's health since we do not allow them inside the hospital. They are concerned he might hand over incriminating evidence against them, no doubt."

"Those schmucks. I'll go check that out tomorrow night," I said.

"Remember not to give yourself away," Dragon warned.

"Hey, you're talking to a vampire, here. Wlodek, Merrill and Gavin would have apoplexy if I weren't discreet," I said.

"You know Merrill?" Dragon eyed me speculatively.

"Yeah. He's my surrogate sire," I said. "You know him?"

"Only peripherally, through Adam."

That was news to me. That meant I might have to be careful

around Dragon in case he wanted to carry tales back to Adam, who might then carry tales back to Merrill. Or to Griffin, who would then carry them back to Merrill.

"You have such a sad look on your face, little vampire," Dragon observed.

"It's nothing," I shook my head. "How much night do we have left?"

"Six hours," Karzac said.

"Good enough," I said, and misted away.

"She said that the first night she was here and then went out to kill sixteen priests," Karzac sighed when Lissa disappeared.

"I could *Look* to find what causes that sadness in her," Dragon offered. "But I hate to pry in case it is too personal." Dragon was referring to the gift that all Saa Thalarr possessed—that of reaching out and obtaining almost any information—it was something they'd been given in order to combat the enemy effectively.

The enemy also had it, up to a point. Neither could penetrate the other's shield to discover where they were. Each battle could turn into a lengthy dance, trying to locate the enemy in order to initiate a confrontation. The winner gained the planet.

If the Ra'Ak won, the planet would be devoured; they and their demon children survived on flesh and blood. If the Saa Thalarr won, they left the planet to its own devices and the Ra'Ak could not challenge again for at least a thousand years.

I didn't want to murder priests in their beds and that's where most of them were. The six I found awake were sitting in an office, drinking and laughing about the prisoners they'd tortured earlier. Those guys died so fast they didn't have time to be afraid.

I could have dumped them in the river nearby, but I didn't. I left their headless bodies inside the office before misting their heads to the temple's domed roof. I left the heads there; all six lined up in a neat row on an outside ledge where they grinned grotesquely at anyone approaching the temple. Then I went looking for their prisoners.

The prison cells were located beneath the temple floor and the captives I found showed fresh signs of torture. A few were near death. Altogether, I found fourteen people—both men and women. I wondered if any of them knew how to drive the vans the priests owned.

"Can you drive?" I stood before a man who sat dejectedly on the stone floor of his prison cell. At least he appeared mostly whole; I didn't think he'd been there very long. His six-by-six cage was at the end of a long line of identical cages beneath the temple's marble floors.

Gabron's library was more than two hundred feet beneath the streets. These cells were around thirty feet down and nobody cleaned —I got that right away. The smell of blood, mildew, excrement and rotten food offended my nose. It was extremely dark there, too, preventing the prisoner from getting a good look at me.

The only light in the entire place was a tiny bulb burning in a single socket at the opposite end of the cages. The walls surrounding the cells were formed of huge, sixteen-inch blocks of stone. There was no way for these poor schmucks to claw their way to freedom.

"I can drive," the man lifted his head and squinted at me, trying to bring my face into better focus.

"Good," I said. "Do you know how to get to the hospital from here?"

"Yes."

"As soon as I get some of the others loaded into a van, I'll take you out of here and you can drive them," I said, misting away to do just that.

I got seven in the first van before going back for the driver. He was shocked when I razored through his chains with claws that he couldn't see; he only heard the metallic chink of them dropping around him. "Go straight to the hospital," I placed compulsion after misting him into the front seat inside the van. "None of you remember who got you out," I added, watching as the driver took off; he pulled away from the garage where the vehicles were kept. Now I had to go down and talk to a second driver.

"I'm not sure this one's going to make it," I said, pointing out one of the women I'd found. God only knew what had been done to her. She was nearly naked, had brands and burns over most of her body and blood just about everywhere. It made me want to kill the six priests all over again—only slower this time.

The driver—a woman this time—shook her head. She'd been tortured but not nearly as much as some of the others. "You won't remember me," I said, closing the door of the second van so she could drive to the hospital. I was thankful the vans were solar powered and made no noise as they slipped silently away from the temple complex.

Misting overhead, I followed the last van until it reached the hospital. It was greeted by a horde of medical personnel under the porte-cochere. I went a bit lower and heard quite a bit of conversation concerning the first van and now this one. A lot of cursing, too, aimed at Solar Red.

The dying woman was taken in first on a gurney and almost at a run. I heaved a mental sigh and headed home. I hoped the authorities wouldn't take the vans; I'd been careful to close doors with my claws but who knew if they might pick up a stray fingerprint here or there? My bed was calling, dawn was getting close and I wanted a shower to get the scent of blood and bits of skin off me.

Karzac was up again, having tea at the small kitchen table when I came in. "Honey, don't you get any sleep?" I asked.

"I received a call—something about fourteen torture victims brought in with some needing my attention," Karzac said, his green-gold eyes studying me. "You wouldn't know anything about that, would you?"

"Who, me?" I pointed to my chest with a finger. Not that my bloody clothing wasn't a giveaway or anything. Carrying torture victims and placing them in two vans had ruined my outfit. Not to mention the flying blood I'd been spattered with after decapitation six priests. I'd put my last bloody set of clothing in the cooled trash collector, along with my used blood bags. This outfit was going in there, too.

"Go get your shower, I'd hate to find you in the bath with cold water running over you when I get home tonight," Karzac smiled.

"Honey, did you just make a joke? I'm so proud of you," I said, smiling brightly. "I'd hug you, too, but you're clean." That made him laugh out loud. Karzac left and I went to get my bath.

~

"Karzac says to tell you the woman didn't make it." Dragon informed me as we walked six blocks to his dojo where he taught self-defense.

"I didn't think she would; she was in terrible shape," I blew out a sigh. "This is probably better for her; she'd more than likely be maimed physically and emotionally if she did live over it. At least she died with nicer people around her."

I didn't want to say what I was about to say out loud while we were on the streets, so I used mindspeech as I explained to Dragon what I'd heard from the vampire prisoner the night before. Dragon received all the information I had concerning the impending Solar Red ritual.

He didn't know how they planned to do the sacrifices, I sent when Dragon asked.

How did you come by this information? he asked.

I attended the Blood Council meeting, I replied.

There are vampires here?

Duh.

I'll take that as a yes.

A good supposition, I agreed.

I cleaned Dragon's office, the showers and the dressing rooms as Dragon taught his last class of the day. There were several women taking the class, some of whom were there to stare at Dragon, mostly. Who wouldn't fall for those wide shoulders and the handsome face—

when he wasn't scowling, that is? Even a couple of the men kept their eyes on Dragon.

I think one of the young women was about to swoon when Dragon put his hands on her. He was all business as he proceeded to demonstrate a particular move designed to escape an attacker. The girl's hero-worshiping gaze didn't seem to affect Dragon at all. Ignoring the batting eyelashes and the attempts at flirting, Dragon helped her complete the move. The man was focused, I'll give him that.

I polished the wood floor when Dragon finished with the class, then rolled up the large mat they'd practiced on and swept and polished that part, too. The studio was one big room with a nice wood floor, half of which was covered with the padded mat, similar to that used by gymnasts. There were no windows inside the studio itself, with mirrors covering one wall.

"My office looks much better," Dragon said, coming out to survey the studio; I'd just finished with it. "I don't suppose you've ever swung a blade in your life?"

"No. Why do you ask?" I carried my broom and floor-polishing machine to the tiny closet where they were kept.

"I wouldn't mind sparring with someone and there isn't anyone available."

"Well, I could probably block okay. I think I could see your blows coming."

"You think so?"

"I can try. I saw you fight with your blades the other night, remember? Just don't expect too much from me."

"I have wooden practice blades," he said, going back inside his office. He brought out four wood practice blades that had decent handles on them. He even showed me how to hold them, telling me to parry with the flat of the wooden blade and not the edge. That made sense; you whack any metal edge, I don't care how tough the metal is, you're likely to nick it.

"Okay, have at it," I said. He came after me. I learned that Dragon could move pretty fast. It was my guess he'd been doing this a long time. A really long time. He was grinning after a while when he backed off for a breather.

"I'd like to see my brother's face if he had the chance to do this," Dragon said.

"You have a brother?" I asked. "Does he do the same thing you do?"

"No. He is immortal, though, and my twin."

"What's his name?"

"Crane."

"Ah. Does he have the decorations going, too?"

"If you mean the tattoos, then yes, he has cranes where I have dragons. Crane has been instructing students in the art of the blade for a very long time."

Dragon got the workout he wanted, I think. I managed to block all his blows. No way I wanted to get whacked, even with a wooden sword. He wasn't holding back after a while, getting comfortable with the fact that I had the strength (and then some) to handle what he could dish out. "We'll do this again," he said, wiping off the practice blades and putting them away.

"Whatever you say, boss. Now, if we're done for the evening, I have a few things to check into." I took off as mist.

The restaurant near the hospital had a bar and I discovered that there's nothing in Solar Red's religion to keep its priests from drinking, or even drinking heavily. There were four of the red-robed assholes sitting at the bar when I wandered in. They were drawing dark looks from some of the patrons, too; a few of whom were off-duty medical personnel.

Karzac, honey, are you still working? I sent. I was hoping he was at home, actually.

I am at home having a meal, he returned.

Good, I sent. *I think you need to turn in early.*

You would have made a good physician, he replied.

Nah, I used to freak at the sight of blood. The perfect person to become a vampire, I know.

The other torture victims you rescued are recovering.

I imagine the priests aren't happy about that. There are four Solar Red priests here at the restaurant, I informed him.

I ordered a glass of wine and sipped it while the priests drank their bourbon straight and glared at anyone who gave them more than a cursory glance. They were still sitting there, ordering more drinks when three people walked into the bar.

What happened next might have been the strangest thing I'd ever experienced. The man was tall—nearly as tall as Gavin, about as wide across the shoulders and Flavio was now the second most gorgeous man I'd ever seen in my life.

This one, though, had a scent about him that I'd never come across. Power radiated from him. He wasn't Ra'Ak; I'd know a Ra'Ak's scent anywhere and it was pure evil. This one—it was like scenting an entire planet at least, maybe a whole universe—with earth, oceans, mountains, snow, deserts, everything.

While I was working out in my brain how a single being could hold all that inside him, the two shorter men with him (at least I thought they were men, they looked a little androgynous) zeroed in on me. The tall man had to hold them back; otherwise, I think they would have run straight to me.

The man brought them to me at a walk and one of them dropped onto the floor right in front of me, started gabbling in a language I couldn't understand and then kissed my feet. That wasn't uncomfortable or anything.

"Honey, what's wrong?" I knelt down next to him and lifted his face in my hand. He was crying, as was the other one. Neither was much taller than I was, but one had dark-brown hair, the other nearly blond.

The tall man they were with had dark, beautiful, exotic features. I almost couldn't tear my gaze away from him to tend to the dark-haired one weeping on my shoes. I had to pull him up—he was kissing my feet again. "What's wrong with him?" I asked the man when I couldn't get the little guy to stop crying.

"Here." He tossed a credit chip onto the table for my drink and motioned for me to follow him away from the bar. I didn't like leaving my drinking priests behind—I had plans for them when they left. This was just too puzzling, though, and I didn't need the attention these three were bringing to me.

A few bar patrons were beginning to stare and whisper. Both small men hooked an arm through mine and escorted me behind the taller one. We found a table in a secluded portion of the restaurant and the two smaller men sat as close as they could get to me while the tall man sat across the table.

"I am Kifirin," the tall, handsome one introduced himself. "These are comesuli, or companions in your language," he informed me, indicating the two shorter ones. "Their kind has not seen a Queen in a very long time." I nearly froze at Kifirin's words.

"How would they know something like that?" I scoffed, not sure at all how the man had come by that information. It worried me, too—it could at best bring me unwanted attention and at worst get me killed. Somehow, I knew (without knowing how I knew it), that compulsion wouldn't work on Kifirin. He held confidential information—and my life—in his strong, long-fingered hands.

"If any mortal would know you were a Queen, they would," Kifirin replied smoothly. "The comesuli still teach their children that a Queen will come some day and rebuild Le-Ath Veronis."

"Le-Ath Veronis?" I had no idea what this man was saying. How did he know what I was and how did these two little guys? They were staring at me with adoration. I had no idea what to do with that.

"In your language, Le-Ath Veronis would translate into *Heart of the Vampire*." His dark eyes studied me, as if he were weighing my character and intentions. I shivered at his explanation.

"That information, loosely tossed about could get me killed," I snapped, angry in an instant. Frantically, I searched for any logical reason why these three would have information on me, as well as what they intended to do with it. All they had to do was hand my information over to four drinking priests in the bar nearby and I'd be on the run.

"As if I would harm one of my own," Kifirin snorted. I swear—a bit of smoke curled from his nostrils. "These two," he indicated his companions, "they would be your devoted servants and would die in your defense before any harm could be brought to you," he added.

"Honey, I don't have any idea what to do with that information," I muttered. A waiter came to our table and offered Kifirin a menu, placing others in front of the rest of us. Kifirin opened his and looked inside.

"In a little while I will come to you again and make an offer," Kifirin said, gazing at me over the top of his menu. "You may decide what to do with the information, then. In the meantime, it would mean the world to these two if you would bite them and take a bit of blood. The comesuli cannot have sex any other way; they have no genitalia."

His words shocked me more than a little. There were people who didn't have genitalia? "But you just said they have children," I pointed out, still unsure what to do. If I were capable of dreaming, that's what I'd imagine I was doing.

"A good Queen," he smiled and kept reading his menu. "They are self-sufficient in their reproduction. They develop a sac on their left side; the child grows inside that. When it is time, the sac detaches and the child makes his way out, similar to a lizard hatching from an egg. Now, these two want the bite."

"I can't bite anyone, this is a public place," I hissed, realizing Kifirin was serious. Meanwhile, the other two were begging with their eyes for the bite. "And stop saying that where anyone can hear."

"I am shielding us; no one will see, hear or approach unless I permit it. Go ahead, it will only take a bit of blood; this is what they were created for—to be companions to the vampires. They had a symbiotic relationship with them on Le-Ath Veronis. It rotates on its side, you know, so that the southern hemisphere is always in twilight. Perfect for the Veronis, wouldn't you say?"

He spoke to the two small men; they rose and came to beg in whatever language they had. They wanted the bite—were desperate for it.

"How long has it been since they, well, had sex, I guess?" I looked across the table at Kifirin. He'd set his menu down.

"These have never had it. It is only a tale to them, a myth, almost. The vampire is the only one who can do this for them."

"You didn't want to take them to one of the others?"

"Little Queen, you are the one I brought them to, with the anticipation that you might grant their wish. This will allow them to carry the tale back to the others. To give them hope."

"Hold on, honey," one of the little guys was rubbing against me, and it was almost like detaching a determined kitten from your clothing. Once they get those little claws into you, they don't want to let go.

"They are begging you, in their language," Kifirin coaxed as the two gabbled imploringly.

"All right," I sighed. "You're sure you have us shielded?" I was taking a big chance; I could see other people inside the restaurant. Why was I believing this? Reality had been suspended, somehow, and Kifirin seemed quite convincing.

"I do have us shielded," Kifirin smiled slightly at me. To be honest, once the little guys had gotten that close to me, I could scent their blood and it smelled spicy sweet, like cinnamon rolls used to smell.

"Come here, baby," I said, and took the dark-haired one by the neck, holding his head in my hand. The worship in his eyes was frightening in its intensity. I kissed him, causing him to moan softly, and then holding him tightly so he wouldn't struggle with the bite, I sunk my fangs into the pulse in his neck. His blood was the sweetest I'd ever tasted; warm and scented, it almost made me climax as well.

His orgasm was explosive. If this was truly the first time he'd had sex, I could see that. I didn't take a mouthful of blood, even, but he certainly got pleasure from it.

Kifirin helped me get the little guy back to his seat afterward. "They replace blood faster than any other species," Kifirin explained. The other one was now waiting, so I did the same for him. If I thought they worshiped me before, they really did now. "Can you make sure they eat something?" I asked. The priests were about to walk out the door and I was standing, preparing to go after them.

"I will make sure they eat before I take them home," Kifirin smiled at me. "Be careful, avilepha. We will see one another again."

"Thanks," I said, leaning down to kiss my two donors again before rushing out the door behind the priests.

These priests I handled differently. I hauled them off to the nearest city guard station, gave them compulsion to go inside and then instructed them to confess their crimes, along with forgetting they ever saw me. They nodded eagerly at me; it was easy to place compulsion since they were a bit drunk. I went home after that.

∼

"Dragon, have you ever heard of someone named Kifirin?" I asked the following evening as we walked toward his dojo. I was planning to meet with Gabron after I did my cleaning; the news had been all over the local stations regarding the four priests who'd confessed to killings and rapes.

The police were holding them, of course, but I figured their cronies might come and either try to get them out or kill them. Of course, the Solar Red temple was labeling the ones who'd confessed as renegades and no longer a part of their order. Regardless, the police now had information they didn't have before.

"I've never heard of someone named Kifirin. Kifirin is the name of the High Demons' planet. Where did you get that information?" Dragon asked.

"I just met someone yesterday who called himself that."

"Lissa, that knowledge is only known to a select few on this side of the universes," Dragon said. "It's likely an accident that he came across that name." I just hunched my shoulders and didn't mention it again.

∼

"Honored One, I know a call from me is likely unwelcome at this time, but I've had two hits on Lissa's information. One I'm sure you or someone you know ordered, but Xenides has thrown his hat into the

89

ring, I think." Wlodek had Tony's call on speaker and he, Charles and Radomir were listening.

"What evidence do you have, Mr. Hancock?" Wlodek frowned deeply as he flipped the gold pen in his fingers.

"Footage from a hidden security camera, records of a box sent to an address in London and a dead legal secretary."

Charles handed Wlodek a shocked look at that news; he'd gotten the box containing Lissa's records five days earlier. Xenides must have been right behind him in his search. "Do you have Xenides on the camera recordings?" Wlodek asked calmly.

"No, Honored One. I don't recognize this vampire. I can send a copy of the digital images, though; I still have the e-mail address I was given before if it's still good."

"How quickly can you send this?"

"I can send it now; it should only take a few minutes," Tony replied. "Why are they interested in Lissa, other than the obvious?"

"That is not something we are prepared to discuss with you," Wlodek replied, reining in his temper. "Send us the images; we will attempt to make identification."

"Sending now," Tony tapped on his computer. "Something else you may be interested in; my contacts have reported sighting Xenides in London, last night. I'll send those images as well."

"Very well," Wlodek said. "Any other information?"

"No, Honored One. I'll keep you posted on any updates."

"Good." Wlodek terminated the call. "Charles, get Merrill on the phone right away," Wlodek demanded. "And pull up those images as soon as they come through."

"Of course, sir," Charles whipped out his cell and was dialing numbers and tapping on the computer at the same time.

"Xenides may be in London; I've called for the jet," Merrill slid into the other side of the booth at the bar. Gavin looked across the table at Merrill.

"Are you ready to go, then?"

"After we pick up our bags. The jet is refueled so we can depart as soon as we arrive at the airport." Gavin rose and he and Merrill walked out of the bar together.

~

"That is Bartholomew." Charles was nearly breathless; he recognized the vampire that had taken the file from Gerald Michaels' office in Oklahoma City. The legal secretary's body was off to the side; he'd killed her by breaking her neck and then tossed her aside as soon as she brought the records to him.

"Our records indicate he walked into the sun two hundred years ago," Radomir muttered angrily. "That is why we stopped hunting him."

"We were led to believe that is what happened," Wlodek said as they watched the footage together. At least there was nothing incriminating done that would indicate the perpetrator had been vampire.

"And now Xenides most likely has Lissa's records. What is he looking for?" Charles asked.

"Probably the same thing we have looked for," Wlodek sighed. "We have already searched to see if she had sisters or brothers and there are none. Both parents are dead and there were no other marriages for either. Lissa's siblings might have had the same talents she holds, had there been any."

Charles didn't say anything. This had happened before, he knew, only not during his lifetime. That was why they had two sets of brothers as misters and mindspeakers—one brother had been turned initially, and when that one had displayed desirable talents, the brother was sought out and deliberately turned to enrich the vampire race.

The practice was a little-known and hidden law designed by the Council—the conscription of a human if their talents would augment the Enforcers or Assassins. Charles harbored the secret belief that even if Lissa had brothers or sisters, that none of them might come up to her level if turned.

"Merrill is on his way," Charles received a text as they reviewed the images sent by Anthony Hancock. Wlodek sat in his chair with Charles's computer in front of him, while Charles and Radomir peered over his shoulder.

"Is there anything concerning Lissa in those records that holds any importance?" Radomir asked.

"Tell him, Charles," Wlodek said as he watched the images again.

"The attorney for Lissa's father had a DNA test run; he paid someone at the hospital to draw Lissa's blood while she was there. Howard Graham wasn't Lissa's father. Of course, this information couldn't be used in court, it wasn't obtained legally and Howard Graham was still guilty of the murder and attempted murder," Charles shook his head. "We even had someone go to Howard Graham's brother and place compulsion to see if he knew anything about any affairs that Harriett Graham might have had, but he didn't know anything and never suspected her of doing anything like that. We've reached a dead end on who Lissa's real father might have been."

"He's likely dead," Wlodek muttered, turning to the images of Xenides that were recorded at Heathrow the evening before. Wlodek cursed softly as he watched Xenides walk right through the doors of the airport and disappear.

"He's after Lissa, isn't he?" Radomir observed. "He either wants her or wants her dead."

"She killed one of his own, right before his eyes in Washington D.C.," Wlodek agreed, leaning back in his seat and looking up at his youngest child. Of course, that youngest child was more than a thousand years old. "Now he wants her, more than likely for his own sick purposes."

"Where is Lissa now, father?" Radomir didn't know.

"Somewhere safe," Wlodek replied. "Xenides has no hope of reaching her for the moment. We may be forced to take steps to ensure this remains true." That statement worried Charles, but he kept his thoughts to himself.

~

Watts ushered the man into Tony's office. Deryn Alford hadn't seen the inside of this office before, so he looked around a bit while Watts discreetly scuttled through the door, closing it behind him. Tony finished tapping out the end of an e-mail, hit send and looked up. "Hey, bro," he said. "Feel like a trip to London?"

CHAPTER 6

"*L*issa," Gabron inclined his head as I materialized before his desk. I'd misted through the place; it was called Blue Desire. I'd learned that much, at least. Kifirin was on my mind again, and the mystery of him and the two companions he'd brought with him chased through my brain, much like a puppy chasing his tail. I wasn't destined to catch those thoughts anytime soon in order to examine them fully.

"Gabron," I nodded back to him.

"Please sit," Gabron held out a hand, offering one of his guest chairs. I sat. "We want to come out in force against Solar Red on the evening of their ritual, as you know," Gabron began. "But there are certain factions within the vampire hierarchy that must be appeased before they agree to participate."

"What kind of appeasement?" I asked.

"The two who wanted to invite you to their home during the meeting?"

"What about them?" I asked.

"They are demanding that you attend a gathering held in your honor."

"They need to lose that idea," I said. "I'm not much on parties."

"Unfortunately we may have to cooperate, to prevent them from passing information to the opposition."

"Good grief," I said. "Don't they have any brains? And what will you and the Council do if you learn that they've done something like that?"

"Oh, if we still live, we'll bring them in on charges. But it will be too late by that time. The city may have already succumbed to Solar Red."

"I'm not going to bed with anybody, not making out with anybody, not sucking up to anybody," I said. "And I don't have anything suitable to wear. Fuckers." I felt like misting away, right then and there.

"You may have to explain your terms," Gabron said. "What do you mean by sucking up?"

"Flattering them," I muttered. "Convincing them they're more wonderful than they are, or even wonderful to begin with. I don't like being coerced," I added.

"Neither do I," Gabron agreed. "Nevertheless, it may keep them happy and give us needed numbers when the ritual takes place. I cannot command you to do this, Lissa, but it will be better for all of us if you accept the invitation. I will make sure they realize that sex is out of the question."

"Please do," I said dryly. No way I wanted to rub against somebody I didn't know. Not to mention what Gavin would think about it. I almost wished he were with me, just to keep the others away.

"If you will come at fourteenth bell tomorrow evening, I will take you to the location," Gabron interrupted my thoughts. "There is also something else I'd like to ask you, little Queen."

"What is that?" I watched his face; he was curious about something and desperate to learn the answer, I think.

"How much Elemaiyan blood do you have? I have an eighth, but that only allows me strong compulsion and mindspeech. I greatly desire to know if you are full Elemaiyan, or nearly so."

As questions go, that one was completely unexpected, bordering on shocking. "What are you talking about?" I blurted. Elemaiyan? I'd never heard that word before.

Gabron was almost as surprised as I was. "You did not know? Only vampires of Elemaiyan descent are able to mist or mindspeak. Others of that race have been reported to have additional gifts as well, but I have not seen these myself; they are only legends here. Obviously, you belong to the Bright Elemaiyan race; the Dark Elemaiya always have black hearts and become criminals when they are turned. I have not seen any of those in a very long time."

"How can you tell the difference?" I asked, feeling frightened by Gabron's descriptions.

"You can't; both races have the same coloring and features. It is only by their actions that you may tell, once they become vampire." I stared at Gabron for several minutes, sure that somehow the two must have different scents or some other way to tell the difference. And why hadn't I heard of them before?

"Where are they from and how do they become vampire?" Those were the next questions on my list.

"They are known as Travelers on many worlds, or Elves, even, although that label is very wrong. The only known race of Elves keeps to themselves and do not wander as these races do. The Elemaiya have the talent for world-walking through gates that they can sense between the worlds. They prefer worlds that are not technologically advanced—they have a power of their own and choose to rely on that."

"And you're saying that I have their blood?" I was skeptical, to say the least.

"You must, your talents indicate this," Gabron's eyes were hooded, now. "You were not aware of this?"

"This is the first I've heard of it," I said. I wasn't sure I should believe any part of it, anyway.

"The Elemaiyan race is a strange one, although our ancestry rests there," Gabron steepled his fingers and watched me as he spoke. "They are capable of reproducing with the humanoid races, as you can see. However, if the child is less than half Elemaiya, the race will not acknowledge it, turning the child out after it is grown."

"So, if one of the parents is half and has a child with a human, then that child is forced to leave? That sounds a little harsh," I said, still not sure I accepted any of Gabron's tale.

"My mother was turned out at age sixteen," Gabron nodded. "She was a quarter as you may have deduced, and her own mother forced her to go. She never recovered from that rejection."

"How long do the Elemaiya live?" I asked.

"They are one of the immortal races," Gabron said softly. "That, in my opinion, explains why they turn vampire so easily; something in the blood accepts it more readily than the other races. I can see that I may have shocked and upset you with this information. Nevertheless, it is true, little Queen. Think on it for a time and if you have questions, please come to me. My mother taught me much about the race."

"All right," I nodded. "I will be here tomorrow evening at fourteenth bell. What should I wear?"

"Wear whatever you like, this is an informal gathering," Gabron informed me. "It was good seeing you again. Would you like me to walk you out or will you leave in the same manner as last time?" He was smiling now, I noticed.

"I'll get myself out," I replied and misted away from him and Blue Desire.

"This is where the perimeter lies," Tony held a GPS locator in his hand; he and his brother Deryn had traveled into Luddesdown and gone past it, following the signal on Tony's small device. "Every signal we received stops here. There were tags in her luggage; I placed them myself and not all of them should have stopped working at once."

"You're serious about this, aren't you?" Deryn watched his half-brother's face as Tony frowned at the GPS screen. Tony had never been involved with anyone before, except casually. He was always too tied up with his work; he always gave that his full attention.

"I want her, bro. Not only for me, but because I think she has the best chance against these terrorists we're hunting." Tony placed a hand on his brother's shoulder. "She's a vampire, Deryn. And not just any vampire. Weldon Harper calls her Pack and she's a member of the Sacramento Pack, too. Now do you know who I'm talking about?"

Deryn's eyes widened as he stared at his brother. Now he knew why they were out in the middle of the English countryside in the dark. They wouldn't find a vampire awake during the daytime and it would be dangerous to move one anyway, during that time. No wonder he'd seen a body bag in the trunk of the rental Tony was driving.

"Bro, you can't be serious; we can't kidnap a vampire—they'd shred us. And if it's the one Dad told Mom and me about, she'd really shred us." Deryn figured he would have to convince Tony to forget this mission.

"All we need to do is find where she is, just before dawn. Then, when she falls asleep, we'll just take her with us. I don't think she'll hurt us, she's not that way," Tony said, climbing inside the car. "Here," Tony tossed his cell phone over when Deryn slipped into the passenger seat. "Find a hotel or bed and breakfast someplace close."

Xenides observed the member of the Vampire Council carefully. Saxom had pointed this one out to his eldest vampire child, telling him to approach her if assistance was ever needed. This particular member hadn't been on the Council at the time—she was selected to take Saxom's seat when he'd been eliminated. *All the better for me,* Xenides snorted softly. He and the others now had a mole on the inside.

"Wlodek has that one closely guarded while she is inside the country," the female Council member paced restlessly. "Merrill is her surrogate sire, but I'm sure you have that information already."

Xenides didn't have that information but his expression failed to reveal that fact. Merrill would be difficult to kill. Saxom had always been wary of him, but Xenides saw no reason to fear. He'd use whatever means necessary to lure Merrill into a trap, like so many others he'd destroyed.

"The girl is susceptible to compulsion; she will be easily manipulated," the female Council member laughed. "The little fool."

"And yet her remaining talents are formidable." Xenides watched the female pace; they'd met on neutral ground—an old hotel on the outskirts of London. Xenides arranged for the room and notified the female afterward, giving the time and place for the meeting.

The Council member's jealousy of the younger female was evident to him. Her petty emotions mattered little. Information was Xenides' objective and he might arrange to have her killed if the death could remain hidden. She'd already given him every scrap of information she knew. No matter. She was contemptible and beneath him and his mission.

"Promise me her death when you are done with her," the female member stopped pacing to offer Xenides a hard look. Xenides smiled.

~

"Grand Master, I wouldn't have come to you if I weren't so concerned." Lucas Alford sipped coffee inside Weldon's study. It was late and Weldon's son, daughter-in-law and grandson were asleep in another portion of the house. Weldon was still awake and talking with the Second from the Denver Pack.

"You think they've gone to London to track Lissa?" Weldon was worried about the same thing, but didn't want to reveal his concern to Lucas.

"Yes. Their mother is terrified and you know what the Council might do if they find out."

"They are not the most forgiving race," Weldon agreed, staring into his own coffee cup for a few moments.

"I don't think we can afford to anger them any more than we already have," Lucas went on. "I have no idea what Tony was thinking when he did what he did."

Weldon didn't know either, and had Tony Hancock not been as highly placed as he was, Weldon might have sought justice for Tony's acts himself. Lissa was Pack and she'd been violated. He'd toyed with the idea of pulling his wolves out of the special division of the FBI. Daryl, Weldon's son, had pointed out that the information garnered through those wolves had been invaluable from time to time. For the moment, Weldon judiciously left those wolves where they were.

"What do you suggest I do about this?" Weldon asked. He had a good idea but waited to hear what Lucas had to say anyway.

"Do you have anyone in the area who might be able to keep an eye on those two? Maybe stop them from doing anything foolish?" Lucas didn't expect anything from the Grand Master, but felt he had to ask anyway.

He'd raised both those boys, although only one was his natural son. Tony was two years old when Lucas met Corinne, Tony's mother. Deryn had come along two years later. There wasn't that much difference in the boy's ages.

"I might have someone," Weldon replied, after appearing to give the matter a bit of thought. "I'll make some inquiries and let you know. We have a bedroom prepared for you, and I'm a little tired myself," Weldon yawned to get his message across.

Kipp and two other wolves would keep watch on the cabin through the night. Weldon had gotten wind of the trouble that might be coming and was taking no chances as a result. Lucas Alford rose and Weldon led him out of his study and down the hall to the guest room.

"You're sure about this?" Rear Admiral Dennis Hafer shut the folder his spy handed over. If the gathered information was correct, Anthony Hancock could be blackmailed or exposed unless the female agent was offered to him. The Admiral had plenty of uses for her; he didn't care who or what she was.

Hancock had allowed his pet research biologist to experiment on six special ops agents. Now, all six were dying of a rare disease. Hafer merely had to leak this information to the press and things would blow up immediately surrounding the Director, the President and a few other top officials. The Admiral smiled grimly. He intended to get what he wanted, one way or another, and he wasn't above using any means necessary to achieve his goal.

"Where is Hancock now?" The Admiral asked.

"Out of the country. In the U.K., I believe," the spy replied.

"Can we have him followed?"

"Easily," the spy agreed.

"There is no need to worry that anyone will attack or compromise the building while we're here or at the manor," Merrill informed Gavin as they dropped their bags in the vestibule. Merrill had ordered their driver to deliver them to the flat they'd used before in London.

Gavin watched as Merrill relaxed his guard once they were inside. It was a four-story brick, but only the first floor was used as living quarters; the rest was used for storage and parking. The underground portion held several vehicles, some of them vintage and worth quite a lot. Merrill pulled out his cell phone and made a call to Franklin. It was still early—not yet nine.

"We're fine," Merrill assured his human child. "How are Greg's treatments progressing?" Gavin listened in on both sides of the conversation—he knew Merrill wouldn't make the call in his presence if he desired otherwise.

"As well as can be expected; Greg's taking medication to keep the nausea down, but that only goes so far. He's doing all right at the moment," Franklin's voice was muted through the cell.

Gavin tuned out the rest of the conversation—Lissa was the one he wanted to speak with, but she'd been sent on a secret mission. Wlodek refused to give details and that frustrated him. He couldn't imagine where she might be that she couldn't risk taking a call now and then. A low growl escaped his throat just thinking about it. Gavin located the refrigerator in the kitchen and helped himself to a bag of blood, grumbling mentally as he drank.

Franklin placed the cordless phone in its cradle and turned to Greg. "You don't think Lissa will mind if I borrow this?" Greg held up her Louis Vuitton carryall. It was one of the bags Charles had given her shortly after the Council found her not guilty.

"Lissa would give it to you if you wanted it," Franklin smiled. Lissa wasn't much on possessions; he knew that. He and Greg were taking their trip to Las Vegas; that's what he'd told Merrill while they were on the phone. Merrill offered the jet and Brock to fly it, but Franklin had already booked first class tickets. The doctors had given a cautious go-ahead for Greg to make the ten-day trip.

"Lissa would give us anything," Greg nodded. "It's just the way she is. I'm still only borrowing the bag." Franklin walked over and kissed his mate.

~

Dragon and I sat in the small office inside Dragon's dojo. The local constabulary had come calling to check our IDs. Our wrists were scanned, the computer records checked and I was doing my best to emulate the vampire mask of indifference.

My cleaning had been interrupted for this and now the cop was asking Dragon questions. He couldn't find a thing wrong with our IDs or computer records; Dragon sent mindspeech, telling me that Pheligar the Larentii was very efficient at this sort of thing.

"So, you purchased this business three months ago? Where did you live before then?"

"My records indicate that I was off-planet. My birth planet is Falchan, as I'm sure you've been made aware. I'm obviously not local," Dragon pointed out. There wasn't any doubt about that; his Asian good looks weren't Refizani by any stretch of the imagination.

"And your reasons for relocating here?" The local cop wasn't giving up. I wondered if he were on Solar Red's payroll, mentioning that to

Dragon in mindspeech. He didn't even bat an eyelash when I sent him my question.

He is, good catch, Dragon returned. I don't know how Dragon gets his information so quickly, but at least we knew what the local cop was digging for. He was about to get a little taste of compulsion.

"Mr. Tatsuya here has answered all your questions," I put my own mojo on, looking the cop in the eye. "He saw a business opportunity and took it. He doesn't do much besides providing eye candy for the women he teaches. I'm his cleaning lady. That's it. Goodbye, Mr. Streetbrick." What a name, but it was on his badge.

"Thank you for your time," the man nodded, his eyes still clouded by my compulsion. He gathered his data recorder, placed it inside a pouch he slung over a shoulder and left.

"That was outstanding." Dragon gave me a hug as he and I stood. I went back to my cleaning and promised Dragon I'd lock up so he could go home and eat something. Changing later after a quick shower in the locker rooms, I headed toward Gabron and Blue Desire.

"Little Queen." Gabron smiled and tucked my hand in his arm. He led me through the same door that Briden had taken me through before, only we took a different route this time.

The vampires held the entire underground beneath the Refizani capital city. Karzac informed me it was called Ordinandis and was quite surprised when I told him I didn't know where I was. Well, Pheligar hadn't handed me a road map or an atlas to the place when he dumped me in Dragon and Karzac's apartment.

"There are more than thirty ticks of solid ground beneath the streets and nothing under the buildings has been tunneled through," Gabron informed me as we traveled a path through warrens and passageways. Every few feet we passed a massive column of natural rock or concrete, supporting the ground above us and holding everything in place. Seems the Refizani vampires had some talented engineers among their numbers.

"So the vampires have created most of this?" I watched Gabron's face. We were currently on level ground so he turned and smiled at me a little.

"Yes. Over centuries we have done this; being careful, always, to make sure there is enough support for the upper ground. If something new is placed and we determine that it isn't solid enough beneath, we either fill that in or convince the authorities to build elsewhere."

"Where are we going now?" I asked.

"There are other meeting places besides the Council theatre," Gabron replied. We walked for nearly an hour before coming to a narrowing and then to a wide, formal-looking doorway. There had to be at least six hundred vampires inside the hollowed-out chamber beyond, all there waiting for us.

Is every vampire here? I sent to Gabron, who turned and absolutely beamed at me when he received my mindspeech.

Little Queen, it has been thousands of years since I was able to mindspeak someone, he returned. *No, not every vampire is here. These are the eldest and our elite. They all wanted to meet you.*

This brought to mind the annual meeting that I'd gone to last year in London, emerging from it engaged to Gavin. I hoped this wouldn't turn out to be something similar.

I was given so many names as we made our way into that huge, hollowed-out chamber that I stopped trying to associate names with scents after a while. "This is one of our hosts," Gabron introduced me to the next one and I held my hand out automatically before getting his scent.

Thankfully, the automatic gesture probably saved us—for the moment, anyway—the vampire was radiating nastiness and it was all I could do to smile and say it was a pleasure to meet him. His name was Mirazal and I was sending mindspeech as quickly as I could to Gabron as I took Mirazal's hand. He kissed my palm, making my skin crawl and then itch furiously.

Gabron, something's wrong and Mirazal knows what it is! I was desperate for him to believe me. The vampires at home would have brushed it off with an *are you sure, Lissa?* Or, just given me a stare while ignoring what I'd said. Gabron did neither. Instead, he smoothly intervened.

"Mirazal, you will tell me now just what evil you and Farimak have planned." Mirazal could no more ignore that compulsion than he could walk in sunlight without being fried.

"Solar Red is coming. Farimak is leading them in," Mirazal parroted. I could tell the words came against his will and Gabron was about to gather the other vampires and get them away when the lights went out.

The lights going out wouldn't hamper vampires, but it was what the sputtering of the lights heralded that created the panic. The caves surrounding us were being imploded; we could all hear the booming sounds of detonations, along with the crashing of rocks and earth as they collapsed around us.

Then, the floor beneath our feet began to shake and dust and dirt sifted down over our heads. Chaos was now prevalent inside the chamber and we were in danger of being trampled.

Grabbing onto Gabron as quickly as I could, I went to mist and lifted both of us over the heads of six hundred frightened vampires. The shaking around us became worse; rock, dust and the occasional brick or small boulder fell among those still standing on the floor, so I sent mindspeech to Gabron.

Are they going to blow this one, too, do you think?

It is possible. He was doing his best to remain calm, even though he was mist and unable to do anything for himself. Many vampires were being trampled underfoot, trying to get out the one wide doorway, which had nearly disappeared beneath rubble from the outside cavern. Once the door was completely blocked, the floor beneath the vampires began to buckle. *Time to take action.*

I'll give the vampires props for not screaming much. There were a few shrieks while the explosions were going off but mostly there was a panicked exodus toward the door, resulting in some being knocked down and injured. I, on the other hand, was just about to see how many vampires I could carry as mist. It turned out to be most of them.

My nose became my best ally that night in gathering vampires. If they smelled tainted in any way, I left them behind, gathering up the others instead. In all, I picked up five hundred forty-seven vampires (I didn't learn this until later when Gabron told me) and carried them, first through the ceiling of the cave and then out and over the streets.

We watched from overhead as a huge bowl caved in beneath us, blowing a tremendous cloud of dust and debris skyward. Any vampire left inside that cavern died. I now had the name of a new enemy—Farimak. He was on my list of the next to die if I had anything to say about it.

Gabron, where do you want me to take you and the others? I'd thought about the Council Chamber but didn't know where it was from above.

My library, he returned. I knew where that was; I'd come out of there and would recognized the building from overhead. I flew in that direction and in less than ten minutes I was above the building, listening to more than five hundred vampires scream mentally as we descended right through the roof.

We then streamed downward more than two hundred feet until I was surrounded by the bookshelves in Gabron's library. Hoping that five hundred vampires could sort themselves out, I dumped them in the widest space inside Gabron's huge collection. Some of them ended up stacked a few deep, but they were alive.

Gabron took charge, thank goodness, and ordered some to separate the injured from the others so they could be treated for their wounds. I helped as much as I could and Briden, who appeared out of nowhere, heaved a huge sigh of relief when he saw that Gabron and the others were all right.

He found water and medical supplies; what was needed for vampires, at least. A few present had some sort of medical experience —they were helping set broken bones. Vampires are a hardy bunch and aside from being a bit grumpy over the whole thing, they came out all right. The broken bones and other injuries would heal during their next rejuvenating sleep.

Gabron pulled me away after a while and all the Council members followed silently behind.

A hidden room behind a heavy shelf was where I was taken; Gabron's palm was what it took to get us inside and away from the others. It looked like a war room to me, with electronic maps of the city shining across a lengthy, glass-surfaced table. Chairs surrounded the table as we all took seats.

"Farimak will believe we are all dead, unless we lead him to think otherwise," Gabron began. That was exactly what I'd been thinking, so I didn't interrupt. "Therefore," Gabron continued, "we will remain dead for the time being."

"How will we feed ourselves? There are more than five hundred, out there." One Council member gestured angrily toward the library itself.

"I have stores set aside," Gabron sighed. "I was afraid that Solar Red would take the city and we would have to provide for ourselves while we fled. I have enough in the chamber behind this one to feed us for nearly a month. It is frozen at the moment, but that can be remedied."

"Then my most persistent worry is averted," the Council member visibly relaxed.

"Your assignment is to go out and inform the others that we will remain in hiding until the evening of the ritual, allowing Solar Red to think they have crippled the vampires," Gabron continued. "With these five hundred or more gone—our most powerful vampires seemingly killed through treachery—the others who are left will be leaderless and abandoned. We must allow them to think this and give no indication otherwise. It is only for a short while, before we will be free again and rid our city of the taint that grows within it. Are there any objections or alternative suggestions?" Gabron surveyed his Council. I think they all saw the wisdom in his words—nobody said anything.

"Good. Go perform your duties. Place compulsion if you must. Lissa and I have an errand to run." All the council members were still covered in dust from the explosions and cave-ins and looked as if they were mighty grumpy on top of all that, but they rose silently and walked out the door to inform the others.

"Lissa, we must go to the Solar Red temple," Gabron turned to me once the others were gone. I'd sat quietly beside him while he talked to the others.

"As mist," I nodded. I think he and I were on the same wavelength.

This was such a welcome change from dealing with Wlodek and the others. I think he and I both knew that Farimak posed the greatest threat to us, and more than likely Solar Red had imprisoned him after the cave implosion.

Who knows what plans they had for him—after all, they'd not shown any sympathy toward his co-conspirator, Mirazal, leaving him to die inside the chamber with all the others.

I also wanted to check out the damage around the cave-in; a street ran overhead but there were buildings nearby. I wanted to see what was being done and if the warrens and caves surrounding the cave-in were in danger of being discovered. Farimak came first, however.

"Are you ready?" I asked Gabron.

"Yes," he jerked his head in a curt nod. I didn't want to be Farimak, right then. Gabron was angry and had held that anger back until now. I turned to mist, pulled him into my mist and went through the ceiling like a rocket.

"She's fine," Dragon patted Karzac on the shoulder. Karzac could *Look* for himself, but was afraid to do so. News crews were already covering the scene and while the general population had no idea that vampires existed, Solar Red was now consenting to do interviews, alerting the population that there was an evil among them and offering to give evidence at the ritual.

Dragon snorted at the announcement; Solar Red was threatening to expose the vampires to give the citizens a common enemy; one that Solar Red would be more than happy to help eliminate in an effort to gain a better hold on the planet.

"They won't even realize the vampires have been living among them peacefully all this time," Karzac grumbled. "Solar Red will describe them as terrible monsters, when they themselves are the ones." He walked into the kitchen to make a cup of tea.

"The population is unsettled and Solar Red will take advantage," Dragon agreed.

It was too bad that Farimak hadn't known I could mist through walls and ceilings. Only the Council had witnessed that little trick and I had the notion that Gabron might have ordered them to keep quiet about it. Now, not only five hundred vampires or more had survived what should have killed them all, but at the moment, we were dropping through the roof of the temple in order to find Farimak—the treasonous little bastard.

It wasn't easy. I even hauled Gabron into the small torture chamber where the Vice-Governor had been held, but Farimak wasn't there. There also wasn't anyone inside the cells where I'd rescued prisoners. Guards were posted in both places, however. They must have been expecting someone more solid—Gabron and I misted right past them.

It wasn't until we started making our way through the offices, (of which there were many) that we found our culprit. He had cuffs on; the same kind that had been on Gabron's prisoner when I'd attended the Council meeting. No doubt, that's where they'd gotten them to begin with. It made me wonder just how much Hartolz had spilled before he'd been caught.

We found five priests and two guards inside the office where our duplicitous vampire was being held. Farimak sat in a chair against the inside wall, with all the guards' eyes glued to him and watching avidly, waiting for someone to come. Someone had come, all right, but with this many witnesses, perhaps we needed to be a bit more subtle. *I have an idea,* I sent to Gabron, and misted outside the room again.

There was an empty office directly behind the one that held Farimak and the others. I dropped Gabron inside it. *I'll be right back,* I promised mentally. He nodded. I had done this twice before, but both times I had been extremely angry. Now it was time to see if it could be done when I wasn't so angry I couldn't see straight.

I'd blown my mist outward the first time and knocked the front out of Galloway Recycling in New Mexico. Then I'd blown the door to my room shut in the same way when Dragon and Karzac were less than receptive to vampire help.

Perhaps the priests weren't prepared for that entire section of the building to get blown outward. I wasn't, either, but that's what happened. We were close enough to the outside of the building that the wall itself now had a huge hole blasted in it, and office windows were all knocked out as well.

Office contents, consisting of papers, bits of furniture and parts of priests now littered the paved courtyard outside. I was going to have to gauge this better the next time, I figured. My little blow-up achieved the desired results, however. The priests surrounding Farimak, along with one of the guards, came rushing out to see what happened.

I misted right through them as they boiled out of the room—the last one turning and locking the door behind him. I laughed mentally as I went right through the locked door, hauled Farimak and the remaining guard into my mist and then went through the wall behind them, gathered up Gabron and got the hell out of there.

CHAPTER 7

The Council was convened again as soon as Gabron and our two prisoners were dropped off inside his map room. Gabron placed compulsion right away, and then straightened his rumpled suit.

The man had been hauled around like a misbehaving child all night and never said a word. The guard sat in a corner on the floor, blank-eyed and slack-jawed. Utilizing compulsion, Gabron had taken away what little intelligence he might have possessed. He'd be killed elsewhere. Perhaps his blood would be taken—I didn't really care.

I stood in the opposite corner and watched while Gabron and the others questioned Farimak. The vampire actually seemed relieved to have them as judge and jury. There was no telling what Solar Red had planned for him, and had likely informed him at length of those plans.

Fear was another of Solar Red's weapons, and Farimak had been terrified when we'd found him. Solar Red hadn't planned a swift death for him; I was sure of that much.

"How much did you tell them?" Gabron demanded. Honestly, I think Gabron was going to deal justice himself on this one. The compulsion he laid was nearly as good as anything Merrill might do.

"They knew about us already," Farimak's answer was surly. "From other planets. They've done this before—revealed the vampires and the werewolves so they could pretend they were protecting citizens from monsters."

That didn't come as welcome news to me. How many vampires had they destroyed? How many werewolves? I shuddered at the thought and wanted to ask Dragon to see if he had an answer. Unfortunately, that would have to wait.

"So, instead of warning us, you were prepared to help them," Gabron's voice held contempt.

"They promised us the run of the vampire community," Farimak whined.

"Did you tell them about me?" That question just popped into my head.

"No. Mirazal was supposed to pull you out; he and I decided to keep you for ourselves."

"As if I wouldn't have anything to say about that!" I crossed my arms over my chest and glared at Farimak.

"We were going to go to the god and ask for help," Farimak muttered.

"Did you see the god?" Gabron was angrier, now.

"No. The priests kept promising that we would, though."

"Trust me; you don't want to see that." I stood there, shaking my head in disbelief at Farimak. "I watched him gulp down priests like candy, you stupid fuck. Then he sent his little soldiers toward the city to bite people and make more little soldiers. That is no god. That is an evil, and you wanted to see it."

Farimak's eyes widened. "You saw this?"

"Yes. I saw that," I nodded. "And if he'd seen me, I wouldn't have survived either. More than likely, those Solar Red priests were waiting for the ritual so they could toss you in front of the crowd and show them just what you are. Then they would have tortured you. You haven't seen what they've been doing to the people inside their little altars and prisons. I have. They cut up the Vice-Governor and branded him across his eyes. The man will never see again. Or be whole. I watched two young girls get raped and mutilated before they died. This is what you want to place in power over the entire planet? Is that what you want?" I tossed a hand in the air in disbelief.

"How do you know all this?" Farimak looked at me skeptically.

"You're more stupid than you look," I muttered and misted right through a wall to get away from his ignorance. Gabron could have this one. He was dumber than a doorknob.

❧

"The Queen has spoken," Gabron said. "Does anyone else have questions for Farimak before I behead him?" A few hands were raised and the questioning began.

❧

Wishing I had Gavin's talent for languages so I'd have more curse words at my disposal, I slammed the kettle onto the burner to make tea. Some sort of normalcy seemed to be required at the moment; it was still an hour before dawn and I was exhausted and wound up at the same time.

"Lissa, you may want to slow down; I don't have time to buy a new kettle," Karzac walked into the kitchen, still half asleep.

"I'm sorry, I didn't mean to wake you." I took a chair at the table and covered my eyes with a hand.

"You didn't. I had to get up to go to the hospital," Karzac assured me, pulling out a cup for himself and setting it beside mine on the kitchen counter. "Tell me what happened tonight."

"Damn, I didn't even get a chance to go check on the damage," I grumped, finally remembering *that*.

"It's a huge hole in the ground. No reported casualties. Not humanoids, anyway. Did vampires die?" Karzac lifted the boiling kettle off the flame and poured hot water over tea leaves in both cups.

"A few," I said, watching him calmly make tea. He set a cup in front of me and we both waited for it to steep. "The bad ones," I continued when Karzac didn't say anything. "I got the rest out."

113

"And how many was that?"

"More than five hundred, I think."

Karzac is a good physician, even if he is a little on the curmudgeonly side. "Are you well? Do you need assistance?" he asked, doing his best to give me a visual once over without appearing too obvious about it.

"I'm okay," I said, sipping my tea. "There were a few broken bones among the others, but there were enough vamps there that had experience with that, so the injured vampires were taken care of. They'll heal with a good sleep."

"How did you get that many out?"

"By turning them to mist. Karzac, Solar Red wants to expose the vampires so the people will be afraid of them and not Solar Red. Are there any werewolves on this planet? They might be targeted, too."

"No. The werewolves were exterminated long ago. There was a race war for centuries and the werewolves lost that battle. It isn't often that the two races can coexist upon the same world."

"Too bad," I said softly. There were many werewolves I liked very much. I'd hate to see them taken down.

"As you say," Karzac nodded and drank his tea. I offered to make breakfast for him but he pointed to the time, suggesting that a hot shower might help before I went to bed. He was right. What I didn't expect, however, was to find Kifirin waiting inside my bedroom when I was done.

"I only want to make sure you are well," he said, his angel's face filled with concern.

"But that doesn't explain how you're here inside my bedroom. Did Dragon or Karzac let you in?" I had fists on my hips, glaring at him.

"Little Queen, you have nothing to fear. Get into bed before you fall over with the sunrise," he pulled the covers back. The bed did look good, but not while he was standing next to it. He laughed as the thought crossed my mind.

"If it will make you more comfortable, I will leave. I only wish to do what others do—is 'tucking you in' the correct phrase?"

"Tucking me in? Kifirin, I don't know what you are. You smell like snow and flowers in meadows. And waterfalls, maybe, with a volcano thrown in. I don't know what to do with you and I need to go to bed or you'll be picking me up off the floor."

"We cannot have that," he was laughing suddenly, and just as suddenly, he disappeared. Well, as exits go, it was a darn good one.

~

"This stack I have been able to eliminate from the suspect list," constable Streetbrick laid a pile of papers onto the High Priest's desk. "This stack contains the questionables."

Seturna Phipik thumbed through the stack of questionables; there were about fifteen of them. "Very well," he pulled a drawer open and held out a flat folder. "The codes are on the sheet; you can transfer the funds to your account immediately."

Constable Streetbrick left the priest's office, feeling elated. He could do so much with the added funds. He was nearly off the property when Seturna Phipik ordered him followed and killed.

The guard who took the order bowed smartly to the High Priest and left the office in a hurry. A second guard was handed the papers containing names of questionable new citizens. "Check every one of these and kill any that seem suspicious to you," The Seturna ordered. The guard nodded and followed the first guard out the door. "Good, imbecilic hounds," The Seturna mumbled to himself, stuffing the list of names that checked out into a desk drawer before turning to other things.

~

"René, I'm afraid I have bad news," Wlodek spoke over the phone. René was in London and checked in regularly with Wlodek through his private number.

"Honored One?" René barely kept the surprise from his voice.

"Radomir just contacted me from Barcelona. He and Russell are attempting to pick up Xenides' trail there, but in the course of their investigations, they were led to your villa outside the city. Local police were already investigating the death of a human housekeeper there—is that correct?"

"Alejandra is dead? Why have I not heard of this?" René was uncharacteristically upset. "I do not understand why Aubrey has not informed me of this. He and Alejandra are quite close."

"That is the difficulty, René," Wlodek said quietly. "The local authorities failed to find the ash, but Radomir and Russell recognized it easily enough—Aubrey was killed as well. Now, I have heard rumblings that you declared Blood Vendetta against Xenides. While I am in agreement with your reasons, Aubrey may have been murdered in order to harm you."

René remained silent for several seconds, attempting to get his emotions under control. His Aubrey—dead. And in retribution for his declaration of Blood Vendetta? Xenides was more of a coward than he'd thought. René growled low. "Honored One," René said after a moment, "I will do whatever I can to bring this criminal to justice. I have attempted to make contacts with others so I might track him. I want him dead. I want him more than dead—I want him tortured, mindbroken and dead."

"René, Aurelius did not teach you to torture."

"Yet this one is responsible for Aurelius' death."

"I will appreciate your efforts to track Xenides—we must cooperate in any way we can to bring this terror down. I curse the day Saxom was made and I curse the sire that made him," Wlodek hissed. René listened as Wlodek expressed his anger.

"Now, Saxom's whelp Xenides is likely carrying out his maker's last command—to destroy all of us. We must find him and his collaborators first, René. I will contact you if I have information that might benefit us both. At the moment, Anthony Hancock is also chasing after Xenides. Perhaps we will profit from his collaboration."

"He desires our little rose. That is why you hear from him." René snorted derisively.

"Nevertheless, he is providing valuable information. We cannot discount that, regardless of his purpose. I will keep you informed. I

suggest you send someone else to your villa to collect Aubrey's ashes
—Radomir placed them in an urn and left it in your suite, there."

"Tell your child I thank him for his efforts," René sighed and
hung up.

~

Lissa? Gabron's voice was echoing in my mind the moment I woke.

Gabron? What do you need? I felt as if my eyes were glued shut and
my mouth had a horrible taste in it.

Lissa, I am sorry to wake you. I only wanted to make sure you were safe.

I'm safe, honey. Is that all?

You call me honey? Why is that?

Honestly, I wasn't sure I would ever get the hang of Refizan, its
language or its people or vampires. *It's an endearment, not an insult.*

You are calling me an endearment?

*Honey, I call all kinds of people honey. We're not going to pick out
matching towels now, I assure you.*

Pick out towels?

Never mind. Where are you? I'll come as soon as I get dressed.

*I will be in my library. Do not feed, I wish to provide for you when you
arrive.*

All right. I turned off the mindspeech and went to find my clothes.

Providing for me turned out to be one of the girls from Blue
Desire. Well, it was warm blood as opposed to cold and most likely an
insult if I were to refuse. "I prefer women," the girl said when Gabron
urged her toward me. Well, then, I'd give her the best orgasm I could.
She enjoyed it right down to her toenails, which were painted pink
and curling when I took from her.

"Thank you," I told her as she planted a kiss I wasn't sure how to
return. Gabron shooed her away after that, so I thanked him, too. It
was polite.

"The guard was only that and had no knowledge," Gabron got right
to business as I sat down on a nearby sofa with him. He might have
wanted me to scoot closer, but I didn't. There was a foot and a half

117

distance between us and I was satisfied with that. Yes, I liked Gabron. And maybe in another life, he and I might get close. Just not this one.

"Farimak was only interested in his own gain and did not bother to listen to conversations and such—he allowed Mirazal to handle those things. You were correct in your assessment of him, Lissa. He was indeed more stupid than he looked."

"Who knows what they might have done to him," I said, leaning back against the sofa, and allowing my head to fall back. I stared at Gabron's ceiling—artificial lights hung from iron chains at regular intervals. They weren't bright lights, but were tasteful and decorative. Gabron scooted closer.

"Lissa, he no longer has to worry about such things," he said softly, reaching out and touching my hair lightly.

"Gabron, please don't ask for something I can't give," I turned my head to look at him.

"Lissa, please don't stop me from trying for something I want very badly," he replied. As replies went, that one was pretty good.

"I need to go to work," I showed him my new implant.

"I noticed that yesterday," he was still touching my hair, curling a short strand around a finger. Just as a mental side trip, I wondered how many frustrated erections I'd caused since becoming vampire. Gavin alone would account for quite a few, I think. It had to be my scent. I couldn't think of any other reason.

"Thanks for dinner, honey," I patted his cheek and misted away.

"Do you think you might help me with demons when you finish?" Dragon was wiped. Off-day was tomorrow; at least he'd get some rest (I hoped). Karzac would be working since he'd been off last time.

"Yeah. Let's go kick demon butt. Slice off a few heads. Toss priests into rivers. That sort of thing." I was sweeping the floor as I spoke.

"Just demons tonight, Lissa." Dragon smiled tiredly.

"Honey, you look exhausted," I said. "Why don't you just tell me where they are and I'll go."

"I'm not that tired. The classes are just getting too large to handle, that's all. I have to start turning students away."

"Don't know how to say no, huh?"

"Not to the females. Many of them are desperate—they have children and they want to be able to protect themselves and their offspring."

"Have those assholes been taking more kids?" I stopped sweeping.

"Up the river," Dragon mumbled.

❧

"I don't believe this. Drive faster," Tony was nearly shouting as his brother drove through the English countryside, speeding toward London. Tony had the small tracking device in his hand; it began beeping half an hour earlier and now they were on the road, following along.

"They must be sending her somewhere else," he grumped as Deryn did his best to merge onto the highway toward London, discovering it was the M20, which soon branched off to the M26, and from there to the M25. "They're going toward Heathrow," Tony said excitedly, pulling out his cell.

❧

Rear Admiral Dennis Hafer sat in the passenger seat while his temporary assistant drove like a bat out of hades to catch up with Director Hancock's car. His assistant operated as a part-time spy, but he was also a Navy man and discretion itself. "I believe they're driving to the airport," the spy commented, weaving in and out of traffic on the M25.

"They can't have caught up with her already," Hafer muttered. They hadn't seen any evidence of it, but how could he know for sure? He was positive they'd holed up at the bed and breakfast they'd rented; Hancock and the other man hadn't done anything except drive around and sightsee for the past few days.

119

Hafer wasn't interested in who the other man was; probably an agent from somewhere that wasn't likely to be recognized. "Don't lose them, man," Hafer grumped as they swerved around yet another slowly moving van.

~

"Is Hafer still following us?" Tony spoke with one of two agents who'd been following the Admiral.

"Like a mosquito after a meal," came the reply. "We've got him in our sights; he doesn't even suspect." The agent had placed a tracking device on the Admiral's rental early on.

"Don't lose him and keep me posted," Tony ended the call.

The drive into London finally caught them up with the Cadillac emitting the signal; Tony got the tag number, running it through his database. It was registered to Franklin Wright, who held a residence in both New York City and a small house in Luddesdown that didn't appear to be occupied, much of the time.

Obviously, Franklin Wright wasn't vampire; he was driving during the day and his identification listed him as sixty-three years of age. No vampire would look that old.

Deryn let Tony out of the car at the airport so he could follow the two men discreetly. They both looked in their sixties, Tony thought. He made another phone call as he watched them check in, discovering his quarry was traveling to Las Vegas. He also saw that one of them carried a bag Lissa had used. Tony was going to give up the search, but not before he misdirected Hafer.

"Get me a ticket to Las Vegas," he told his agent on the phone. Hafer would have the information almost as soon as the ticket was booked, Tony figured. Then, when he knew that Hafer would also be traveling to Las Vegas on an alternate flight, he would leave the airport, have Deryn pick him up and they'd drive straight back to Luddesdown.

~

The woman was terrified when she was brought in. Wlodek might have felt some sympathy for her—she couldn't be more than twenty-five, if that, but she did have connections to Xenides. Gavin and Merrill had managed to pick her up, along with Llewellyn, a long-time thorn in Wlodek's side.

Llewellyn was nearly as old as Merrill and was a holdout for the old ways. He'd refused, time and again, to acknowledge that the Council served any useful purpose at all and had scoffed repeatedly at the laws created to govern the race. Wlodek suspected Llewellyn of killing humans upon occasion while drinking from them; he was also a holdout on the bagged blood issue. Wlodek lost contact with him for the past century and only now had the rogue resurfaced.

"It was a fluke," Gavin explained as the girl was directed to one of the cells inside the high security prison complex maintained by the Council. "Merrill and I heard a rumor that a man died outside a pub only recently, his throat slashed. The authorities said the man bled to death. Of course we went to investigate, in case Xenides might have had a hand in it."

Throats were often slashed to hide the fact that blood had been removed from the victim before they died. If a pint or two was missing, who might go looking for it amid all the other blood that was in the alley or on the carpet?

"Explain, please, before we question the girl," Wlodek nodded to Gavin and Merrill, taking a seat behind the desk in the office.

"We didn't find evidence of vampire involvement in the murder," Merrill said. "Gavin and I went inside anyway, to ask a few questions. Gavin went to speak with the bartender while I sat down to wait."

"That does not explain how you captured these two," Wlodek observed. "How was this accomplished?"

"With this." Gavin held up his money clip, handing it over to Wlodek when the Head of the Council reached for it.

"What are you doing with Llewellyn's money clip?" Wlodek asked, examining the gold clip that had two rows of round diamonds on the end. It also had the initials LLM engraved on it, for Llewellyn Leroyce Millard.

"It's not Llewellyn's," Gavin coughed softly. Vampires didn't embarrass easily, especially old vampires, but this, well...

"Then whose is it?" Wlodek's dark eyes studied Gavin. Merrill almost snickered.

"Mine," Gavin confessed. "Lissa bought it and had it engraved for me."

"It's because he keeps asking her if she loves him," Merrill did chuckle, now. He'd listened in on enough of Lissa's phone calls to know. "She had this made up for him. The initials mean Lissa Loves Me."

"And this is how you managed to collar a vampire I've been hunting for more than two hundred years, along with Xenides' human toy?"

"That pretty much sums it up," Gavin nodded. "Xenides instructed the girl to meet Llewellyn at the pub; he was going to be carrying something with his initials. I bought a pint for myself and Merrill so we'd fit in after questioning the bartender; the girl saw the money clip when I pulled it from my pocket to pay for the pints."

"Of course Gavin didn't know what the hell she was talking about when she called him Llewellyn, but I overheard from the table we'd taken. When Llewellyn walked in thirty seconds later, I had him under compulsion immediately. Gavin grabbed the girl, placed compulsion and here we are."

Merrill wanted to laugh; it was absurd in the extreme and couldn't have been more perfect. He might have collared Llewellyn when he spotted him, but the girl was a bonus. Neither he nor Gavin would have known to take her if she hadn't thought Gavin was Llewellyn.

"Quite fortuitous," Wlodek wanted to smile, too, but held back. "I will ask Flavio and Susila to come in and sit with me while we question the girl. Llewellyn will be questioned and then brought before the Council. I will try to arrange this so Lissa may attend."

Merrill nodded; he knew Wlodek wanted to use Lissa's nose in this matter; there were no records on Llewellyn's sire and he wanted to know if Llewellyn had Saxom's taint about him.

Merrill pondered that for a few moments. Lissa could smell

Saxom's taint. His eyes flew wide and he gasped. Wlodek turned quickly to him. "What is it?" he asked.

"Our girl has been holding out on us," Merrill was smiling again. "Because she's afraid, more than likely."

"How have we frightened her this time?" Wlodek steepled his fingers.

"Because we're all male," Gavin interrupted, causing Merrill to gape, almost. Gavin gave Merrill a level look. "It's true," he said. "She has no reason to trust any male. I have been thinking about this for some time, now. Her father—well, the one listed as her father, nearly killed her, after killing her mother. What have any of us done to earn her trust?"

"She doesn't trust vampires in general," Merrill offered.

"I wish to go back to the point Merrill was making," Wlodek turned back to his eldest child.

"Lissa doesn't just smell the taint from Saxom's get. If Saxom stood in front of her, she'd recognize him. She can smell the blood, Honored One. More than likely, she could tell you who your vampire children are, even if you'd never told her."

Wlodek raised an eyebrow at Merrill. He and Merrill knew exactly what that meant—that Lissa knew that Wlodek had turned Merrill. He swore softly. "Do you mean to tell me that all these turns that we suspect are someone else's—that she might be able to give us the truth of the matter?"

"I think so," Merrill nodded. Wlodek swore again, a little louder, this time.

"I beg you not to punish her for withholding this information," Gavin said.

"We will not," Wlodek huffed. "But this information is not to leave the room. Just as she can tell the ages of vampires, that information remains with us as well."

"Agreed," Merrill smiled. Gavin nodded.

"We just have to find a way to let her know that we know, without frightening her or making her fear that she will be punished for this," Wlodek toyed with a pen on the desk. It was a simple ballpoint—not the gold fountain pen of which he was so fond. "Will you attend the questioning of the girl tomorrow evening?" Wlodek asked Merrill and Gavin. They both agreed on ten as the appointed time.

～

We found twelve demons near the river this time, headed straight into the city. *Do you think they brought them in by boat?* I asked Dragon through mindspeech.

It's possible, he returned, drawing his blades. I'd carried Dragon in as mist again and we set down off to the side. The wind was blowing behind the demons; Dragon told me they could scent us if we came from that direction. Taking them completely by surprise, we had half of them down before the rest turned, snapping and snarling, to fight us. Dragon carried on a mental conversation this time, while he lopped heads.

Baby demons still look humanoid, he informed me. *And they're stupid. They only know to follow their master's orders and will only turn away from their intended target if they're attacked. They will transform to their demon shape after three weeks or so. It takes that long for the demon to incubate and assert itself. Then the outer skin splits, allowing the young demon to emerge.*

And they're so attractive, I sent, my sarcasm evident even in my mindspeech. Dragon grinned as he decapitated the last demon with one quick swipe of a blade.

We went back to the apartment as mist, but found that we had callers. Karzac stood in the doorway, trying to convince two men to leave. They were asking for Dragon. That meant we had to go back out, rematerialize and walk up the stairs to the second floor where our apartment was, surprising the two men.

"Ah, Sursee Tatsuya," one of the men nodded. "We wish to speak with you in private."

"What do you want?" Dragon asked, shouldering them aside so he and I could enter the apartment. They followed us right in without an invitation. Karzac scowled and muttered as he closed the door behind them.

"Anything you wish to say to me, you may say in front of my roommates," Dragon growled. He didn't like uninvited guests, I could tell.

"Well, uh, we wanted your help," one of the men said uncertainly.

"We want to get rid of Solar Red," the other man blurted.

"I don't know what you expect me to do about that," Dragon said. "It is time for you to leave." He walked back to the door and opened it.

"We just thought that with your talents, you might be able to help us," one of the two said as the other man grasped his arm and pulled him toward the door.

"Hear this," I was in front of them immediately. "What you propose is dangerous, and it will get you killed. You will forget this idea," I laid compulsion. "And you will not approach Sursee Tatsuya again. Go home and protect your families. Go now." The two men nodded like bobble head dolls and walked out of our apartment. Dragon shut the door. "Fuck," I sighed, bumping my head against the doorjamb afterward.

Lifting my head, I looked at Dragon. "How far is the next city upriver?"

"Less than fifty miles," he said.

"How much night do I have left?" I asked Karzac.

"Four hours," he replied.

"Good enough," I said, and misted away.

~

There were fifty priests at the Solar Red temple. Sleeping or not, they all died and the children they held in underground cells were gathered up, all six of them, and taken to the nearest hospital. The oldest was twelve, the youngest three.

I remained invisible while sending them through the sliding glass doors of the emergency room. Nurses and aides ran toward them; the children were all crying as they walked through the door dressed in tatters, the two oldest bearing evidence of torture.

These dead priests I left in their beds, their blood soaking into their sheets as I misted home. It took ten minutes, going as swiftly as I could, to return to the apartment. Once again, Kifirin was in my bedroom after I took my shower. I didn't say anything to him; I merely tossed my bloody clothing into the garbage bin with the used blood bags, walked around him to get to my side of the bed and crawled in. He chuckled softly when I covered my head completely with the blanket, shutting out the sight of him.

"Is this how you made the monsters go away when you were little?" he asked gently. I flopped the blanket back down and glared at him— he was now sitting on the side of my bed.

"The monster was real when I was little," I snapped. "I didn't have to make any up."

"I know," he said softly, reaching over to stroke my cheek. "Go to sleep, Lissa. The monster will keep watch, now, and make sure your sleep is undisturbed." Dawn came before I could ask him what he meant.

Paul Winthrop hadn't traveled into Kent before and he found he liked it very much. The countryside was lovely. Silently he thanked the Grand Master for calling him again, even if it was to track down the two that, in Weldon Harper's words, "shouldn't be there bothering Lissa."

He had photographs of both men and understood that one of them was a high-ranking official for U.S. security. Paul snorted at the thought as he drove his small car down the two-lane road. The town of Luddesdown couldn't be that big; it wasn't even on most maps, so he shouldn't have any difficulty finding both of them. One was a werewolf, too, just as he was, so the scent would certainly give him away.

"Yeah," the local pub owner's accent was thick as Paul asked about any guests from the States. "Those blokes staying at Thorne House, between here and Gravesend. They come over for a pint every night, just about."

"About what time, you think?" Paul asked.

"Bout sevenish, I'd say."

Paul checked his watch; it was nearly six-thirty. "Do you serve food here?"

"Yeah. Fish and chips. Nachos. Those blokes love the nachos." The local grinned. Paul noticed the bartender's nose was crooked, as if it had been broken more than once. Paul was lucky; His nose had been broken several times, but werewolves generally healed quickly from any injury and his nose was still straight.

"Then I'll have the fish and chips," Paul decided. "With a pint of your best." The local grinned again and went to work.

Paul's plate was mostly empty; just a few stray chips remained when two customers walked in—one human, one werewolf. The werewolf scented him, just as Paul did the same. He motioned for both to join him. The werewolf grabbed the arm of his human male companion, almost dragging him to Paul's booth.

"Have a seat," Paul nodded toward the opposite, empty side of his booth.

"Sit down, Tony," Deryn hissed. Tony sat, sliding toward the inside; Deryn took the outside. Paul wiped his hands on the paper napkin he'd been given as he studied them with hooded eyes.

"The Grand Master asked me to track you two down," he said. "Said you were off hunting something that could land you in a spot of trouble."

"Now, how the hell does he know that?" Deryn asked, frowning at Paul. "And who are you, anyway?"

"Paul Winthrop," Paul held his hand out over the table. Deryn took it. Deryn was worried the local Packmaster had come to find the werewolf who'd invaded his territory without checking in. "Member of the Newtown Pack," Paul added. "Wales."

"You're the one who helped catch that killer—the one who was taking those children," Tony turned his attention to Paul.

"I try to keep that quiet," Paul said. "I'm sure you know already that the man we brought in was only half the story. Lissa helped catch the other half, from the States."

"Didn't hear about that," Tony lied. He was now examining Paul closely. "Do you know where she is? Where we might find her? I really need to talk to her."

"Send her e-mail," Paul suggested.

"I don't think she's answering my brother's e-mails," Deryn sighed.

"What did you do, then?" Paul frowned at Tony. "To muck things up with her?"

Deryn glanced at Tony, too. Tony refused to talk about it the whole time they'd been searching for Lissa. "Can't say. Top secret," Tony insisted.

That caused Paul to snort. "So, you fuck up and it's top secret, then?"

"That pretty much covers it," Tony nodded. "I don't suppose we could get your help?"

"I'll not be giving Lissa grief over the likes of you, I'm thinking." Paul drained the last of his pint. The barmaid, who'd come on duty in the last fifteen minutes, walked over to take Deryn and Tony's order. Paul asked for another pint.

"Well, are you going home, then, like the Grand Master wants?" Paul asked, watching Tony and Deryn finish off their second pints of the evening.

"Probably not," Tony said, thumping his mug on the table. His cell phone rang. He thumbed the call. "Hancock, here," he said.

"Xenides has been sighted again in London," Ken White said without a greeting.

"Fuck," Tony muttered. "Where in London?"

Agent Kenneth White, one of the few vampire agents in the Special Paranormal Division of the FBI, gave the name of an old hotel on the outskirts of the city. "Be careful, Mr. Hancock. That one is dirty business."

"I'm certainly not going home now," Tony snapped, ending the call. Of course, his brother and Paul heard every word of the phone conversation. Paul and Deryn were hearing the name Xenides for the first time, however. Tony looked at both werewolves. "Who wants to drive to London?"

∾

"Yes, I saw that one," the hotel maid nodded, pointing to the taller man in the photographs Tony presented. The cleaning staff was invisible to most people who came to stay. Xenides hadn't bothered with compulsion on her as he had with the staff at the front desk—he hadn't seen her. "He was here a little over a week ago," the woman went on. "Stayed for one entire day and night, then checked out the following evening. I got to clean his room, first thing the next morning."

"Did he meet with anyone?" Tony asked, tucking the photographs in his jacket pocket.

"A woman came in. Pretty. Long, dark hair. Looked Asian."

"I don't suppose you got any names?" Tony asked hopefully. "Or any other information?"

"No. They shut themselves up in the room around eight, for about an hour. I don't think she was here for the usual, if you get my meaning."

Tony got her meaning. The two hadn't had sex. That meant an accomplice to him.

"Was he driving anything? Did you notice?"

"Didn't see that. Sorry." The woman shook her head.

"Thank you for the information. Don't let anyone else know that you told us anything." Tony passed the woman two fifty-pound notes before he, Deryn and Paul left.

"Did you get anything?" The desk clerk asked as Tony and the others passed his desk on the way out.

"She didn't remember the man," Tony lied smoothly and kept walking. As soon as Tony, Deryn and Paul drove away, the desk clerk placed a call to a cell phone.

"Three men were here asking questions. None of my staff

129

remembered anything," the desk clerk said after the initial greeting. He hung up when the voice on the other end expressed his pleasure at that information.

～

"I know I'm not the most desirable person to hear from," Tony informed Charles the moment he could punch Wlodek's number on his cell from inside the rented vehicle. "But we have a report that Xenides was seen at the Hobart Hotel. It was also reported that he met a woman there who had long, dark hair. She appeared to be of Asian heritage. We don't have information on what the meeting entailed. This happened more than a week ago."

Hair rose on the back of Charles's neck when Tony gave the description of the woman. "I'll get this information to Wlodek," he said, breaking the connection.

"Honored One, I know we're about to interview the girl, but this is important," Charles spoke before coming to a complete halt inside the holding facility's office. "Anthony Hancock called. He says that Xenides was seen at the Hobart Hotel a little over a week ago. He met a woman there with long, dark hair who appeared to be Asian." Charles hadn't paused for breath, getting the whole thing out as quickly as he could. Wlodek showed no emotion at the news; Gavin and Merrill were just as stone-faced.

"We will delve into this immediately," Wlodek replied after considering Charles's report. "Have Flavio and Susila arrived?"

"Not yet, Honored One. Wait, I think I hear them now." Charles left the office to check, leading both vampires in a few moments later. Susila smiled slightly at Merrill, who nodded.

Susila was Scandinavian by birth and was nearly as old as Merrill. She and Flavio took seats on either side of Wlodek. Merrill and Gavin sat behind them, in opposite corners.

"Have them bring the girl," Wlodek nodded to Charles, who trotted down the hall to let Radomir know.

CHAPTER 8

The girl was bound with handcuffs for the interview; compulsion had already been laid for her to be respectful. That didn't keep her from leveling a threat, however.

"You are all dead," she giggled hysterically. "You have no idea what Xenides is." The girl was Spanish but spoke in English, with an accent. It didn't matter; all presiding over her questioning spoke fluent Spanish.

Wlodek barely lifted an eyebrow. "And what is Xenides?" he asked. "You will tell the truth."

"I went looking for vampires. Thought it would be fun. Used to dress up, you know, in the costumes? Xenides doesn't allow that. I found vampires," she repeated.

"What has he done to make you think this?" Wlodek watched the girl carefully. Charles was already tapping quietly on his computer.

"He killed one of the two girls he had before he found me. He made me kill the other one. He forced me to drink her blood. He taunted me. 'You wanted to be a vampire,' he said. He laughed. 'Be a vampire,' he said. I drank some of her blood. It was hot and sticky."

"Have you killed anyone else?"

"I killed a vampire. Xenides gave me a stake and told me where to find him. I killed him. He turned to ash while I watched." The girl giggled again.

"Did you know the name of this vampire?"

"Aubrey Wallis," the girl replied. Gavin shifted in his seat.

"Where did you kill him? Do you know why Xenides asked for his death?"

"Aubrey was in Barcelona, at a villa outside the city. Xenides forced the gardener to give him a key to the house. I used that to get in."

"Why was he killed?"

"Because Xenides heard that someone named René is hunting him. Xenides said he was giving a warning to René."

"How long were you with Xenides?"

"Less than six months. It seems like an eternity."

"Did you commit other crimes?"

"I stole some things—money, some jewelry. I also robbed Aubrey's villa and killed his housekeeper. She was a nosy bitch and wanted the money back. I stabbed her with her own kitchen knife."

"What else did you take from there?"

"Gold. More jewelry. I tried to get into the safe but it was locked and I didn't have the combination. I had to leave it."

"Did Xenides ask you to rob Aubrey or kill the housekeeper?"

"No. I was attempting to get away from him, so I made those decisions myself. I didn't know he was preventing me from escaping. He laughed at me when I was compelled to return to his side."

"And how did you come to be separated from Xenides?" Wlodek flipped the gold pen in his hands.

"He wouldn't let me travel with him. He said my image would be displayed on a security camera outside the villa after I killed the housekeeper. He didn't want to be arrested with me if the police came looking. He told me to meet someone named Llewellyn at a bar. Llewellyn was to take me out of the country. I thought that man was Llewellyn." She pointed to Gavin.

"As you now know, he is not," Wlodek said. "Are there any other questions?" Wlodek turned to Susila and Flavio.

"I have nothing," Flavio said.

"Nor do I," Susila replied.

"Did Xenides ever speak about what he was doing, or whether he was looking for someone in particular?" Merrill asked quietly. The girl turned to him; she could barely see him in the corner. The light was very dim inside the room.

"He wanted someone he called the little princess. He wanted her very much. He made me jealous sometimes; he talked about her so often."

"Did he say why he wanted her?" Merrill went on.

"He kept saying he would make them pay. That is what he said."

"Did he ever explain whom he meant?"

"No. He only said them."

"Did he ever mention the name Saxom? Or Meletius?"

"He said those words together. Saxom Meletius. Is that a first and last name?"

"Possibly," Wlodek nodded. "Do you remember what he said when you heard those words?"

"He said he would raise a monument with those words on it, when the others were dead. He said it was to honor his father."

"Did he talk about how he would kill the others?"

"He said he was going to kill humans first with tainted medicine, so the others' blood supply would be cut off. He laughed and said that the others depended on donors who were paid in some of the poorer countries. He was trying to kill the donors with the bad medicine, I think." Wlodek's fingers stilled, the pen held tightly in his grip. The tainted flu vaccine wasn't aimed at humans only. It was aimed ultimately at the vampire community.

"I have heard enough," Wlodek nodded. This time everyone agreed. "Gavin, will you take this and then inform your cousin, or do you wish for Radomir to do this?"

"I will do this," Gavin rose from his chair.

"Why will he inform his cousin?" The girl was curious. "What are you going to do? I will plead guilty to all charges. I know there is no death penalty in England."

"René is his cousin and Aubrey Wallis was René's child," Wlodek's face was set in a frown. "The death penalty or lack thereof, applies only to human laws. We are not humans here." Wlodek allowed his lengthy fangs to slip out. The girl screamed.

～

I wandered into the living room the following evening, finding Dragon asleep in the large easy chair. Karzac hadn't come in from work, yet. I went to put the kettle on quietly to make Dragon a cup of tea. He was awfully fond of the stuff.

Dragon drank tea from a darker blend, which was kept in a separate container from the leaves Karzac and I used. I drank tea to warm my body; it wasn't such a hardship to eliminate it later.

Dragon woke as I was pouring hot water into his cup. He thanked me when I handed it to him a few seconds later, waiting for it to steep the proper amount of time. "I was watching the news, little vampire. Most of the program was about six children who arrived mysteriously at the hospital in Limrok, upriver. Not much about the fifty dead priests, though."

"What explanation are they giving for the cave-in the other night?" I asked, shrugging off fifty dead priests.

"They say that a water pipe that burst several years ago washed out the earth beneath the street and that it finally collapsed as a result."

"I suppose that works as an excuse," I sipped my own tea. I was still dressed in my pajamas and hadn't bothered to change, yet. Karzac came in a few minutes later. "Honey, you look like you've been in a war," I said. His hair looked wild. He sat down wearily so I fixed him and Dragon something to eat.

"You cook?" Karzac stared up at me when I handed him a broiled steak—I knew he liked his medium.

"I cooked for a few years before I got attacked by a bloodsucker. Eat before it gets cold." I set the salt and pepper shakers beside his plate. He and Dragon ate everything on their plates, vegetables and all. I washed up afterward and then went to dress—I wanted to check on a few things, including a collapsed street attributed to water damage.

Three Solar Red priests stood as close to the collapsed street as they could get; the local authorities had roped off the area and were now bringing in truckloads of sand to fill it in after the water pipes had been replaced.

I went to stand next to a group of normal humans about twenty feet away from the priests. I could still hear what they were saying even from that distance, although they were whispering so as not to be overheard.

"We were told there would be only ash left behind," one of them said, sounding pleased.

"It's true. Hepturna Kandith says the same thing; he was on Orliff, where a similar strategy was employed."

"The authorities went looking for bodies, but there wasn't anything," the third priest laughed softly. "I like that. No evidence to clean up." They turned to go. I walked in the opposite direction, turning to mist as soon as I was out of sight and spinning quickly to fly toward the temple, coming upon the three priests.

They died quickly; only my claws had materialized to cut their throats. Gathering them into my mist, I sped toward the collapsed street. Plunging into the crater beneath a huge pile of dirt that had been packed in already, I left the bodies buried about halfway down. Shooting skyward again, I misted toward Gabron's library. His washroom was my first order of business before I sought him out—my fingers and claws were still covered in blood.

"I have heard that all Solar Red priests are being called to the main temple since the massacre in Limrok," Gabron took my hand and kissed it when I found him.

"Do you know when they're coming and how?" I asked.

"Most likely by river; it's the easiest and least expensive way," Gabron said, leading me to the sofa in his library and convincing me to sit. I'd seen a few other vampires wandering around or reading, but figured most of them were out in the caves somewhere.

"How are the others doing? Are they feeling their confinement, yet?"

"A little. But we vampires are a patient lot. Many of them are plotting revenge. If they get their claws into Solar Red, those priests will not last long."

"Gee, that's too bad. The baby-killing torturers might get what's coming to them," I said sarcastically. "Sick, sadistic fuckers."

"Lissa, at times I am shocked at the words you say, and I am quite old." Gabron was almost smiling.

"I feel old too, even though I'm not. At least by vampire standards."

"How old are you?" Gabron ran the tip of a finger gently around the edge of my ear. That wasn't erotic or anything.

"Forty-nine."

"And how long have you been vampire?"

"Two years, almost." Gabron's fingers stopped, and then resumed after a few seconds. "We keep our vampire children confined for six years," he said, leaning closer and blowing a cool breath against my neck.

"They do it for five, where I come from. As you can see, I'm a little different. Not that they don't tell me what to do and where to go, most of the time. They sent me here to keep me out of a bunch of other trouble, I'm sure."

"What is this bunch of other trouble?" Gabron was nuzzling my neck, now. I tried to push him away. He just lifted my hand and kissed it.

"A pack of rabid vampires. I think most of them might be Dark Elemaiya—isn't that what you called them? The Head of the Council there thinks I'm susceptible to compulsion and I haven't let him know otherwise."

"He thinks this? Lissa, if you were one of mine and withheld that information, I might consider punishing you."

"Been there, done that," I said. Gabron was back to nuzzling my neck. "Is there a picture of you next to the word persistent in the dictionary?" I asked.

"In the what?" He nipped my neck gently.

"Never mind. What kind of punishment do you hand out for stuff like that?"

"Confinement, mostly. Perhaps a few days with the manacles on. Mind you, we only activate them if there is an infraction."

"Uh-huh. Things are different where I come from." I misted away before he could sink his fangs in my neck.

∾

Admiral Hafer and his assistant stood at the rental car center in Las Vegas. Someone had called earlier with the news that Anthony Hancock had never gotten on the plane at Heathrow. Admiral Hafer could curse quite well and was doing so now. They'd wasted valuable time searching Las Vegas for Hancock. "Get me back to London," he shouted as his assistant pulled out his cell to make the call.

∾

"You know I have no interest whatsoever in these so-called priests." The Ra'Ak Prince watched his subordinate pace before his desk. The desk itself was made of rare wood, inlaid with gold and gemstones. He'd taken it from Belifindus, after his subjects had devoured or turned the population.

The Belifindans had become quite greedy and wasteful, eventually earning their planet the undesirable status of *Not Worth Saving*. The Saa Thalarr had not bothered with it and the Ra'Ak had taken it quickly. The Prince appreciated the spoils from that world.

Most possessions were left to rot on the worlds taken; there was only so much space for wealth and riches, when the most coveted thing on the planets was the life that existed there.

"I only allowed you to take these priests as a diversion—it is generally a good thing to unsettle the population before we take it. Panicked prey is always more amusing."

"I'm telling you there is something there that we should not disregard," the subordinate ceased his pacing to get the point across to

137

the Ra'Ak Prince. "I cannot detect it and it is killing the priests easily. Fifty were killed in one night. Silently. Their prisoners were taken away, the locks still locked on their cells. This is no Saa Thalarr; I would have sensed it. That is why I do not believe they are there. I want others with me on the night of terror."

Both Ra'Ak held to their humanoid shapes—it was easier to communicate this way and the subordinate felt more comfortable. If the Prince took his serpent form, the subordinate's life would be in danger. "How many are you requesting?" The Prince gave the subordinate a sly look. The subordinate had no way of telling whether this meant the Prince was considering his request or whether he was toying with him.

"At least three, since we don't know what we are facing. The Refizani have allies; perhaps the Karathian Warlocks or the strongest Wizards have been called to assist. Neither would cause our senses to react."

"It would be worse if the Karathians were involved," the Prince appeared to be considering the request. "Although if these are Grey House Wizards, it might also go badly. Very well," the Prince conceded. "I will allow you to take three with you. Mind you, I expect the children to be brought here for the feast afterward."

Children were always devoured; they were never turned to Ra'Ak spawn. They were simply too small and the others would merely fall upon them and kill them.

The subordinate bowed gratefully to the Prince, departing immediately to select his three before the Prince had an opportunity to rethink his largesse.

"I have never visited Merrill's home, but I know that it is very close to Wlodek's," Ilaisaane glanced at the two vampires Xenides sent to her. She had no desire to allow them anywhere near her home so she'd met them at a neutral site.

A pub in Luddesdown was where they sat, which to her seemed

the back of beyond. Ilaisaane preferred her comforts and city life. If
the occasional human offered a meal, she didn't turn that down,
either.

Saxom had taught her in secret after killing her sire, working
diligently to bring out her desire for power. She yearned for
Wlodek's position, but killing him would not guarantee the seat in
the center of the Council. There were too many others nearly as
powerful. She would have to fight her way through all of them and
frankly, the odds were not in her favor. She was determined to use
guile instead of force. Xenides might be a stepping-stone to the seat
of power.

"Avilepha, what are you doing?" Kifirin appeared out of nowhere.
Again. I was sitting on the banks of the river, tossing stray stones into
it. Dragon's dojo had been cleaned already and I toyed with the idea of
going back to the Solar Red temple, but held off for tonight.

"Tossing rocks into the river," I said, flinging another pebble far
out into the water. More than likely, I could toss one to the far bank
with no trouble, although the river was more than a quarter of a mile
wide at this point. I'd deliberately taken myself upstream in case any
boats came down, carrying priests. This bend of the river hid me well
from the city's population, should the priests float past. Their deaths
would come swiftly if they did.

"I was hoping you would be interested in other activities," Kifirin
sat next to me, gazing across the river at something even I couldn't
see.

"What activities?" My small pile of river stones was nearly
depleted; I considered rising to hunt for more.

"I know that the Blood King here informed you of the Elemaiya,
both Dark and Light."

"He called them Bright and Dark," I agreed, tossing another rock. It
plunked into the water halfway across the river with a satisfying
splash.

"Very good. That is what the Elemaiya call themselves," Kifirin smiled slightly, pleased with my knowledge.

"Gabron said his mother was a quarter Bright Elemaiya, making him an eighth. He says I must be of that race as well." Kifirin radiated warmth. It wasn't hard to sit next to him; the air around the river was very cool and mist rose from the water itself.

"He is wise," Kifirin acknowledged with a slight nod.

"So, you think Gabron's right?" I looked up at Kifirin. His face definitely belonged to an angel.

"He is correct," Kifirin informed me.

"And you know this how?"

"I know a great deal. What I wish to ask is whether you would like to accompany me for a visit to both the Bright and the Dark Elemaiya. I know you have a very good nose—perhaps you would like to get their scent. It could help you in your future dealings, both with those races and the vampire race as well." Kifirin placed an arm around my shoulders. Truly, I wanted to huddle into his warmth. I stayed still, instead.

"Someday, perhaps you will follow your heart and your instincts," Kifirin told me. "Do you wish to go or not?"

"I do," I said, rising easily and dusting off my loose trousers. "I'm not going to be sorry to leave this clothing behind," I muttered. Calling it shapeless was a compliment. "Where are we going?"

The question didn't have time to leave my mouth completely before Kifirin had us somewhere else. And by somewhere else, I mean on another planet somewhere else. The smell was completely different. I wish I knew how he did that, along with Pheligar, and most likely Dragon and the others of his kind.

"It is called folding space," Kifirin informed me, leaning his mouth next to my ear and breathing softly against it. His breath was quite warm. "Do you see the lights, avilepha?" He lifted a hand and steered my chin in the proper direction. There were lights off in the distance. They looked like fairy lights to me, winking softly just outside a grove of trees. Kifirin and I stood in knee-deep grasses on a world that didn't appear to have the least bit of technology.

"The Bright Elemaiya prefer this type of world; their gifts are not forced to compete with machinery and electronics."

"What gifts are those?" I turned to gaze into Kifirin's dark eyes.

"They have the ability to world-walk, between the gates. They can also relocate, but that is a limited gift. A few have mindspeech or the ability to shield or glamour. Fewer still have shape-shifting abilities. The rarest of all have either foresight or the ability to turn to mist as you call it, and the rarest of the misters are capable of turning others to mist with them." Kifirin was watching my face as he described the Elemaiyan gifts.

"Can any of the misters see other misters? While they're mist themselves?" I had to know and Kifirin seemed so knowledgeable about them.

"Ah, there you have hit upon it," he smiled. "I knew this about you already, m'hala. Only the most powerful among them have ever had that gift, and none of the full or half-bloods possesses it in this time frame. The Elemaiya, both Bright and Dark, have revealed their shortsightedness by upholding their laws on the dilution of the race. The gifts still come to those less than half, and they are too blind to see it."

"But how did I come by that blood?" My mother never said anything about this—if she knew about it, that is.

"Avilepha, someday soon, perhaps, one who knows will tell you. It is not my information to give. Come; let us walk among them—they will know not to harm us." Kifirin took my hand and we wandered toward the lights.

Two guards stood with tall, sharply pointed pikes at the entrance to the camp; I didn't miss their gasps as they pulled aside and bowed as we walked past them. The Bright Elemaiya were not very tall as a whole—I didn't see any of them that stood more than five-ten or so, with most shorter than that. They were also slender of build, with ears that were slightly pointed. I thought they were lovely to look upon, with pale, clear skin and mostly blue or vivid green eyes. Their hair colors ranged from blond to dark brown, with reds here and there, most of it hanging down in long braids to their waists or below.

"May we offer you food and drink?" A female had come to stand before us, a crystal cup in her hands, which she offered to Kifirin.

"Queen Friesianna," Kifirin acknowledged her, but neither bowed nor debased himself in any way. He gripped my elbow, letting me know to remain upright as well. Kifirin accepted the cup with his other hand, drank and then passed the goblet back to the Queen.

I got her scent, along with all the others I'd been getting. It was a different spice and one I now recognized—Henri and Gervais had it in a small amount, as did Robert. I could only assume that Robert's brother, Albert, had it as well. The others that had it, surprisingly enough, were Merrill and Gabron. Gabron had been telling me the truth about them, and that made me wonder just how often the Elemaiya had children with a human.

"I beg you to introduce your companion," the Queen spoke again as she took the cup from Kifirin.

"I do not choose to do this," Kifirin snorted, causing a tiny curl of smoke to come from his nostrils. The man had to be a furnace on the inside. The Queen took that as a sign that he was displeased, which made her back away a step. "We merely wished to look upon your kind, and we have done so." Kifirin folded space again, pulling me away from the Bright Elemaiya.

"These will not offer anything but they will cower, just the same," Kifirin said, pulling me through a second meadow. This one had recently been mowed and stacks of hay lay here and there. This world not only smelled different, it was in a different season.

The Dark Elemaiya didn't have their encampment so brightly lit, but Kifirin led me toward it purposely. The moment we passed the guards at the perimeter, I smelled it. These beings held a portion of the taint that Saxom's misters had. I knew these had the potential for evil within them, like a seed that could sprout at any time with deadly results.

The Dark Elemaiya weren't much different from the Bright ones of their kind—in appearance, anyway. It was the scent of them and the darkness in their spirits that I recognized.

"Have we displeased you, High Lord?" One of the inhabitants came and bowed low before Kifirin. He kept an eye on Kifirin and on me while he bowed.

"No more than your Bright kin, King Baltis," Kifirin replied.

"We will not change our laws," the Dark Elemaiya lifted from his bow.

"That is your choice," Kifirin replied. We folded space again.

~

"René, the human who was compelled to murder Aubrey is now dead," Gavin accepted the glass of wine that Devlin held out to him. He and René sat at a small table in Gavin's kitchen; René had agreed to meet Gavin at Gavin's apartment in London.

Devlin sat down with a sigh to sip his own glass of wine and looked mournfully at René. René, as Devlin's sire, reached out and rubbed Devlin's shoulders to comfort him.

"Dare I hope that you accomplished this for us?" René asked calmly, sipping from his own glass.

"I did," Gavin gave the barest of nods.

"Then I thank you, cousin."

"There is something else," Gavin said. "The human did this at Xenides' bidding. She said that Xenides learned that you were hunting him, René. He had Aubrey killed as a message to you."

René cursed softly; first in Latin, and then in French. "I should know better than to convey my intentions to anyone," he breathed. René had no desire to reveal his conversation with Wlodek regarding Aubrey's death—even Gavin had no idea how closely René worked with Wlodek at times. Instead, he turned his head to stare at Gavin's kitchen walls. The room had not been updated in more than four decades. "You should allow Lissa to redecorate your dwelling," René observed.

"René, do not avoid the subject. Either stop hunting Xenides or let everyone think you have stopped hunting Xenides." Gavin forced his cousin's attention to return to the business at hand. "After he is dead and turned to ash, I will allow Lissa to do whatever she likes with this place and will permit you to help her select the décor, if she is willing."

"Will you truly allow me to speak with her?" René was surprised.

"Only if she wishes. She was very afraid of you, René."

"I know this and that was not my intention. Much has happened between us, but she was gracious and amusing afterward, don't you think? The French King would have loved her."

"The French King would have died when he put his hands on her," Gavin growled.

"Cousin, I did not intend to raise your ire."

"The fucking French King is dead! Why are you even discussing this?" Devlin rose from the table in an agitated manner and stalked off.

"We should go," René rose from his seat as well. "I thank you for what you did."

"René, if you get wind of Xenides, I would appreciate the information," Gavin said. "All of us would very much like to see him die."

"But I want the satisfaction of seeing him die first-hand, cousin." René walked out of Gavin's kitchen.

"Merrill, I'm sorry I couldn't call earlier, but Hafer is so suspicious, he'll hardly allow me out of his sight." Daniel Carey spoke on his cell while standing on a street corner. He'd left his hotel room and now stood next to a convenience store in London. "I had to tell him I ran out of shaving cream to get away."

Daniel Carey had only recently been transferred to Hafer, at Hafer's request. Shirley Walker was holding Daniel's Second position in the Corpus Christi Pack in the hopes he'd be transferred back.

Daniel not only flew planes for the Navy but he'd also operated undercover in the past, under Hafer's command. Hafer asked for him personally and Daniel had no reasonable excuse to refuse.

He'd met Merrill four years earlier when the Saxom treachery occurred in south Texas. Daniel and Merrill remained in contact ever since. The minute Daniel learned that Hafer was after Lissa, he'd notified Merrill.

"That's not a problem; Lissa is away at the moment, helping out our special friends." Merrill and Daniel had both assisted in the destruction of Saxom's demon army, with the aid of the Saa Thalarr.

"So, even if Hafer could move heaven and earth, he still might not find her?" Daniel almost laughed aloud. He'd met Lissa briefly, when she worked with William Winkler. He hadn't tried to get close; he didn't want to raise Winkler's suspicions.

Daniel also didn't want to get Lissa killed and hadn't informed Merrill either, until later. Merrill understood his reasons very well—he'd have been obligated to inform the Council, although Gavin already had her under surveillance.

"He won't find her at the moment," Merrill answered. "She isn't scheduled to be back for a few days, at least."

"Good," Daniel replied before hanging up.

"You're not the first one to ask those questions," the bartender at the pub informed the vampire. "I don't know of anyone fitting that description who lives around here and I know everybody, I think. You might want to ask over in Chatham, or Gravesend, there are loads of farms and manors scattered about. They may be travelin' over there to do their business." The bartender wiped the bar off with a cloth as the vampire watched.

"I'll do that," the vampire responded. He'd laid compulsion for the man to tell the truth and the man didn't know anything. He went to his companion, who rose from the booth to go. Ilaisaane had left earlier; she hadn't given them any helpful information at all.

"I got a call—Llewellyn and Xenides' latest girl have disappeared," Quentin dropped the obligatory tip onto the table before walking away from it.

Julius, his companion, snorted. "Probably ran off together, if this is the same Llewellyn I know."

"Xenides suspects the same and says he really doesn't care, he'll just find another girl. This one was getting out of hand anyway and he was already planning to kill her." They'd stepped outside the pub; no one else was around to listen in on the conversation. "He just won't get the blood, that's all." They climbed into their rented vehicle, preparing to find a resting place for the day.

"What about Llewellyn?" Julius asked.

"Xenides says to kill him, if we see him."

"With pleasure," Julius smiled in the darkness and started the car.

CHAPTER 9

Bad news waited for me when I woke. Dragon pulled me down on the sofa and nearly sat on me as Karzac, who'd arrived home early for a change, turned the sound on for the news.

"Yes, vampires are no longer a myth," the newscaster announced as footage was shown, over and over again, of Briden, with cuffs on his wrists and ankles, being forced from a building—Blue Desire—and then screaming and jerking as the rising sun burned him to ash.

"No!" I shouted, struggling against Dragon, but he held on too tightly and whatever he was doing kept me from turning to mist. I was crying before it was all over. "Please tell me they didn't force information from him. Please tell me that," I wept. Gabron and the others were in the caves under Blue Desire and Briden knew that.

"They were unable to get past the compulsion laid on him," Karzac muttered angrily, turning off the program. "Three others were also dragged out and burned; now the entire city is hunting vampire."

"Poor Briden," I was still wiping tears when Dragon let me go. "Where are they looking? Have they found any?" I was set to go to the rescue if that happened.

"All of them have disappeared; underground, most likely. Most of the brothels in the city have closed—none of the population realized

147

that vampires were running those businesses." Dragon was scowling even more than usual. "I shut the classes down early—people were afraid to walk home in the dark."

"So they think that vampires are just going to kill people now, since they've suddenly been discovered among them?" I said sarcastically.

"They'll come to their senses as soon as Solar Red stops goading them and spreading wild rumors," Karzac mumbled.

"And how many are going to die in the meantime?" I whirled to face him. "The vampire population is small. By design. Poor Briden." I headed back toward my bedroom, slamming the door behind me.

I dressed; I'd gone out before still in my pajamas. I wanted to pay Gabron a visit, to make sure he was all right. I misted away before Dragon could stop me, too.

"Gabron?" I found him sitting on the sofa in his library, his head in his hands.

"Lissa, they burned my child."

"I know, honey. It was all over the news." I went to sit beside him, rubbing his back carefully.

"Have you ever been burned Lissa?" He turned blood-red eyes toward me.

"Yes. I almost died that way. Intentionally." Gabron drew in a breath before wrapping his arms around me and weeping.

I misted both of us away after a while, to the banks of the river where I'd been throwing stones the night before. I don't think Gabron understood the English when I sang *When the River Meets the Sea* for him, so I translated it afterward. A large boat came down the river while we sat in silence afterward.

"Those are Solar Red priests on the deck," Gabron stood to get a better look as the ship floated past.

"So much the better, my friend," I said, turning to mist and turning Gabron with me. He was with me as I turned the large boat and all its occupants to mist and then floated it high above the land nearby, finding the largest and rockiest expanse I could before rising at least five hundred feet and dropping it.

The boat, when it hit the rocky surface, made a terrible noise. The metal hull groaned like a giant, dying animal, the sound echoing across the water while the ship broke apart after it struck the ground.

A tremendous cloud of rock and dark earth rose around it; some of the stone fragments and dirt flung outward hit the river, it spewed so far. None of those sailing aboard the vessel survived.

With only my claws visible, I scraped a ghostly message on the half-buried hull. *The vampires are not the problem*; I wrote in the Refizani language before misting Gabron back to his library.

I expected a lecture from Dragon and Karzac when I returned to the apartment, but Dragon drew me into a fierce embrace and kissed the top of my head instead. We then watched the news as authorities and news crews arrived at the ship.

The message I left on the ship's hull was broadcast everywhere. Even several highly placed government officials came out and said the same thing I had. "Think about it," one of them pointed out. "These creatures, according to legend, were once of our race. Have you heard of them before? Have you been attacked by them before? There is no evidence of this, yet Solar Red are now trying to divert the attention away from themselves, finding a new enemy for you to hate. I hope you all sit down and think seriously about this before hunting others. I was personally horrified when I saw those poor creatures burn. What was their crime? Is there evidence against them? Never have I seen the Refizani people exact revenge on someone who may very well be innocent. Show me the crime that any of these committed and we will look into the matter. I am much more interested in the tales that the six children from the city of Limrok are telling. They were all held inside the dungeons of the Solar Red temple; we have found evidence of them within those cells. What was the temple's purpose in holding children? Even our Vice-Governor is healing from wounds he claims he received at the hands of Solar Red priests. Whoever is killing these Solar Red monsters, and yes, I am calling them monsters, is a hero, in my mind. We have all become afraid to speak out against them, but that time must end. We must rise up as a people and demand that they leave our planet. They have no place here. Their beliefs are not ours. Do you worship at their temple? What have these priests done for you, other than make you afraid?" The man stood behind an official-looking podium, making this speech.

"That is the Governor of the Realm," Karzac said softly.

"Can we have him, when you're done?" I asked. "Personally, I think he needs a bodyguard or ten."

Dragon and Karzac went to bed shortly after that, while I stayed up for a while. Kifirin showed up out of nowhere to keep me company. This time I didn't hold back, huddling against him when he sat beside me on the sofa.

"Avilepha," he put his arm around me to hold me close. I let my forehead drop against his shoulder—his body was warm and comforting. "Lissa," he said after a while, speaking softly, "did you know that a Queen of Le-Ath Veronis always had a small circle of advisors around her, all of whom were her lovers? I have seen as many as twelve in that role, in addition to the comesuli that served her."

"Did she love all of them?"

"They—there have been several Queens. And yes, they did. One even had two King Vampires in her circle."

"Gabron is one of those, isn't he?"

"As is your surrogate sire." That almost made me gasp.

"You know about him?" I asked.

"Avilepha, I have done all my research where you are concerned." That reply made me want to ask him what he was, but wasn't sure I wanted to hear the answer. I watched Kifirin smile. "Kiss me," he said softly, and lowered his head to take my lips with his. His mind invaded mine, just as his tongue invaded my mouth. I drowned in him, almost. His desire was mine—his thoughts were mine. I learned what avilepha meant. He'd been calling me *my love*, the whole time I'd known him.

"I do not intend to displace your other lover," he said, breaking the kiss. "When I place my claiming marks it will be painful, but it will only happen the one time, hala avilepha. A vampire's skin will not scar, except from my claiming. My marks will show everyone that you are mine."

I blinked up at him in a stupor, addled by whatever it was he'd done to me. The kiss had left me boneless; a lump of clay in his hands, with no will of my own.

"Come, lean down just a little," he held my neck in one of his hands, and then cradled my cheek against his chest, holding me securely. I watched in a detached manner as the skin on his arms darkened; it was nearly black and covered with scales before it stopped changing. He then he blew a hot breath on the back of my neck, right over the nape. I was comfortable—relaxed, actually, and totally unprepared for what happened next.

Large canines, upper and lower, gripped the back of my neck, their razor-sharp length sinking into my flesh until they nearly surrounded my spine. I cried out with the pain of it. *It will be over soon*, he soothed mentally. *Try to relax, do not struggle. Your spine will not be damaged.*

My fingers were curling and uncurling in my lap; I was held back, somehow, from forming claws or turning to mist. *Hush, it is nearly done*, he sent as I whimpered from the agony. My neck was on fire and the sensation ran the length of my spine. The pain renewed itself when Kifirin removed his teeth; I cried out again and attempted to fight my way out of his lap.

He wasn't having it, gathering me up instead and kissing my neck, touching it with fingers that were now cool, taking the pain away. Somehow, an ice pack appeared in one of his hands and he held it against my nape.

"It is only the once," he repeated gently. I was crying. "Hush, my little love," I was wrapped up in his arms, which were now their normal color. "The Thifilathi must be satisfied in the claiming. I will not hurt you again. The loving will be gentle and careful, and only if you wish it, from now on." I blinked up at his angelic face, the hurt and betrayal showing on my face as more tears fell.

"When the High Demon claims his mate, he spends the rest of his life apologizing for the pain of it," he said, wiping tears from my cheeks and then kissing them away.

"Is that what you are?" I almost sobbed on the words.

"No, avilepha. The High Demons were made in my image." Kifirin kissed me one last time before placing fingers against my forehead and sending me to sleep.

$$\approx$$

"Ilaisaane, we have evidence that you were seen with Xenides," Wlodek toyed with his favorite pen. Ilaisaane sat before Wlodek, chains on her wrists. Merrill, Gavin, Flavio and Radomir were also in the room. Ilaisaane had been lured in on the pretext of judging a human companion.

She had come to the holding facility with Flavio, whom she thought would be judging along with her. She was placed under compulsion by Merrill, whose power was stronger, even, than Saxom's had ever been. She'd heard of King Vampires but had never suspected that one actually existed. Until now.

"I saw him," her words were unwilling, but Merrill had commanded that she tell Wlodek all she knew concerning the vampire. "He wants Lissa very badly." She couldn't keep the contempt from her voice.

"You voted against her, as I remember," Wlodek said casually.

"That little bitch—she should have been killed," Ilaisaane spat. "No female should hold those abilities, especially one so young and stupid."

"And yet she told me that I should keep an eye on you," Merrill interjected. Lissa had told him that the dark-haired woman should be watched, along with two males, Cecil and Nestor. She hadn't known their names, but she'd described where they sat.

Merrill thought Lissa was suspicious of all the members who'd voted against her, until he realized that she hadn't included Jarl in her list—he'd also voted against her. Lissa was certainly correct where Ilaisaane was concerned.

"You sound jealous," Wlodek observed.

"I am. Those abilities should have been given to someone deserving, who could use them effectively."

"Xenides wants her for those abilities, doesn't he?" Wlodek continued.

"Of course. He can get sex anywhere." Gavin growled at Ilaisaane's words.

"What have you told Xenides?"

"I told him that Merrill was her surrogate sire and that Merrill's home was near here. I didn't know the exact location, so I couldn't give him that. He and two siblings, Julius and Quentin, are now looking. I hope they find you soon," she snarled at Merrill.

"Charles!" Wlodek shouted. Charles appeared in the doorway quickly. His laptop was balanced on one hand while he typed in the names Ilaisaane had given with the other.

"The only Julius and Quentin are listed as Corvinus' turns, Honored One."

"Are those the ones?" Wlodek turned to Ilaisaane.

"Saxom was clever, wasn't he?" Ilaisaane laughed softly. "Of course those are the ones."

"What was your relationship with Saxom?"

"He taught me, after he killed my sire," Ilaisaane admitted. "We were lovers for a while, but he was obsessed with someone else. Someone he couldn't have. That blonde bitch you had in the cave four years ago." Merrill growled this time. Ilaisaane shrank back from his anger.

"Do you know how to use one of these?" Tony unboxed one of the crossbows he'd purchased. The arrows were wood; he'd taken a page from the books of the enemy when they'd first appeared in New Mexico. He also had portable flamethrowers shipped in. This was the way a werewolf or a human could fight a vampire.

"I haven't seen one of these in a while," Paul picked up the crossbow and bent the bowstring back, locking it in place. He placed one of the wooden arrows in the arrow groove and pointed it toward the wall.

Tony had taken them to a shooting range to practice. Paul pointed the crossbow at a paper target and pulled the trigger, hitting the outline of the man on the left side of the chest.

"Not bad for someone a hundred and twenty, now is it?" Paul grinned. Tony's cell rang. Deryn and Paul both listened in.

"Those two have been asking around in Chatham," Tony's spy informed him over the phone.

"You know to stay far away from them," Tony gave the warning yet again.

"Of course. They're at the Cock and Pig Pub, right now. We're about to drive on past, they just walked into the place."

"We can be there in fifteen minutes," Tony snapped the cell shut. "Bro, you know how to use this?" He tossed the flamethrower to Deryn.

"I'll figure it out on the way," Deryn grinned. They ran toward the car; Paul drove, Tony made another call. Charles answered and handed the phone to Wlodek.

"Do you have someone in the Chatham area? Those two vampires are in the Cock and Pig Pub in Chatham, according to my sources," Tony informed Wlodek.

"Russell is nearby," Charles offered—he'd heard Tony's words.

"Get him on the phone," Wlodek ordered curtly. Merrill handed his cell to Charles, who punched in Russell's number. Russell answered right away.

"Are you anywhere near Chatham?" Charles asked.

"About twenty minutes away," Russell replied.

"We may need you as backup," Charles informed him. "Two of Xenides' siblings—Julius and Quentin—are there, according to our sources. Anthony Hancock and two werewolves are on their way there, now."

"We've got someone coming to assist," Wlodek informed Tony. "Do not confuse him with the other two."

"Not a problem, I have photographs of the two I want," Tony replied and cut off the communication.

❧

"Look, there it is," Deryn pointed out the pub. Paul pulled over to the side of the street quickly.

"I wish Lissa were here," Tony grumbled.

"Just hold the bloody thing behind your back," Paul instructed, as Tony loaded the crossbow before stuffing several more arrows in a deep pocket of his trench coat.

"Who do you think you're talking to?" Tony grumbled. "I'm ex special ops, you know."

"Then straighten up and act like it," Paul said, walking across the cobblestone street toward the pub.

Only two humans sat at the bar, their backs turned to Tony, Deryn and Paul as they entered. Julius and Quentin sat in a corner booth near the back. Deryn grinned and held the flamethrower behind him as best he could while Paul jerked his crossbow up and fired, hitting Julius square in the chest with a wooden dart.

Julius began to jerk and spasm in the booth, attempting to pull the bolt out of his torso. Quentin lurched from his seat, fangs and claws out. Deryn fired the flamethrower; Tony added a dart in Quentin's chest when Deryn shut off the flames. Quentin dropped to the tiles, still burning. The humans at the bar, along with the bartender, hit the floor.

"Honored One, I only had to place compulsion on three humans; they think a smoking incident caused the fire damage," Russell grinned as he spoke with the Head of the Council. Russell walked toward his car as he spoke; he'd gotten the human and the two werewolves away already.

"Julius and Quentin didn't have time to blink, I'm sure. I got the bartender to sweep up and dispose of the ash; I have the clothing." Russell tossed the singed apparel into the back seat of his car before climbing into the driver's seat.

"Is there identification?"

"Yes, but some of it is charred a bit."

"As expected," Wlodek said. "Bring it. We're at the holding facility." Russell agreed and terminated the call.

～

My neck ached when I woke and it was difficult getting out of bed. I didn't remember getting myself into it, to be honest. Kifirin must have done that. I wanted to have a talk with him. Well, a yelling session might be closer to the truth.

He'd put his teeth in my neck. What the hell was that about? I'd acted as if I were drunk the night before and, like a fool, allowed him to do as he pleased. I walked into the bathroom across the hall and used a hand mirror to check the back of my neck—sure enough there were four large red dots, spaced about three inches apart on both sides of my neck. Kifirin had called them claiming marks. Maybe I should reciprocate. The schmuck.

I hunched over as I walked through the rain to Dragon's dojo—he was finishing up when I came in to clean. "Hey, Dragon," I gave him a quick hug before grabbing the dust mop to sweep the wood floors.

"Lissa, if you had been in my army when I was Warlord on Falchan, I would have slept better," Dragon grinned and let me go.

"Warlord, huh?" I smiled back at him. "Was it good to be you?"

"Sometimes. When Crane and Pheran Tiger weren't chewing on me."

"Dude, those two must be something. I wouldn't want to chew on you and I'm a vampire."

That caused him to laugh—something that didn't happen often. Dragon had his shirt off and all his tattoos gleamed with sweat; he'd been working out again. He grabbed a shirt from his office and slipped it on. He was hungry, he informed me, and wanted to get something to eat before going home for the evening. I told him I'd lock up as he was leaving.

"Is the proprietor still in?" A man walked in the door about five minutes after Dragon left. I hadn't made it to the front door to lock up and now somebody was there. Cursing mentally, I set my dust mop aside and went to talk to the man.

"No, sorry. He left earlier," I told the guy. He was around five-ten or so, with very short, nearly-black hair and a three-pronged tattoo beneath his left eye. The scent of him was what held me, though, and I worked desperately to school my face into the vampire non-expression. "Would you like to leave a message?" I asked as politely as I could.

Dragon, I sent, *we may have trouble.* I went to find some paper when the man said that he would like to leave a message. I wouldn't have done anything, and been content just to let him go out the door and on his way, if he hadn't tried to place compulsion on me after writing out the message.

"You will make sure your employer is here tomorrow evening; I wish to speak to him personally," the man said. The compulsion was the slimiest I'd ever had to deal with, and it just slid off like all the others.

"Of course, sir," I moved forward to take the message, slicing his head off with my claws before the fucker could even blink.

No, I hadn't expected him to dust in humanoid form but he did, just as much as if he'd been the giant serpent he could change into. The worst part? Even though I'd known he was Ra'Ak, he wasn't the one I'd first seen in the meadow, eating the priests.

I was pounded and blasted against the back wall when the guy turned to dust, his fist-sized particles rocketing outward at a tremendous rate of speed. It's a good thing I automatically went to mist in about a blink; otherwise, I would likely have died.

Dragon came running in only a moment later as I struggled to stand while the floor wobbled in my vision. The rest of the dojo looked like a hurricane had swept through it.

"Are you all right? What happened?" Dragon demanded immediately.

"One of your Ra'Ak friends," I replied, working to get my breath back. "I surprised him by relieving him of his head."

"He wasn't in serpent form?"

"No." I dusted my butt off; I was covered in all kinds of debris. "And he wasn't the one I saw in the meadow, either." Dragon's shocked look caused me to stop trying to clean myself off for a moment.

"You're sure?" Dragon asked after a while.

"Yeah. Different scents," I tapped my nose. "Here, he left this note for you and then tried to place compulsion on me to get you to be here tomorrow night to meet with him." Dragon took the note from me; I still held it in my right hand.

"That one thought you might be what you are," Pheligar appeared at Dragon's side, peering over his shoulder at the note.

"Do you think he told his other scaly friend?" I asked, coming over to stand next to Dragon, too. I had to stand on tiptoe, just to look at the note. It was requesting a meeting for business purposes. Well, business was going to be a big fight, in my opinion; I'd just beaten him to the punch. Or the claw, as it were.

"They seldom share information such as this," Pheligar said, looking around at the mess in Dragon's dojo. "It is a coup for one of their kind to destroy a Saa Thalarr. He would gain much honor from his Prince had he been successful. Lock the door, young vampire. I will take care of this."

That night, I got to see a little of what the Larentii are capable of doing. Pheligar barely waved a finger and things were whole and complete again. He cleaned everything up with half a thought. Those wizards in children's novels might have been impressed, even—I certainly was.

"Little vampire, we will speak of this night again, when the assignment is over," Pheligar informed me, laying his hand on the top of my head before disappearing just as swiftly as he'd appeared in the beginning.

"Come home with me, I want Karzac to look you over," Dragon said, pulling me out the door. "Did you get hit by any of the debris?"

"Some, but I went to mist pretty fast and the rest just sailed right through. Of course, it probably turned to mist while it was going through, but it rematerialized once it got past me."

"That is quite the talent you have," Dragon said as we made our way home.

Dragon had a sandwich while Karzac checked me over. There were a few bruises, the worst one on my ribs on the right side—a big chunk had caught me there.

"What are these?" Karzac found Kifirin's bite marks.

"I'm going to smack Kifirin," I grumbled. "He put his teeth in my neck."

Dragon was there so fast I barely saw him move. When he saw the marks, he started cursing. I later learned it was in Falchani, his native language.

"Only High Demons do this," Dragon shouted.

"He said he wasn't a High Demon," I looked into Dragon's dark eyes. "He said the High Demons were made in his image."

"There is nothing to be done about it now." Pheligar was back and looking at my neck. "Finish the assignment. We will sort this out later."

"Sort what out later?" I asked, but Pheligar was already gone again. Dragon was rubbing his forehead as if he had a headache. Karzac went to fix that.

Pheligar stood next to Griffin and both faced Belen, whose race was held in such secrecy that none could speak its name. The Saa Thalarr had dubbed his kind the Nameless Ones, so they could be distinguished from their subordinates, nicknamed the Powers That Be for the same reason. Thorsten, of the Powers That Be, stood not far from Belen. Pheligar and Griffin had requested the audience with Belen; Thorsten had no choice but to allow it.

"She actually said Kifirin?" Belen stared at Pheligar. Belen didn't often resort to corporeality, but it helped when dealing with the others.

"Yes," Pheligar nodded respectfully to Belen. "I have *Looked* for myself and it is true. The High Lord of the Dark Worlds is awake."

"Not awake now. He has come back on the timeline. He wakes in the future," Thorsten offered.

"Regardless, he is awake," Belen said. "Time has no meaning to us, as you well know."

"He did this so he can take action to rein in his creations," Griffin snorted.

"How is that?" Thorsten glared at Griffin. Thorsten supervised the Saa Thalarr and their Larentii Liaison, Pheligar. He and Griffin had clashed on more than one occasion.

"When he created the Dark Worlds, as you were creating the Worlds of Light to keep the balance," Griffin said, "Kifirin's rules as he laid them down were that he would not interfere with those worlds. He has held to that promise, much to our regret. He slept for a time, we all know that, and the Ra'Ak took all the Dark Worlds down, except for the High Demons' planet—the Ra'Ak are afraid to approach it. Now, Kifirin is awake and attempting to deal with this situation in the only way he can without breaking his rules and his word. One of the laws governing the Dark Worlds is that of mate protection. If he uses the excuse that he is protecting his mate, which is now Lissa," Griffin grimaced at that admission, "then he can do almost anything. And since she is from this side of the universes, he can come and protect her here, as well."

"But should he ever take her to the darker worlds, she will not be able to return," Thorsten folded arms over his chest. Belen looked at him thoughtfully for a moment.

"No. That will not be," Belen said. Griffin heaved a huge sigh of relief. Belen glanced at the oldest of the Saa Thalarr, who was now retired. "What are you holding back?" Belen asked. A small smile played around Griffin's mouth as he explained fully and in detail, just what it was he had held back for a while.

"So, back again to cause trouble?" I was throwing more rocks into the river, wondering how long it would take—and how many rocks—to impede the river's progress toward the ocean. Kifirin had appeared at my side, sitting next to me on the river's grassy bank. It was late fall on Refizan; the grass was nearly dead, its brown length pliable and beaten down from recent rains.

"My claiming marks are quite lovely," Kifirin observed, first thing. "Did you see how straight and evenly spaced they are? I had no wish to mar your beauty." He touched the nape of my neck with gentle fingers.

"That'll go over so well with Gavin, when I explain it to him like that," I muttered sarcastically.

"Avilepha, that will not be a problem. Not with me."

"Yeah? You may not be jealous, but Gavin is. In the worst possible way."

"I will take care of that," Kifirin informed me.

"You're not going to hurt him, are you?" I was just about to leave him sitting there alone; my anger was rising so swiftly.

"Love, sit down," Kifirin had his hands on my hips and was not only sitting me down but also pulling me against his side at the same time. "Your lover is in no danger. Not from me. Anyone who cares for you will also receive my care."

"You really don't care that Gavin exists and that I'm engaged to him? That is so bizarre," I huffed.

"I will see to it that he tolerates me and will not be jealous," Kifirin nuzzled the top of my head, the ever-present curl of smoke emanating from his nostrils. "The Saa Thalarr also cannot experience jealousy. It is removed from them when they are turned."

"I heard Dragon say something about that—about what he was before," I said.

"My brothers who watch over the lighter worlds select good candidates and they are remade," Kifirin informed me. "There are seven Saa Thalarr and six healers."

"That doesn't sound like a lot."

"More will come. The Ra'Ak are becoming restless, and the rules set down will be ignored by those most disobedient children. Had their black cousins not allowed their copper relatives to exterminate their race, they might have been held in check. Treachery and deceit have become second nature to the copper ones, however," Kifirin sighed.

"I killed one, earlier," I said.

"I know this," Kifirin smiled at me. "I might have come, had you needed me. You did not."

I mulled his words over for a moment. He'd said he might have come. What did that mean? I shook my head in confusion.

Tony stared at his surroundings. He doubted that many humans had stepped inside Wlodek's mansion, and if they had, they might not have walked out again. Yet here he was—an invited guest, along with Deryn and Paul.

Merrill, who was there, had greeted Paul politely while saying very little to Tony at the same time. Tony ignored the snub; instead, his fingers itched while he examined the books in the bookcases lining the walls of Wlodek's study.

"We appreciate your assistance with Julius and Quentin," Wlodek remarked. Tony turned toward the Head of the Council—he couldn't believe he was seeing Wlodek in the flesh. He looked to be of Greek origin, although his name said otherwise.

Wlodek's face could have graced any number of ancient coins. The suit he wore cost in the thousands and had never seen a rack in its life. An authentic Monet, one of the artist's many paintings of water lilies, covered the wall opposite the bookcases. Another painting that also looked to be expensive—a portrait of Napoleon—hung in the short space between bookcases.

"It's a David," Wlodek caught Tony looking. "It was a gift." Wlodek didn't elaborate past that. "Now," Wlodek turned to business. "While we are still incensed over your treatment of Lissa, we are offering an olive branch of sorts. We wish to combine our efforts to search for Xenides. We will also include your terrorist, Rahim Alif, in our search. We do this in good faith, since you have provided us with valuable information thus far. It is imperative that we bring this traitorous vampire down. He desires to kill all of us; not just the humans, as previously thought."

"Then I have a favor to ask," a smile spread slowly across Tony's face.

∾

"Merrill," Daniel Carey met him on the corner, away from the small hotel where he and Admiral Hafer were staying. Anthony Hancock had asked Wlodek if there was any way that Admiral Hafer could be removed from the equation, with the use of compulsion.

"Hello, Daniel. It is quite a pleasure to see you again," Merrill held out his hand and Daniel took it. "What must we do with our decorated officer?"

"Not only does he want Lissa for his own purposes, he wants to bring several people down, including Anthony Hancock and the President," Daniel explained. "We can't afford the chaos this will cause; we have enough trouble as it is." Merrill nodded in understanding. The economy everywhere was in crisis. Something like this could cause worldwide panic.

"I believe I can help with that," Merrill smiled. "Lead the way, friend," he nodded toward the hotel. Daniel pulled out his key and headed for the door.

∾

"It must be the Karathian Warlocks; they are powerful enough and willing enough—if the price is right." The Ra'Ak was back and pacing before his Prince.

"And there we thought all along it would be the High Demons who'd step in and hinder our progress," the Prince grumbled. He thought about going to serpent form and killing his subordinate, simply because he was angered.

"I always heard that the one who made us committed an error,

163

placing Karathia on the boundary between the Light and Dark Universes—half light and half dark, as it were," the Ra'Ak continued his pacing. "Now, the local government is pressuring my priests to leave the planet. And things were going so well, too."

"We can overpower these sorcerers, when the time comes," the Prince replied. "Take two more with you. There can't be more than a handful of the sorcerers on the planet, there won't have been enough money to pay them, otherwise. Five of you should be sufficient."

"Thank you, my Prince." The Ra'Ak bowed gratefully and made his way quickly out of the Prince's study.

~

"My child may not have died in vain," Gabron said. Grief still bound him but he was grasping hope where he found it. "The authorities have pulled legislation together formally condemning Solar Red and are drafting a bill to outlaw their presence. Of course, this may not happen soon enough, little Queen." Gabron had me in the crook of his arm on the sofa. I'd barely managed to get away from Kifirin earlier; he wanted to neck a little more. Gabron would settle for necking, period.

"Honey, maybe we should do something as a memorial. What do people normally do when someone dies here?"

"Not much—just a simple service. They no longer bury the dead; they are cremated."

"Where I come from they sing, and someone, perhaps several people, talk about the person's life," I said. "And they place flowers as a memorial."

"They place flowers?"

"They do."

"There is a flower market, not far away." Gabron rose from his seat. "Will you take me there, little Queen?" He went to a table nearby, opening a drawer. "We seldom use coinage now, but it is still good, and accepted," he said, pulling a heavy bag from a drawer. "Get me inside the flower shop, Lissa."

We went to the flower shop, Gabron guiding me with mindspeech. We misted right through the door, Gabron indicated the flowers he wanted and we ended up with half the shop, I think.

I allowed the bag of money to drop onto the counter; it didn't even set off the alarm as we misted away. The streets were deserted in front of Blue Desire when we landed and materialized; Gabron and I placed the flowers, scattering them around the doorway.

"Should we write something?" I asked. There was a wide expanse of sidewalk in front of the business.

"What do you suggest?" Gabron asked.

"Here," I said, pulling out a claw and scraping a message on the sidewalk.

"I like this," Gabron said when I finished. The quote was off the cuff but heartfelt all the same—*I will hold your name in my heart as I strike down your enemies*, I'd written. I reached down, pulled one of the blossoms off a bouquet, and handed it to Gabron, giving him a kiss. "Come on, honey," I said, and misted both of us away.

CHAPTER 10

"I don't suppose you know anything about that?" Karzac pointed at the video screen, where a news crew had recorded images of the flowers and the message I'd scratched into the pavement.

"It was a moment of weakness. It won't happen again," I promised.

"Probably for the best," Karzac nodded and went to find something for dinner. "Need to make a trip to the market," he grumbled, looking inside the fridge.

"If you'll write a list, I'll get it on my way home tonight," I offered. Karzac seemed quite happy with that suggestion and went to find a pen and paper.

"Please don't let any more Ra'Ak in the door tonight," Dragon said, reminding me to lock the door behind him when he left.

"Will do, boss," I agreed, locking and bolting the door after he left. The dojo was a mess; dirty towels were all over the locker room so I ran those through the washer and dryer while I cleaned everything else. Kifirin appeared as I was finishing up. It seems he was planning on coming to the market with me afterward, so I took a quick shower before we left.

"I like these," he pulled a package of cookies off a shelf.

"Are we buying for you?" I asked, grabbing the box of cereal that Karzac asked for.

"I could hope so," he smiled beautifully.

"All right," I took the cookies from him and tossed them into the cart. Several women were inside the store even though it was late, and they were all staring at Kifirin.

He didn't dress like the locals at all—he had on dark pants in a raw silk and a white knit shirt with an open collar. For shoes, he wore black leather boots. He wasn't far off from Earth fashion, to be honest. And he looked really good, of course, on top of that. His smile alone could cause most females and a few males to experience orgasms and lose consciousness, I think.

Several other Kifirin-related items went into the basket. He helped me carry it all back to the apartment after we paid, shocking the hell out of Dragon and Karzac as he waltzed right in and helped me put everything away.

"Uh, Dragon, Karzac, this is Kifirin," I introduced him.

"Saa Thalarr," he nodded at Dragon. "Healer." He took Karzac's hand and shook. "Have no fear; your secrets will remain safe. My silence will protect Lissa as much as it will protect you."

Dragon wore an inscrutable look on his face as he nodded slightly to Kifirin. "Now, if you will excuse us," Kifirin took my hand and folded us away.

"Hey, I didn't see you take those," he held the cookie package in his hands and was munching away. He laughed at me and offered me a bite.

"You know I can't eat it," I grumbled. He hugged me instead, one hand draped around my shoulders, the other shoving the rest of a cookie in his mouth.

~

"I have learned my lesson," René lied casually. He and Bartholomew sat at a table in an upscale London restaurant. Few knew that Bartholomew still lived and René was one of those few. He just hadn't bothered to inform anyone before of this fact. He'd sent a text message to Gavin, however, when Bartholomew agreed to meet him for a drink at the usual place.

"So, Xenides has nothing to fear?" Bartholomew secretly thought it laughable that René imagined he might take Xenides down to begin with.

"Yes. I have no desire to end up like my dear, sweet child."

"Aubrey was never a good turn to begin with," Bartholomew snorted softly. René schooled his expression so Bartholomew wouldn't know the contempt in his soul for the black-hearted bastard.

Bartholomew's heart was as evil as Xenides', but he lacked Xenides' creativity and focus. René had done some thieving for Bartholomew in the past; the reward at the time had been too great to refuse. Now René knew that those excursions on the wrong side of the law had been funded by Xenides and possibly by Saxom himself. Gavin had given important information after René had taken Devlin home a few nights earlier. René had called him and they'd had a lengthy chat.

"Aubrey's death has certainly curtailed further thoughts of revenge," René offered smoothly. "I hope this hasn't damaged our business relationship. I would still like to work with you in the future. It has definitely proven lucrative in the past."

"Of course not, René. Your talents in that area are most formidable," Bartholomew smiled and sipped his wine.

They talked for perhaps another half hour before Bartholomew rose to leave. "Don't worry about it, I'll get this," René sipped his wine and waved off Bartholomew's offer to pay. "Don't forget to contact me, my friend, for future business."

"I knew you'd see things my way," Bartholomew said before leaving the table. He pulled out his cell as he was about to exit the restaurant, hitting a number on speed dial. It was answered quickly.

"He has called off the hunt in favor of future business prospects," Bartholomew informed the vampire on the other end before terminating the call. He was slipping the phone inside his suit coat pocket as he was snatched away from the door of the restaurant and compulsion was laid a bare second later.

$$\sim$$

"Back from the dead?" Will grinned as he placed chains on Bartholomew inside Merrill's Range Rover.

He, Gavin and Merrill had gone after Bartholomew when René informed his cousin of Bartholomew's whereabouts. Gavin had taken Bartholomew's cell phone first thing; he'd turn it over to Wlodek. Merrill placed compulsion; Wlodek hadn't wanted to take any chances with the rogue vampire.

Bartholomew didn't enjoy the ride to the holding facility. He'd been given permission to blink but that was all. Gavin glared at him the entire time, as if he'd like to execute him right then without waiting for the Council to pass judgment. Gavin's cell rang. It was René, so he answered.

"We have him, thanks to you, cousin," Gavin said. René's sigh of relief was heard by every vampire inside the Range Rover.

"Thank you, cousin," René returned. "If you need anything else, let me know." Gavin ended the call and continued glaring at the prisoner.

Wlodek, Charles and Radomir were waiting when Bartholomew was unloaded and forced inside the underground bunker that housed the holding facility. "The reports of your death are greatly exaggerated, are they not?" Wlodek watched while Will and Gavin pushed Bartholomew into a seat inside the office. Wlodek had read Mark Twain, along with a great many other authors one might not expect.

"You will truthfully answer everything any vampire in the room asks you," Merrill commanded. If Bartholomew could still sweat, he would have. He could only nod and he did.

"First, tell me how you managed to make everyone believe you walked into the sun," Wlodek commanded. "Whose ashes were those?"

"Lucius," Bartholomew replied sullenly. "He wanted to turn us in."

Wlodek's eyes became red; Lucius was a friend and had disappeared suddenly. Wlodek was afraid that Lucius' human lover had staked him at the time, but he'd never found the girl either, after Lucius' disappearance.

"Did you kill him and Jovana?"

"No," Bartholomew smiled a little. "Jovana staked him. I used his ashes and wrote the note."

"Where is Jovana now? What happened to her?" Wlodek always worried about her but Lucius was in love with the human female and she'd been approved by the companion vote—his and Oluwa's had been the only dissenting votes.

Bartholomew almost laughed. "Saxom turned her," he said.

Wlodek cursed in Greek. "Is she enslaved to Xenides, now?"

"No," Bartholomew smiled.

His answer caused Merrill to stand swiftly. Lissa had said something not long ago, about the possibility of Saxom turning females, along with the fact that Saxom had known what to look for as far as misters and the like had been concerned.

"Is she a Queen?" Merrill demanded.

"Oh, yes," Bartholomew smirked. "You don't want to meet up with her. Even Xenides is afraid of her. Why do you think he wants your little princess so badly? Jovana has become a bit of a problem for Xenides and he wishes to be rid of her."

"So, Saxom was the only one who could control her?" Wlodek asked.

"Yes. A shame isn't it, that you managed to kill my sire?"

"That's a matter of opinion," Wlodek snorted. "Do you have any idea what he was planning, or with whom he had allied himself, there at the end?"

"He promised us that we would all be kings," Bartholomew hissed.

"You would have been dead," Wlodek replied. "There was no room in his plans for any of you. He only made you to be his pawns, to get him what he wanted or to take his revenge, should he die. It's too bad you can't see that for yourself."

Bartholomew growled, but Merrill's barked command kept the

disrespect behind his teeth. "How many children did Saxom make?" Merrill demanded.

"I only know of forty-seven, but Xenides always hinted there were more. He wouldn't give me the information when I asked."

"Give me names. Immediately," Wlodek snapped. Bartholomew began ticking off names.

~

"This Queen business worries me. Where is she?" Merrill paced restlessly. He'd never met Jovana; he only had Wlodek's account of her. According to him, she was self-serving in the extreme, in addition to being beautiful with thick, platinum blonde hair and a fair complexion. Lucius had been smitten, no doubt about that.

"She made me gag every time I saw her and she was in her forties the last I saw of her, shortly before Lucius disappeared." Wlodek sat in the office at the holding facility. Gavin and Merrill were the only ones remaining; he'd sent the others home after settling Bartholomew in a cell next to Llewellyn.

"Then Saxom had a hand in all that; he could have overridden Lucius' compulsion easily," Merrill observed. "And if Bartholomew is correct, she can turn to mist and use mindspeech, in addition to being immune to compulsion."

"At least we know what she looks like, but who will we send after her?"

"I'm the only option," Merrill sighed.

"I wish to settle the dilemma of Lissa," Wlodek said. "Xenides and Saxom's turns present a terrible fate for her, if they get their hands on her. I know," he held up a hand when Merrill started to speak. "But you and I know that there may be ways around your compulsion. Therefore, I have taken the liberty of presenting this option to the Council, with the exception of Ilaisaane, of course. Their opinions coincide with mine. We feel that her marriage to Gavin should take place as soon as she returns and then she will be confined and placed under the strictest of compulsions unless she can be of assistance to

171

you, Gavin or one of the Enforcers. Then we will allow her to work in controlled circumstances. Her susceptibility to compulsion is a glaring weakness, as you both know. Otherwise, there is nothing we could do to control her. Our enemies know this too, now, thanks to Ilaisaane."

"You know what this will do to her, Wlodek. Lissa will walk into the sun the first chance she gets." Merrill wasn't happy with Wlodek's and the Council's decision.

"That will be the first compulsion I place," Gavin growled. He knew what this would do to Lissa as well, but he couldn't deal with the sight of her blackened body again. The attempted suicide earlier in the year had left a terrible mark on his soul.

"That is what I hoped for, and you know the Council will loosen the law for a spouse's compulsion," Wlodek nodded. "That is why we wish to move the marriage up."

"Then why wait?" Merrill tossed a hand in the air. "We can do it now, in absentia. Honestly, I have no desire to stand here and watch her weep while you force this on her."

"Merrill, this is for her own good," Wlodek declared. "And for the good of the race, as well. Tell me this is not so."

"What is good for the race and good for Lissa are two separate things in this case," Merrill argued.

"She will be treated gently and with care," Wlodek argued back. "I will make sure that Charles is available, whenever possible. Radomir and one of the other Enforcers will accompany them to keep her safe."

"We'll be her jailers," Merrill growled. "We already are, only this will be worse. Are you saying that she'll never have any freedom? That she'll be under the Council's thumb from now on? That all her decisions will be Gavin's to make?"

"I will not be that terrible," Gavin was now growling at Merrill's accusations.

"This argument will stop immediately!" Wlodek thundered. "We will hold the ceremony here and now. Gavin, if you do not already have the ring, you will provide it when she returns. She will be brought to me and I will inform her of what her life will be. She already despises me. Nothing will change in that respect."

"I already have her ring, it is at Merrill's home," Gavin muttered.

"Very well," Wlodek said, reeling his temper in a little. "I declare your marriage to Lissa Beth Workman Huston active, Gaius Livius Montanus, now known as Gavin Montegue, for a period of one hundred years. I expect you to treat her well. My blessings on your union."

Gavin had stood for the pronouncement, and now he bowed deeply to Wlodek. "My thanks, Honored One," he said. Merrill was still frowning and wanted more than anything to speak with Griffin about this, but his friend was not available.

"You do not have anything to say, Titus Marius Merula?" Wlodek glared at Merrill. Merrill hadn't heard his Roman name in a very long time and wasn't sure he appreciated Wlodek using it now.

"What can I possibly say? You have decided; I cannot gainsay it now." Merrill had his arms crossed tightly over his chest. Wlodek knew he was furious. "I know the race must be protected and I have never felt so angry over having to do so. I hope you are prepared for what will come," Merrill handed Gavin a grim look. "She may never smile at you again, unless you place compulsion." He went so swiftly out the door he lifted papers off the desk in a swirl and eddy.

"We will do our best to make her smile," Wlodek said softly. Gavin was staring at the door that Merrill had just flown through in his haste to leave.

"I'll need a ride, Honored One," Gavin turned back to Wlodek. Wlodek nodded.

∽

"Attack me, Lissa!" Dragon grinned as we sparred with wooden practice swords.

"Honey, I don't want to hit you," I said.

"If you hit me, maybe I deserve it," his grin widened.

"Unbelievable," I said, blocking his blows. I could see them coming easily.

"Come on; just give me a small attack."

"I sure hope Karzac is in the mood to fix you up," I grumbled and went after him. When I whacked him the second time, he laughed and stopped the bout.

"Until now, only my brother has managed to get a blow in," Dragon said. "Feel up to turning to mist and getting us both home so we can clean up there?"

"Sure," I said. I'd already cleaned the dojo; Dragon had stuck around and rested a little while so we could spar. The door was locked and he'd had an alarm installed the day before.

Things with Solar Red were turning strange; the priests were withdrawing from the public for some reason and nobody could figure out why. Perhaps it was because of the legislation that had been drafted condemning the religion, but I wasn't so hopeful that the current political climate was the reason. Yeah, I didn't trust those Solar Red guys. Not at all.

We cleaned up our practice blades and returned them to the racks inside Dragon's office before going to mist and heading home. Karzac was just finishing some sort of stew that Dragon apparently liked; he filled a bowl and ate before going to clean up. I went to take a shower and drink a little extra blood; I wanted to go pay the temple a visit and see if I could tell what was going on.

"Honey, are you okay?" I asked Karzac when I came out, clean and a little damp around my hair, which was growing out nicely. He was sitting at the kitchen table still, his empty bowl in front of him.

"I am fine, but looking forward to this being over," he said, his green-gold eyes betraying a bit of concern. Dragon was now in the shower after eating two huge bowls of stew. "I never thought that returning to my home world would be so exhausting."

"They just run you ragged, don't they?" I rubbed his back to comfort him. He smiled up at me, and Karzac doesn't smile very often.

"If we could ask for the M'fiyah, I would certainly consider it," he said.

I had no idea what he was talking about, so I gave him an extra pat. "I'm going to mist over to the temple and see what those red devils are up to," I said. "Go to bed early, doc." I misted away.

~

Life is strange, even wondrous at times, but there are days when you experience something so horrible it leaves its mark upon you and the memory lingers, vivid and terrible, for the rest of your days. That's what I witnessed that night.

I found a group of perhaps fifty priests, dressed in their finest red robes, gathered around a single man. He looked like a man. He just wasn't—he was Ra'Ak—I could tell by the scent. He was performing some sort of ritual that would have made me gag if I'd been in solid form.

A Ra'Ak, in humanoid form, still has the long, snaky tongue that they have in their other form—I learned that right away. He was kissing those priests, one at a time, his tongue going right down their throats and staying there for seconds. *Dragon, he's kissing them—the priests*, I sent, still trying to quell a non-existent gag reflex.

What? Who's kissing the priests? Dragon's voice came back to me.

A Ra'Ak. He's sliding his tongue down their throats, I returned.

How many priests?

About fifty.

Lissa, the Ra'Ak can only do this if they refrain from manufacturing poison for three weeks. This Ra'Ak is virtually helpless. Do not think him unguarded, though. Be assured there is another there, somewhere. Do not approach him. Come home now. We will deal with this. Dragon wanted me to leave. Honestly, I was glad to—I couldn't stay and watch this much longer. It took a few minutes to get home and I was heaving the moment I came back to myself.

"Bend you head down," Dragon said, after getting me seated on the sofa. I got my head down to the vicinity of my knees and breathed for a few minutes. "Don't think about it," he ordered. I was trying. Really.

That image was going to stay with me for a while, I think. A really long while.

"It's the Ra'Ak's kiss," Dragon said, raising me up after I stopped gagging. "It's the way they create demons, who in turn can create other demons. They sometimes do this to the willing, who think they'll become Ra'Ak. The truth, of course, is that it will be survival of the fittest from this point forward. Perhaps one in ten thousand demons survives to become Ra'Ak. They stay in demon form for around twenty years before they make the final turn, and even then the Ra'Ak weed out what they determine to be weak or unsuitable candidates. Their chances of survival are very small."

"But what if these schmucks go out into the city and just bite anybody they see?" That's what the others were trying to do that we'd killed so far.

"A true dilemma," Dragon nodded. "However, I cannot help but believe they were trying to trap you tonight by doing this. Did you ever see the other Ra'Ak?"

"No. I didn't smell him, either."

"Then he was heavily shielded. They can do this, just as we can, but generally they do not bother. We can't sense them while we're shielded, and we know the moment we drop our shields they can sense us, not having their own shields up, as it were." Dragon was frowning as he sat beside me on the sofa.

"You don't have a fun job," I muttered.

"I can't imagine that you do, either."

"You got me there," I agreed. "Maybe I'll go see Gabron instead."

"What about Kifirin?"

"He does what he pleases," I said. "It's not as if he left his phone number or anything."

"No, he just left these." Dragon touched the marks on my neck.

"Yeah. I still feel like punching him for that."

"I can't advise you, one way or the other on that," Dragon told me and rose from his seat. "I have to go to bed or I'll be worthless tomorrow." He yawned when he stood.

"Goodnight," I said, rising as well.

~

"I feel ill, just thinking about it," I told Gabron later. He hadn't heard of the Ra'Ak before but he was hearing about them now. I'd described them, both as serpent and humanoid, and what they'd done to the priests earlier.

"You'll be able to tell when you kill them," I said. "They blast out in these fist-sized chunks, like a giant sandstorm. Their spawn do the same, only their particles are more like normal sand and don't do so much damage."

"Will they consume or bite vampires?" Gabron asked.

"I don't know. I'll ask and let you know later."

"The ritual is only a week away," Gabron reminded me. "The others are becoming restless; they want out of here and are counting the days."

"I understand that completely," I nodded. I knew exactly how it felt to be confined or under house arrest. "The good news is that the whole vampire scare has died down, I think."

"If they knew that you were the one dropping large boats from great heights and that you were also vampire, they might rethink that," Gabron smiled.

"Hey now, I only go after the bad guys," I grumped.

"I know this," Gabron chuckled softly and put his arm around me.

"Someone I met recently told me about a world called Le-Ath Veronis," I said, settling into Gabron's embrace. "He said those words translate to Heart of the Vampire. He also says that the planet rotates on its side, so the southern hemisphere is in constant twilight. I was told that vampires lived on that planet in a symbiotic relationship with a race of companions that can only have sex with the bite of a vampire. They replace the blood taken faster than any other race and they taste good, Gabron."

"That sounds like a pleasant dream," Gabron nuzzled my hair and then sucked on my earlobe.

"What would you say if I told you I met two of that race? That I drank from them? It was as good as eating cinnamon rolls."

"Some blood is sweeter than others," he nipped my earlobe now before moving down to my neck. I didn't move, even though I knew what was coming. He placed the kiss and then his fangs were in my neck while I writhed in his arms with the climax.

Gabron got his, too; he took my blood, I took his, and he enjoyed it. Very much. I went home immediately after; I didn't want to hop in bed with him in a moment of weakness. "You'll allow the little King to do this and yet you hold me at arm's length?" Kifirin was in my bedroom (of course, where else would he be?) when I came in just before dawn.

"We didn't do the run up the middle," I said, pulling the covers down on the bed.

"You're using football analogies?"

"You know everything, don't you?"

"If I want to know it, I will."

"Then you know I'd like to toss you on the bed right now and have my way with you," I grumbled. "Just to keep that shit I saw earlier out of my head."

"I will accept any reason given to have sex with you." He walked over and leaned down to kiss me.

How does he do it? How can he make me boneless enough to drop to the floor, almost, just with a kiss? I didn't have enough brain cells afterward to figure it out. Yeah, I didn't think there was enough time before dawn to do the nasty.

I was wrong.

"The claiming is complete." Kifirin was smiling down at me when I woke the following evening. I slapped a hand over my face. How was I going to explain this to Gavin? It was bad enough that Gabron and I had done a blood exchange, now Kifirin and I had gone all the way and if I was reading the signs right, we were about to do it again.

I still didn't have an explanation for what happens when he kisses me and why it only escalates from there, until I want him to bury himself inside me. I was like a crazy woman or some animal, the way I went after him just before dawn.

Kifirin's smile was bigger, now. "It is the linking, your mind with mine. You feel my desire. It is primal. Did you not enjoy it?"

"Honey, if I enjoyed it any more, I'd duct tape myself to you and you'd never get away," I grumbled.

"Exactly what I wanted to hear," he said, leaning down to kiss me.

∼

"Mr. Hancock, this is René de la Roque," Russell introduced René to Tony, Deryn and Paul. René's eyebrow lifted slightly; he'd never worked with werewolves before. After a moment, he realized he relished the idea. René had always been something of an adventurer at heart.

"You're going to help us track Rahim Alif?" Tony asked, taking René's hand. René didn't mind contact with humans, as some other vampires did.

"It will be a pleasure; his vampire associate had my sire killed and then murdered one of my children," René answered. "Anything I can do to hurt him, I will do gladly."

"Are you prepared to travel?" Tony asked René.

"Of course."

"Good. Pack a bag; we're leaving for Paris tomorrow evening. My contacts report a sighting of Xenides, and we believe Rahim Alif is there as well."

"Perhaps you would like to stay at my home tonight, then?" René offered the invitation. "You will be safe and undisturbed. I have human servants who can cook for you, if you wish."

Tony looked at Deryn, who shrugged. "Sure. Thank you for the invitation," Tony said. "Just give us a moment to collect our things."

∼

"Grand Master, we're on the move again," Paul informed Weldon. He was standing on the expansive marble porch that ran nearly the length of René's manor outside London. The lawns were beautiful; Paul could see stables in the distance and when the wind was right he could smell horses. "We hear Lissa is out of the country, so Tony has focused on what he should be focused on—the rogue vampire Xenides and the terrorist Rahim Alif."

"Has the Head of the Council calmed down a bit?" Weldon asked.

"Yes, Grand Master. In fact, he was so appreciative of our efforts, killing the two in the pub, that we were invited to his home. You should see it, sir. Just one or two paintings off his walls and you'd be living like a king."

"I understand he's had a couple thousand years or more to acquire all that," Weldon snorted. "I'd rather be where I am, thanks. Have you and Deryn found a place to run for the full moon?"

"We'll be in Paris, Grand Master. If you could get us the hook-up there, I'd appreciate it."

"I can do that," Weldon said. "I'll call or send a text as soon as it's set up."

"Thank you, Grand Master." Paul closed his cell and sat down, propping his feet up on the chaise. The sun was out today and it was the perfect time to be sipping coffee and staring out over the English countryside.

"Your son and step-son are safe from the Council; they're going after terrorists and rogues, now," Weldon informed Lucas Alford over the phone. Lucas was back in Denver; he was Second to the Packmaster there and his presence was required for the run on the full moon.

"At least that's Tony's job," Lucas growled. "Any word on how long they'll be gone?" Deryn had taken a leave of absence from his job as a Lieutenant for the local police force.

"No, he didn't give me a time frame," Weldon replied. "If I get anything, I'll pass it along."

"Thank you, Grand Master," Lucas said, terminating the call.

Wlodek had to coax Merrill back; his eldest was still angry. Wlodek knew Merrill was the one who should place compulsion on Ilaisaane before he allowed her to leave the holding facility. Wlodek had her cell phone and knew Xenides had tried to contact her already. Wlodek allowed the call to go to voice mail.

"Xenides will know something is up if he wishes to meet with her and she fails to appear," Wlodek informed his oldest child. Merrill was barely speaking to him and the situation was quite tense. "We should place compulsion not to turn over important information, including whom we currently have as prisoners here before allowing her to leave. She will report to us when it is safe to do so, and once Xenides is eliminated, we can bring her in again. Charles already has the transcripts and the information will be distributed to the others, once she is recaptured."

"I will place compulsion," Merrill growled as he followed Wlodek down the long hall toward Ilaisaane's cell.

"You will behave normally; you were merely here for a companion hearing, after which we allowed the companion her freedom," Merrill commanded Ilaisaane. "Ian will drive you home, Flavio has other business." Ilaisaane nodded blankly as Radomir and Ian removed the chains from her wrists and ankles. "You will contact us discreetly if you are asked to meet with Xenides or have contact with him for any reason. Under no circumstances will you betray any of us to him or give out further sensitive information. Do you understand?" Ilaisaane nodded. "Good," Merrill sighed. "Ian, you will not repeat any of this information to anyone, or release any sensitive information concerning Ilaisaane or any other member of the Council. You will not give out information on any Enforcer or Assassin. You will also not repeat anything concerning myself or Lissa," Merrill instructed the Enforcer. Ian nodded. He'd had Merrill's compulsion before; it didn't concern him at all. It was a way to keep them all safe.

Wlodek handed Ilaisaane's cell phone to her; Ian and Radomir walked her out of the building and she was already chattering and complaining before they reached the door. "Will you share a bottle of wine with me or will you remain angry, child?" Wlodek asked Merrill.

"I will go home, Father. It's best for the moment," Merrill replied stiffly. "I'll see myself out of the bunker." Wlodek watched his eldest child walk away and sighed.

CHAPTER 11

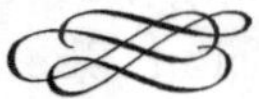

Gabron was upset that I wouldn't allow him to bite me again and that I wouldn't bite him in return. The ritual was two days away and he and I were both tense. Dragon and Karzac were, too, as they fully expected the Ra'Ak to make an appearance, just as I did.

I was also keeping an eye on the newscasts; I waited for someone or several someones to be kidnapped so the sacrifices could be made. Solar Red had to be planning something; the priests had stopped coming out of the temple, making me wonder what that meant.

Dragon advised me not to go back there; the boat I'd taken from the river and dropped had killed all the priests from the satellite temples—more than six hundreds of them, in fact—along with two hundred additional guards. More priests had been stationed in the outlying cities than even Gabron suspected.

Journalists hinted that the official eviction for Solar Red could come from the government any day. I worried that everything would happen simultaneously, with disastrous results.

I was cleaning the dojo while Dragon finished with his last class. "Are you going to the ritual?" A female student asked as she wandered into the dressing room. I was busy straightening up and cleaning out showers.

"Is there something of interest there?" I asked. Of course I would be going, but it was to lop priests' heads off, starting with the ones who were turning to demon.

"Everyone got a flyer," she said. "They're giving out gifts."

"You're kidding?" I couldn't believe this—why did people always turn out in droves if something was being given away? "Stay away from there," I placed compulsion. She nodded blankly just as three more women came in to shower and dress.

"Dragon, one of those women said she got a flyer of some kind, saying that Solar Red was going to hand out gifts," I said after the last of his students left and we'd locked up for the night. "If a ton of people show up, that's just fodder for those demon fuckers. And, if the vampires come out, it'll make it more difficult to fight."

"They've thought this through," Dragon rubbed the back of his neck. "I'm not sure what we can do about it, though, without calling their attention to us." We walked home, both of us silent, worrying about the ritual and what might happen.

Karzac was already there and waiting when we arrived; he'd roasted fowl for his and Dragon's dinner, so they ate while I cleaned up. I didn't want to go out again, honestly, but Gabron would be expecting me. My visits broke up his self-imposed confinement. I carried the news of the flyers and the people who'd likely attend the ritual as a result and he wasn't pleased with the information.

"This will make things so much worse," Gabron paced. "I must warn the others; we will have to take care if we attack the priests."

"Dragon says the ones that are demon won't bite a vampire—they don't like the taste. They'll just try to kill us instead. They move fast, Gabron. Be sure to tell the others so they'll be ready for that."

Xenides sat in a corner of the royal suite at a luxurious hotel in Paris. He'd chosen a Louis XIV-style chair so he'd be in shadow. He watched, feeling quite bored as Rahim instructed his subordinates; their target on the full moon was another hotel nearby.

Xenides smiled at the thought—Anthony Hancock had become a thorn in his side. If Rahim saw things the same way, so much the better. Word had it that Hancock and the little princess were close, so he could achieve both his goals—destroying Hancock would likely bring the princess to Paris to investigate. Xenides listened as Rahim carefully explained his objectives.

Xenides spoke some modern Arabic, but had never bothered to learn the language completely. Rahim spoke fluent English, in addition to French and Italian, so they were able to communicate quite well.

Rahim instructed his two suicide bombers regarding their target the following evening. His goal was to produce an explosion that would generate the greatest amount of damage. Rahim ended his spiel with the usual "Death to the infidels." His subordinates repeated the phrase and stole away from the room, one at a time.

Both were dressed in western-style clothing and appeared to be tourists on a holiday. Rahim had seen to that. He was very good at what he did—Xenides was happy to have him under his thumb. "Soon our glory will be multiplied," Rahim smiled at Xenides after his second subordinate left the suite.

"Of course it will," Xenides agreed. "Just make sure your sheep do as they're told." Compulsion was thick in Xenides' voice.

~

"Bro, you need to stick close to Paul; at least he can howl in French," Tony teased Deryn as Paul and his brother made ready to leave the hotel in order to run with a Pack outside the city.

"Bro, you need to stick to human shit; you couldn't give a good howl if it would save your life," Deryn teased back. Tony shook his head at Deryn's words as Paul and his brother walked out the door. Deryn and Paul's dinner would likely consist of rabbit and other small prey. Tony was on his way downstairs to treat himself to a nice, thick steak.

～

I sat on the roof of the apartment building and watched as a quarter moon rose over the horizon. Worried couldn't begin to describe how I felt and Kifirin's absence the past few days only added to that.

Dragon was also tense, although he hid it well most of the time. Karzac had gone to work at the hospital, after telling us he would be available if needed. I felt we were about to go to war in two hours; the ritual would begin at that time and I could hear people on the streets below, already walking toward the temple.

I'd finally gotten my hands on one of the flyers. It promised a huge sum of money, to be given away by a lottery of sorts. The flyer encouraged the population to come early so they could receive their tickets.

Tickets. Monsters were handing out tickets. That was a terrible joke and made me wonder for perhaps the hundredth time what their real intentions were. No doubt, I'd know before the night was over.

Dragon didn't want to go until the last minute, in case the Ra'Ak was there and looking for us. Probably a good idea. I had plans to mist us both there anyway, so they wouldn't see us walking past the guards that would undoubtedly be posted.

Little Queen, we are leaving our underground prison, Gabron sent. He'd informed me the evening before that the vampires would scatter and come at the temple from all directions in small groups.

I hoped things went well for us; my skin had been itching for the past two hours. I was afraid to mention it to Dragon—he and I could both go down, along with Gabron and his vampires. My knees were up to my chin and I was only waiting on Dragon now.

I watched as vans containing news crews drove past on the streets below; they were one of the few independent businesses that actually possessed their own transportation. Whatever happened was going to be recorded. If it was my death, along with Dragon's and the others, I hoped somebody would let Gavin and Merrill know.

Wlodek had allowed my participation in this—had he known how dangerous it might be? Ever since Dragon let me know that the Ra'Ak was shielded against us, we had no way of telling if or when he'd appear. My nose was no longer a help in the matter. I was flying blind just like everyone else and it frightened me. I hate surprises. Especially lengthy, toothy, snaky ones.

"I have a harder time than you do, scaling the sides of the building without using any power," Dragon hopped onto the roof and gracefully navigated the narrow surface to sit beside me. He was as lithe and sure as any jungle cat walking a high limb.

"Merrill and Gavin can just float around," I said, lifting my chin off my knees. "I had no idea Gavin could do it; of course I didn't know he was vampire when I first met him either," I added.

"You didn't know?" Dragon wore a confused expression as he blinked at me.

"I hadn't been vampire very long; the one who turned me never intended for me to live and I managed to get away before he could kill me," I said with a shrug. "I had no idea what I was doing and nobody to teach me the rules. The Council sent Gavin—he's an assassin—to get rid of me. He sort of got sidetracked, though, and stayed to watch the werewolf I was working for. I couldn't ever figure out how he got onto roofs and over walls without making any sound. I didn't find out he was vampire until he placed compulsion and hauled me off to the Council."

"You're susceptible to compulsion?" Dragon sounded surprised.

"Not anymore. I haven't been since the end of my first year as a vampire. I haven't figured out why, yet, but it's the truth. The other vampires back on Earth still think compulsion works. It doesn't." I snorted at the thought. "They'll probably kill me if they find out."

"Surely not," Dragon scoffed.

"You don't know them," I said, leaning my chin on my knees again. "They don't know half the stuff I can do. Some of it, they're just too blind to see."

"What else can you do that they don't know about?" Dragon was looking off in the distance, toward the temple. He and I were only killing time, now.

"I can tell who sired whom, as far as vampires, humans and just about any other race goes," I replied.

"Do you know who made Merrill, then? Kiarra has wondered but she won't go *Looking*, she thinks it would be an invasion of privacy. She likes Merrill a lot." That statement made me laugh humorlessly.

"That's nothing to how Merrill feels about her," I said without thinking. I slapped a hand over my mouth afterward, but it was already too late. Dragon put his head back and laughed. I mean out loud. He then placed an arm around me and squeezed.

"I'll keep that to myself. Do you know who made him?" Dragon asked his question again.

"Wlodek did, only he has no hold over his vampire child. Do you know what a King Vampire is?"

"I have heard that term before. They hold the strongest compulsion and no other vampire can force them to their will. They are generally strong; stronger than most others, even from the start, and the only vampire they cannot control is a Queen."

"Yeah," I said glumly. "Merrill is a King Vampire and even he can't place compulsion on me. The minute they learn they can't control me like they think they can, they'll get Gavin or one of the others to sharpen their claws and I'll be headless and ash in less than a blink. They sort of forced me into an engagement with Gavin and I always worry that Wlodek will just tell him to kill me while I sleep, since he wakes before I do and I fall asleep before he does. One of the drawbacks of being a young vampire."

"You're terrified your own fiancé will kill you while he's in your bed?"

"He was all set to kill me when he dragged me in front of the Council, although he swears he loved me then. Now tell me how that works," I huffed.

"I can't explain that," Dragon sighed. "Have you talked to him about this?"

"Most of the time we don't talk. He yells and I listen. The yelling is generally in foreign languages I don't understand. He's insanely jealous, so I don't know what to do or say about Kifirin. Kifirin keeps telling me it won't be a problem, but he's never met Gavin before. Honestly, I don't know what happened with Kifirin—normally I'm able to resist. This, though, I can't explain it."

"The M'fiyah," Dragon said softly.

"Karzac said that word too. What does it mean?" I looked up at Dragon, who was still staring off in the distance.

"It means mate recognition, as nearly as I can translate it from the original Neaborian. Some of the immortal races are predisposed. That means the moment you see your intended mate, or mates, you recognize them, somehow. It's nearly impossible to resist them, most of the time. What did Karzac say to you, when he used the word?"

I would have flushed, if I could have. "He, uh, said if he could ask for that, he would consider it."

Dragon smiled at my words. "That is a real compliment, coming from Karzac," he said. His arm was still draped around me and he hugged me closer.

"So, no M'fiyah for you or Karzac, yet?" I asked.

"Sadly, no. But Griffin, who sees farther and better than anyone I have ever met, says it won't be long now. So I am waiting." Dragon smiled down at me.

"Is that what Adam Chessman had with Kiarra?"

"Yes. And it was something to see, little vampire. She was the last person I would have believed to be caught in that net, yet she was landed and gasping like a fish when she saw him the first time."

"So, you think that Kifirin and I?" I didn't finish my question.

"I think so," he nodded. "I can't imagine that one such as he would have been interested otherwise, and as you say, you have fended off others in the past. The M'fiyah is the only explanation I can think of."

I blew out a sigh. Was that it? Kifirin and I were destined to be together? That still didn't help at all with Gavin and what his feelings would be over the whole thing. Honestly, I didn't know what to do about either one of them.

I wanted to go to bed with Kifirin, no doubt about that, but I was still waiting to love him, I think. And Gavin? I still cared about him, for the most part. I just needed to stop being afraid all the time. Of him, of Wlodek and the Council, of Merrill, even, to a lesser degree. I knew where that fear came from; it was from my past and I thought I'd beaten it. Becoming vampire had brought it back with a vengeance and I was struggling against it again in my second existence.

"Let's go, little Queen," Dragon said softly, lifting me to my feet. I stood beside him, dusting off my loose pants with a hand before turning Dragon to mist with me.

The crowd was enormous outside the temple; I estimated at least a hundred thousand or more. Karzac told me the total population of the capital city was around three million, but a hundred thousand was a huge number of people.

Some football stadiums, and that was in the European sense of the word, might be able to hold that many. The people were all milling around outside; I saw a few red robes around, passing out slips of paper. I assumed those were the tickets.

I misted Dragon and myself next to the temple wall on the back side, in an empty spot where we wouldn't be seen as we materialized —most of the crowd activity was toward the front. I smelled vampire, too, but didn't go looking for them. Their actions were out of my hands—Gabron was giving those instructions and I was content with that.

Dragon and I made our slow way around the octagonal temple toward the front, but it was difficult at times; the multitude was pushing against us as more and more people joined the crowd, anxious to find a priest and receive a ticket for the drawing.

I'm thinking about using compulsion like a shotgun, and just yelling for everybody to get the hell out of our way, I told Dragon in mindspeech. He smiled and nodded his understanding as we were squeezed by yet another knot of people.

The noise as we went through the crowd was nearly unbearable, too. All of them were talking; I even heard some shouting, here and there. I did my best to ignore all of it, concentrating on arriving at the four main entrances into the temple and getting there before everything was scheduled to start.

What truly frightened me, however, was the number of parents I saw who'd brought their children. That almost stopped me in my tracks.

Lissa, focus, Dragon sent. *We can only do as much as we can do.* My mouth was dry, even though I'd had my blood—as much as I could drink, anyway. I think I was praying silently by that time that somehow the children would be spared if their parents fell.

I nodded at Dragon's mental message and we moved on. Eventually, I ended up behind him; his shoulders were so much wider and he was so much taller than I was that it was easier for him to make a path for us. I was tired already, I think, just pushing our way through the throng toward the front gates. I took a few deep breaths, preparing for whatever came, when three priests slipped through the front doors. One of them had an amplifier and microphone with him.

He's not demon; young demons do not have speech capabilities, Dragon sent to me. That was good information to have. If I'd been close enough, I could have smelled whether he was demon or not but I wasn't that close and my nose was filled with the scent of too many Refizani bodies crowding around me.

"Good evening, citizens of Refizan," the priest with the microphone began to speak. "We will allow you into the temple in moments, but as you might imagine, we can only take so many. Do not fear; we will bring you all through eventually. Everyone will have an opportunity at the prize."

He and the two other priests stepped back inside the doors. A few minutes later, the doors swung inward. Priests, stationed at all four entrances, allowed the waiting crowd to push inside. Thug guards were positioned at the doors, too, just to make sure none of the people got out of hand. Dragon and I were shoved forward, passing priests who had the stink of demon on them.

I know. Dragon sent to me as we were pushed farther inside the temple.

Gabron, I sent a mental shout, *the priests at the doors are demon.*

We are placing compulsion at the edges of the crowd, telling them to go home, he replied. I sent up a mental thanks.

Get as many of the children out of here as you can, Gabron, I begged, before cutting off communication. The huge, heavy doors were closing behind us. We'd been forced into the center of the temple floor; it was bare, I noticed.

They had allowed perhaps two thousand of the waiting people in on the first round and there was a semi-circle of priests at the front, before an altar. Five more men, not dressed as priests, stood behind the altar. That semi-circle of priests? All demons; I recognized some of them as the ones receiving the Ra'Ak's kiss earlier. They were completely silent and had no expressions on their faces. In fact, they were gazing at the crowd as if—*as if they were hungry.*

I looked around me swiftly. Men, women and children surrounded me, all hoping to win the lottery, I suppose. It might be a lottery, but the priests were about to be the winners, I had no doubt about that. I ducked down, hoping that the attention wouldn't be on me when I turned to mist, watching in horror as more priests by the hundreds came through side doors and stood behind the ones already lined up at the altar. It made me think of cockroaches escaping the walls, there were so many.

Most of these were demon; their scent overwhelmed me as they crowded the front of the temple. Obviously, the Ra'Ak had been busy; more than Dragon or I had imagined. It made me wonder just how many Solar Red priests were still humanoid.

I'm mist, I mindspoke Dragon and rose high above the crowd in the temple. Several priests stepped forward. People were about to be eaten or turned to demon and I was at a loss as to what to do about it.

I am safe from them, Dragon sent. I had no idea how that was possible. When the first screams of the people came as demon priests fell on them, ripping and tearing their flesh with teeth that didn't belong in any human mouth, I became desperate and did what I might not have done otherwise.

"I am on my way," René informed Tony via cell phone as Tony sat in the hotel restaurant, waiting for his order to be taken. René had spent the night in a safe house not far away; he preferred not to stay in hotels if he could avoid it.

"I am in the restaurant, Le Chat Gris, downstairs," Tony said. "Come by, I'll buy a glass of wine for you and we'll talk."

"I will be there in shortly," René replied, terminating the call. He was riding in a taxi; he'd managed to get one to take him to the hotel.

Tony drummed his fingers impatiently on a menu as he watched a waiter walk toward his table. The waiter was almost there and Tony was just about to ask for *un steak saignant* when the front of the restaurant blew inward. In the blink of an eye, although to Tony it appeared to move in slow motion, he was blown away with the rest of it.

I was mentally screaming for Gabron, shouting *they're eating them*, as I wound my mist as tightly as I could before releasing it, blasting the roof and the walls of the temple outward. People were screaming inside and out as chunks of brick and mortar came raining down on everyone.

The priests inside—the demon ones, anyway, took that as a sign that their dinner might be getting away and stepped up their assault. The guards began shooting into the crowd; total chaos was a mild description of what was actually happening. The crowd was panicked and running—if they could. Many of them were trampled in their haste to get away. The vampires had done a good job, however; only half the original crowd remained when I blasted the temple.

The only ones making their way toward the temple floor (only a waist-high ring of wall now stood around it), were the vampires. I saw them as I hovered high overhead, taking stock of the situation. I couldn't see Dragon any longer, the mass exodus was so confused and disorderly.

Demon priests were tearing apart any humanoid they came across, devouring the pieces swiftly as they moved to attack the next one. A news crew situated atop a nearby building was recording it all—and sending a live feed to citizens across Refizan. The noise was almost unendurable, with each of the remaining fifty thousand people screaming at the top of their lungs as they fled.

I dived downward, intent upon helping the vampires who were now reaching the demon priests—more than two thousands of them —all dressed in the red robes of their order. Demon priests were dusting as they met up with the vampires, whose claws were out as they sliced heads off viciously. I saw one vampire go down trying to protect a mother and her child. I went there, first.

"Fuckers!" I screamed in English as I removed the first head before completely materializing. Another priest took his place and he dusted, too. The mother was running behind me, getting away from there as quickly as she could.

Karzac and many of the hospital's employees were glued to the video screen, watching in horror as people were running away, some of them not getting far before being torn apart by priests in their red robes.

"They're eating them!" One of the nurses wept as they watched the carnage. Karzac schooled his face; he'd seen this before, just not to this degree or on his home planet. The cameras, some of them, now focused on the vampires who were fighting the priests, allowing the people to run away as best they could.

"Those are the vampires," another physician said, the awe in his voice unconcealed.

"Those monsters are exploding when they're killed," someone else observed.

"Come, I think we're needed there more than here," Karzac said. "Leave half behind. Those who are willing, come with me." He gathered up as much in the way of supplies as he could and headed toward the door. Several followed his lead. "Look, there's a female vampire," someone said as Karzac made his way through the sliding glass doors of the emergency room. Karzac smiled grimly at the comment.

Most of the Refizani citizens had gotten away; the majority of what was left were priests and vampires. The five who'd been standing behind the altar were still there as well, only they'd moved toward the back wall, content to watch as the vampires fought Solar Red.

Dragon, when I saw him off to the side, was whacking priests with bricks and bits of wood. He didn't have his blades; those would have been too obvious when we'd come in. Nevertheless, he was doing pretty well with what he had, driving priests toward waiting vampires, who were only too happy to remove heads.

I was getting blasted by demon sand time and time again as I moved among them, slicing off heads. I might have been nicked here and there, but the heat of the battle was too intense for me to notice.

A knot of vampires flanked me after a while and I found Gabron fighting at my side. He was fiercely efficient, moving so swiftly no demon priest held the tiniest chance against him.

Emergency vehicles were now making their way to the temple, with sirens announcing their presence. Briefly, I wondered what they could do for the ones bitten by demons but had little time to reflect on that dilemma—more priests came and they were joined by demons that had already sloughed away their humanoid appearance. They boiled out of the underground caverns beneath the temple like angry ants from a mound.

Lissa! Dragon's desperate mindspeech came just as the most recent wave of demons was followed by a huge monster. He had to be at least twelve feet tall with the same ugly, grayish-brown skin that the smaller demons wore.

Dragon had said they stayed demon for twenty years or so before becoming Ra'Ak. This had to be one of the older ones. I had to go to mist to fight this one; he was sweeping vampires away before him with wide swipes of huge arms—they couldn't get close enough to do any damage.

Coming up behind him, I gave him one good slash to the back of the neck with my claws, severing his spine. He went down with a terrible howl, falling first to his knees before crumpling, crushing two remaining priests beneath him. They'd sought his side as protection from the vampires and died for their trouble.

Finish him Lissa! Dragon shouted encouragement, so I swooped in, letting only my hands and claws materialize as I swept the remains of the head from the torso. The huge demon dusted almost as violently as the Ra'Ak that I'd killed days before.

Vampires were blown outward with the dusting and some didn't rise again quickly enough—demons were falling on them, which caused me to scream and go after them.

That was the moment the Ra'Ak chose to reveal himself. The one I'd seen in a field outside the city materialized first; he was one of the five men who'd stood behind the altar and watched as demon priests attacked humans.

Then, the other four turned as well—Dragon had five Ra'Ak to contend with, instead of the one that was supposed to be there. Dragon, I learned quickly, wasn't given that name because of his tattoos. I watched, completely amazed as he shouted at the Ra'Ak before becoming a huge dragon; his lithe, well-muscled body covered with red scales tipped in black.

Dragon was now facing five Ra'Ak, who were just as large. No way could he fight them all. No way could he take them all down. I almost went rigid from the fear that gripped me.

❧

René was doing what he could without revealing himself and the strength he was exerting, tossing aside rubble and debris from the bombed hotel and searching for survivors. He shouted for medical personnel and anyone else who would listen, anytime he heard the faintest heartbeat or sniffed out the least sign of life.

Fire crews were nearby, putting out small fires here and there, so René was completely soaked by spraying water. He ignored any discomfort—he knew Tony was somewhere amid the destruction and he was desperately searching for the man. He also knew that Deryn and Paul had gone out earlier to run with one of the local Packs, so they would not be buried with the others.

"*Aidez moi!*" René's French was flawless as he shouted for assistance. Two paramedics came as quickly as they could, stumbling around unstable debris to get to René's side. As soon as they arrived to help the woman René had uncovered, René placed compulsion to forget him and continued his search for Anthony Hancock.

Dragon told me that even brushing against the Ra'Ak in their serpent form would poison anyone; that even their scales held poison, along with their teeth and spines. What could I do? Watch helplessly while Dragon was taken down? *Stay away from the snakes!* I shouted at any vampire who could hear me.

I didn't know if Gabron was still alive; I'd lost sight of him minutes before. Well, as potential deaths go, I was far from home and I had no idea how deadly the poison was or how quickly it would react. It might be a horrible way to die, but could it be worse than the sun on a vampire's skin? *Been there, done that.*

I misted toward the monsters—and Dragon, too—he was fighting the Ra'Ak as well as he could, but the best he was doing at the moment was getting out of their way as more than one charged him at once, their teeth bared, ready to kill.

CHAPTER 12

Tony moaned; he couldn't feel his legs and he knew he should be in pain, buried as he was beneath broken furniture and debris. He lost moments as his consciousness became a fleeting thing, coming and going with the sounds of shouting and sirens, followed by periods of blankness.

He didn't have the strength to call for help; he could only lie there and hope, when he was coherent, that someone would find him soon. He heard the groan of metal twisting and then a crash as a heavy weight was lifted off him. "Mon Dieu," René's voice came and then René was kneeling beside him.

"My friend, this is quite serious," René looked into Tony's eyes. Tony blinked up at the vampire; they'd become friends in a short amount of time.

"How?" That one word was all Tony could muster. He was begging René to tell him how bad his injuries were.

"My friend, I will be truthful. You may not live," René said softly. "Much blood you have lost, here."

Tony watched the vampire's face and knew the truth of René's words. "Don't let me die," Tony begged. René looked about him, checking to see who was close. All the others were busy elsewhere.

"I must take you away from here and honestly, the move itself may kill you," René said, removing the remaining debris from Tony's body.

"Try," Tony moaned. "Please." René gave a curt nod and moved to place his arms beneath Tony's body.

~

You can't fight what you can't see. That night, it took on a double meaning. While I was mist, the Ra'Ak couldn't see me, and I was mist until I got right in their faces and sliced through their eyes.

I'd discovered their weakness; hit their eyes and they fall and writhe like the serpents they are. They scream in pain, too, lashing out with their lengthy tails, uncaring as to what they hit or crash into as they struggle and thrash about.

Vampires and priests alike were rushing away—the ones who'd gotten hit initially were screaming and dying from the poison. I had three Ra'Ak blinded before the last two learned something was attacking them; they began searching for me while trying to fend off Dragon at the same time.

I got one additional eye, causing the one I'd hit to scream and hiss, still looking for me with his remaining good eye. Dragon's huge, tooth-filled head snaked in and snapped that Ra'Ak's head off. The monster dusted, his chunks hitting his brothers and anyone else nearby. Now, only one sighted Ra'Ak remained; the others were still twisting and writhing in pain upon the temple floor.

I misted in quickly, hoping to get in a hit with my claws as the Ra'Ak snapped out at me. I barely managed to get out of his way. Dragon took the opportunity to snap the head off one of the three blinded Ra'Ak while the sighted one went after him again.

Dragon recoiled and shifted away, even as the one he'd just killed blasted out fist-sized chunks, the bits traveling right through my mist. The remaining vampires were now chasing the few priests that still lived; they'd begun running away from the temple to escape dusting Ra'Ak.

I tried for the eyes of the sighted Ra'Ak again; he snapped at me, leaving Dragon an opening to bite off yet another blinded head, which infuriated the sighted one. He roared—that loud a sound hurt me even in my misted form. Dragon lunged in next, but the creature managed to slide out of the way at just the right moment, leaving Dragon exposed. The Ra'Ak, seizing the opportunity, counter-attacked, snapping at Dragon's unprotected neck.

I think I was screaming, whether mentally or physically I cannot say, as I flew toward the Ra'Ak, slicing his eyes first with one set of claws and then the other—I had to come to partial corporeality to do it, running headlong into that horrible, spiked head.

My subsequent, pain-filled shout bounced across the floor of the temple, echoing up and out; I don't think there was anyone within a quarter mile that didn't hear it. Ra'Ak poison truly was as bad as the sun and I was screaming, along with the blinded Ra'Ak, as I dropped toward the floor.

The bone-jarring landing never occurred, however. A very large, black hand reached out to pluck me from the air. I almost didn't have the sense to notice that the fingers on that huge hand had very large claws; I was in too much pain. The scent, however, was very familiar.

Kifirin.

Setting me down nearby as gently as he could, he turned toward the Ra'Ak. I whimpered as I watched him. At least twenty feet in height he was, and winged. Kifirin was covered in black scales, was completely naked and smoke was curling from his nostrils. Even the Ra'Ak, blinded as he was, must have recognized the scent because he cowered.

"Ra'Ak!" Kifirin roared. "You have injured my mate! I am aggrieved!" He reached out with one giant hand, gripped the Ra'Ak's neck and squeezed. The Ra'Ak dusted immediately, but the chunks dropped harmlessly to the ground instead of blasting outward.

Kifirin roared, shaking the ground with the force of the sound before going after the other sightless Ra'Ak, executing him just as swiftly. Karzac, who'd come from nowhere, was suddenly at my side.

"I will do my best to neutralize the poison," he assured me, but the poison was already working its way through my body; I couldn't feel parts of it now.

"Karzac, I think it's too late," I whimpered.

"No, hush," he said, while light formed around his hands.

"How bad is it?" Dragon was suddenly at Karzac's side, light enveloping his entire body. That was Power with a capital P, I think.

"We will deal with this," Pheligar was suddenly there as well, helping Karzac. "Little vampire, do not be afraid." Karzac reached out with two fingers, placing them against my forehead. I was out in an instant.

∾

René, who had the ability to fly just as his cousin and many others among the older vampires did, carried Tony to a nearby rooftop. The scene below had been so chaotic and noisy that his exit with Tony in his arms had not been noticed.

"My friend, if all goes well, I will be your sire from this point forward. You will be my sixth turn, child." Tony was losing consciousness along with his blood; the femoral artery in his right leg had been severed and he would be dead soon if René didn't act quickly.

René lifted a wrist to his mouth and bit into it savagely. "Drink, child," René placed compulsion as he held his wrist over Tony's mouth. Tony opened his mouth, allowing the blood to drip inside it. He swallowed. And then swallowed again. René was mentally ticking off seconds; he'd done this before without the aid of a watch. He was well-versed on turning.

∾

"Little King," Kifirin raised Gabron from the pile of Ra'Ak dust— Gabron had gotten hit and knocked temporarily unconscious with the dusting of one of the monsters.

201

"Where is Lissa?" Gabron gazed about, somewhat dazed from the wounding.

"She is safe." Kifirin was no longer in full Thifilathi form; he looked humanoid again. Kifirin had watched with a bit of concern mixed with a little humor; even the Larentii was there, helping his little Queen. The Larentii held quite possibly the best and most powerful healing abilities, although the Saa Thalarr and their own healers were quite talented as well. His little Queen was in good hands, if Kifirin himself couldn't get to her. He was satisfied with the way things were.

"Who are you?" Gabron asked.

"I am Kifirin," the High Lord of the Dark Worlds replied. "Little King, one day I will come for you and your vampires here, and you will help my little Queen rule Le-Ath Veronis. You have all proven your worth this night."

"Lissa mentioned that world. Is it true, then?"

"Very true." Kifirin smiled. "Come. Let us gather your vampires before the news crews descend like a flock of crows." Gabron laughed and allowed Kifirin to set him on his feet.

Altogether, three hundred of Gabron's five hundred vampires that fought with him died that night. The two hundred that survived were counted as heroes by the population of Refizan, although no one could find them afterward to offer thanks. Certainly no interviews were agreed upon.

Since Refizan had space travel, however, the footage recorded made its way offworld and was seen on many other worlds; eventually coming to the attention of many vampires. Those vampires all witnessed the female vampire who, with the help of a Dragon and another creature that some named High Demon, (because that was the closest they could come to a true identification) destroyed five huge, snake-like creatures, along with thousands of smaller, flesh-eating monsters.

The footage that received the most play was of Lissa killing a twelve-foot monster and then blinding four of the five large serpents so they could easily be defeated.

~

"You will take us," René laid compulsion and the cab driver could only nod mutely as René loaded the bloodied man into the back seat of the cab. They would be driving to René's home in the French countryside; it was less than two hours away.

"You will be well-paid for your time and efforts, and reimbursed for the damage to your vehicle. You will tell everyone that you took one of the injured to the hospital after the explosion."

The cab driver was still nodding as he placed his car in gear and drove away, heading toward the countryside outside Paris. René held his youngest child's head in his lap. Anthony Hancock had stopped breathing the moment René pulled his wrist away, forcing Tony to stop drinking. That was a very good sign. Very good indeed. René lifted his cell phone to make a call. Wlodek answered.

"Honored One, I have just made my sixth turn. We will see if he survives," René informed the Head of the Vampire Council.

"Very well," Wlodek replied and René could hear the scratching of a pen over paper. "Please provide me with the details so I may begin the registration process."

"This one was a victim of the hotel bombing in Paris this evening," René began. "The femoral artery was severed and death was imminent. I managed to get him away without being seen; the rest of the site was in chaos and there were none to pay attention to us. All has gone well so far, Honored One. He will replace my dear, sweet Aubrey."

"Very well," Wlodek was still writing. "Do you have a name?"

"Anthony Hancock," René replied. Wlodek dropped his pen. René smiled.

~

"The poison has been neutralized," Pheligar declared. He'd still been working over Lissa's body while Dragon folded all of them away from Refizan. Karzac was satisfied; Lissa and Dragon had managed, with the help of the local vampires, to take down the five Ra'Ak and their demon force. Griffin was now there, as was Belen, who was shining brightly, half corporeal, half light.

"Do it now, then," Belen instructed. Griffin nodded and peeled back the sleeve of his shirt. With the giving of Griffin's blood, Belen was ensuring that Lissa could walk both sides of the realms—light and dark. She would not be confined solely to the Dark Realm if Kifirin transported her there. Griffin was smiling as he made his preparations.

"Dragon, will you help me?" Griffin asked. Dragon nodded and lifted Lissa's limp body into a sitting position. It was daylight where they were and Lissa would normally be asleep anyway, although Karzac had not removed the healing sleep. At the moment, the shield disc that Pheligar had installed was protecting her from sunlight.

"Karzac, will you wake her, please? She'll be sluggish but this is the best time for me to do this; she won't resist." Griffin drew a line on his left wrist with a finger of his right hand, leaving an opened vein in its wake. Blood was already welling up.

"Lissa, wake," Karzac commanded. It took a few seconds before Lissa sleepily opened her eyes, blinking in a confused manner at all the blurry images around her. She hadn't been awake in daylight in a very long time and the light hurt her eyes.

"Hold still, little one," Pheligar soothed. The Larentii nodded at Griffin.

"My blood is a gift to you, Lissa," Griffin said, reciting an ancient vow in the Neaborian language. "You will take no harm from it. There are no bindings or conditions, it is freely given." He held his bleeding wrist under her nose.

"Drink, Lissa." Dragon's command was better than any vampire compulsion. Lissa was tired and needed the blood; Pheligar had purposely not fed her after her healing. This blood would do. Lissa drank from Griffin's wrist until she'd gotten enough. Griffin drew his arm back and healed up the gash himself, vanishing the extra blood with merely a thought.

"Go back to sleep, Lissa," Karzac crooned to her. She dropped off immediately.

~

I woke the moment the sun slipped below the horizon, my eyes just popping open. My waking was never that quick. Ever. I was blinking up at a pale aqua ceiling and wondering where in the universe I actually was. This wasn't a ceiling I'd ever seen before.

"Nothing to worry over, little vampire," Karzac was at my bedside. I turned my head to look at him.

"Where are we?" I asked. He smiled.

"You're in Dragon's aerie," he replied. "We often stay here; there are no other humanoids here and Dragon can go flying through the mountains as much as he likes without fear of detection."

The walls behind Karzac were mostly bare and there was no furniture, except for the bed. "Dragon was on campaign most of his life as Warlord on Falchan, and the less you have, the easier it is to get yourself from one battle to the next," Karzac was reading my thoughts.

"I don't feel terrible," I said, attempting to sit up in bed.

"You shouldn't. With the Larentii helping with your recovery, you should feel quite fine."

"Then I owe him a big thanks," I said.

"He wants you to stay here for three days and rest before we take you back," Karzac informed me. "We have blood for you in the kitchen, if you are thirsty." I found that I was dressed in pajamas; something I would actually pick out for myself, if I were able. A stretchy, sleeveless top in a pale pink, with pink and white striped bottoms.

Experimentally, I swung my legs over the side of the bed. I wasn't stiff or anything, which was remarkable. Karzac led me down a flight of polished wood steps to the kitchen and living area below, where I stared in amazement at an open wall.

"The glass windows slide back, allowing us a full, unhindered view of the mountains and the valley," Karzac said, coming to stand next to me. He was right; the mountains were so close I could almost reach out and touch them, and the valley below was shining in the moonlight.

This must be incredible in sunlight," I whispered reverently.

"It is. Blood first, or tea?"

"We'll do blood and then tea," I said, following Karzac into the kitchen. They had solar powered everything, I learned, as Karzac handed over a bag of blood from the fridge and then put the kettle on the stove to heat water for tea. I took my blood back to the open view and stared out at the scenery while I drank my dinner.

Dragon flapped up in dragon form a few minutes later, changing to his normal shape as he landed on the balcony outside the house. Karzac handed him a cup of tea as he came in and he grinned at me before sipping his tea.

"I see why you like it here," I said, sitting on one of the cushions scattered about the room. There was no carpet here, just a nice rug in the center. Everything else was covered in wood flooring. I figured it was bamboo—the pale, natural color blending well with the cushion colors and the few sculptures and paintings.

Karzac brought my cup of tea and settled down with a cup for himself. Dragon got his favorite darker blend; I recognized the scent. Karzac and I got our usual.

"Several bodies are still missing," a reporter for the BBC stated, microphone in hand as she stood roughly a block away from the pile of rubble left after the hotel bombing in Paris. "The explosion and fire may have completely destroyed some victims and there is now little hope in their recovery. Among the missing is Anthony Hancock, an American who was Director for the National Security Agency and

Homeland Security Joint Office," the female journalist went on. "The American President has ordered all flags flown at half-staff to honor their fallen hero, who, according to sources, was once a special operative for U.S. Intelligence."

If Wlodek hadn't already informed Merrill and Gavin of what had truly happened to Anthony Hancock, Merrill might have been upset. He could only imagine what the news might have done to Lissa. As it was, Griffin had informed him that she would be home the following day.

Franklin and Greg had returned from their trip to Las Vegas and although the trip had been good for them, Merrill could see that Greg was weakening. The chemotherapy had already resumed earlier that day. Merrill worried over his human child Franklin; he wasn't saying anything, but Greg's illness was taking its toll on him as well. Merrill was going to wait a few days before making his offer again.

Merrill was also concerned for Lissa; Wlodek instructed that she be brought to him in two nights so he could inform her of her marriage to Gavin while she was absent. He also planned to tell her that she was now going to live under Gavin's thumb for the rest of her days.

Merrill wished to ask his sire just how he intended to break the news to her, but was too afraid of the answer to ask the question. They would all find out together. Gavin promised to stay at his London apartment until Lissa was informed; Merrill didn't want the news to come to her sooner than necessary.

Gavin was restless himself; he would be taking over Lissa's teaching, although she would still be living with Merrill. Merrill had accomplished that, at least. He'd argued with Wlodek that Lissa did better when she was around Franklin and perhaps helping to care for Greg would take her mind off the fact that she was a captive and would never be otherwise.

Griffin, when he'd come to give the information to Merrill of Lissa's impending return, had been curiously tight-lipped over where Lissa had been or if she'd been any help at all to Dragon. Merrill shrugged it off; he'd ceased any attempts to decipher Griffin's actions long ago. If Merrill was destined to know, he would be informed. If not, then Griffin had his reasons.

"Father, try this," Franklin was suddenly at Merrill's elbow, offering a small slice of cake to him. "They served this at the French restaurant at the hotel," Franklin added. Merrill lifted the fork and dipped up a little of the cake.

"This is very good," he replied, taking the plate from Franklin and cutting off another piece of the dessert.

~

"There is nothing to fear," René was there when Tony took his first breath as vampire. Tony had his own bedroom inside René's chateau; Aubrey's had been closed away and neither René nor Devlin could bear to go inside it.

"Here, child; you are hungry, I know." René handed over the bag of blood, showing Tony how to clip off the tube at the top to drink. Tony accepted the bag with shaking hands; René rubbed his back soothingly as Anthony Hancock drank his first blood meal as a vampire.

~

Deryn had given up hope of finding Tony and was trying to explain to his weeping mother over the phone that Tony's body most likely had disintegrated in the blast. The restaurant had been near the front of the hotel, after all, and that's where Tony was seen last.

Not for the first time did Deryn curse the full moon that had taken him and Paul away. They hadn't learned of the bombing until nearly dawn, when they made their way back to the hotel, finding the area surrounding it blocked off and ambulances and fire trucks everywhere.

He and Paul had gotten around the police; they were werewolves, after all, and had sniffed around, finding nothing. Nothing alive, anyway. There was plenty of blood and bits and pieces of bodies, which they didn't touch.

The authorities received notice that Rahim Alif's group was responsible, which led Deryn and Paul to believe that Tony was their intended target. Deryn also informed the Grand Master, since Paul was there at his request.

Weldon hadn't been happy with the news. Deryn and Paul were now determined to hunt down Rahim and had taken steps toward that goal. They'd already examined the remains of the van the suicide bombers had driven, but Alif's scent wasn't in it.

Tony would have been the one to have that sort of thing on file, Deryn knew, but that option was no longer open to them. Deryn finished the call to his mother; she'd become too upset to talk and Lucas, Deryn's father had come on the line, saying a few words to his son before hanging up to take care of Deryn's mother.

Deryn and Paul checked into another hotel—they'd had to buy clothing to replace what was lost in the blast. Deryn fluctuated between anger and depression much of the time. Paul was doing his best to keep the younger werewolf focused and moving.

Gavin sat at his ancient kitchen table, fingering the wedding ring he'd bought with Lissa's engagement ring. It was a simple gold band, thin and shaped to fit around the other ring she wore. He had mixed feelings about the whole thing—excited, because Lissa would truly be his—concerned, because she would be upset.

Until he placed compulsion, Lissa would likely be angry and weeping when she was informed of their marriage. There was a way through this—there had to be. She would come around and be happy; he would see to it. They would stay with Merrill, at least for a while, until things settled down and she accepted what was.

Gavin also heard from his cousin René. René informed Gavin that Anthony Hancock's turn was successful. He'd wakened and had been fed the first time. Gavin almost warned René to keep his new child away from Lissa, but that would be another blow to her; he knew she would be upset if she watched the news and learned of his apparent death.

Hancock was newly turned; he would be easily controlled. Only a slight compulsion would be needed to warn him away if his feelings for Lissa survived the turning.

~

"This is a gift for Lissa, because she saved us," Karzac informed the other healer as they made their way through the National Naval Medical Center, located in Bethesda, Maryland. Both were dressed as physicians, with official nametags and other necessary ID. The rooms holding six agents infected with vampire blood were close together, making it easier for the two healers to do their work.

"Take the last three, I'll take the first three," Karzac whispered. Joey Showalter, who'd once been vampire and Merrill's last turn, grinned at Karzac and headed toward the first of his three assignments.

~

"Little girl, it's time to go home." Griffin had arrived, appearing out of nowhere just like the rest of his kind could do. Dragon had gotten some clothing for me from somewhere—it wasn't the shapeless Refizani crap, either. I didn't want to insult Karzac's home planet by saying that out loud and Dragon just grinned as he handed over a pair of jeans and a pullover shirt.

"I owe you, little vampire," Dragon said, hugging me. Karzac had left earlier; he said he had work to do and I'd gotten my good-bye hug from him, then. I patted Dragon's back before I let him go and in a blink, Griffin had me inside Merrill's kitchen.

Franklin and Greg were both there and hugging me, almost making me cry. I'd missed them and I told them that. They'd gone to Las Vegas while I'd been away; I discovered quickly.

"You went and didn't take me?" I pretended to be hurt.

210

"We'll take you next time, you'll love it," Greg promised. I wasn't sure there would be a next time for Greg; he was thinner and weaker, I could tell, and his scent was changing—the disease was taking over.

"We stayed at Caesar's," Franklin said. "And it was wonderful, even though it was crowded. We lost a ton of money; won a little of it back and ate ourselves sick."

"We flew over the Grand Canyon, went to Hoover Dam and saw all the tourist traps," Greg added. Well, they'd gone to the Liberace Museum, I just knew it.

"So, what did you do?" Franklin asked. He'd just finished making dessert and was serving some up for Greg and himself.

"Went to Refizan," I said.

"Where is that?" Greg asked, dipping into his dessert.

"No idea. Nowhere close, I know that," I said, smiling. "I met vampires there. And I learned some things. Really important things. Wlodek is going to flip when I tell him."

"What about the vampires?" Greg asked.

"The one who was in charge, his name was Gabron," I said. "And he's about three times as old as Wlodek."

"What's this?" Merrill came through the back door, taking off his trench coat as he came in; it was raining out, apparently.

"The Head of the Council on Refizan. He's about three times as old as Wlodek," I repeated. "And he gave me some great information. I know what Saxom was looking for when he was making misters and mindspeakers."

That caught Merrill's attention right away. "What was it?" he demanded.

"Have you ever heard of a race called the Elemaiya?" Merrill went still. He had, I could see it in his face.

"Yes," the answer was guarded.

"Well, there are Bright Elemaiya and Dark Elemaiya. I got a good scent on both—all of Saxom's misters and mindspeakers had Dark Elemaiyan blood. Our misters and mindspeakers all have Bright Elemaiyan blood. Gabron says they're Travelers—the Elemaiya, that is. He says they can world-walk, through gates between the worlds, whatever those are."

Merrill stared at me for a few seconds. "There's a gate nearby; Griffin uses it at times," Merrill admitted. "He told me that he has sealed it off so only Saa Thalarr and a few others can use it now."

"You mean that if he hadn't, those guys could just come right in?" I asked.

"There may be other gates; he says that some worlds have more than one, but this one is on my property. That's why he sealed it off." Merrill came over, wrapped me in an embrace and rocked me gently. "We missed having you around, little girl," he said softly, kissing the top of my head.

"Well, too bad you weren't where I was," I said. "The vampires could have used your help, I think. There was this terrible religious cult that called themselves Solar Red. They practiced human sacrifice and turned themselves over to demons and the Ra'Ak," I babbled.

"And what were you doing in all of this?" Merrill frowned as he held me away from him.

"Lopping off heads; both priests' and demons'," I replied. "You should have seen what I did to their temple, there at the end. And those Ra'Ak? There was only supposed to be one. There were five of those suckers. I thought Dragon was going to die so I blinded four of them, Dragon killed three of those, and then Kifirin came in and got the last two. Oh, and that doesn't count the one I killed while he was in humanoid form. I can smell them, if they're not shielded."

Merrill stared at me, hard. "I'm going to have a talk with Griffin," he muttered and stalked away.

"What did you do to their temple?" Greg whispered as soon as Merrill was out of hearing.

"I blew it up," I grinned and hugged him. He laughed.

～

"Lissa, dress nicely, sweetheart, Wlodek wants to see us," Merrill knocked on my bedroom door the following evening. I was brushing my teeth; I'd already had my dinner and dressed in jeans and a pullover. Now I was going to have to change.

I'd tried to phone Gavin but the call had gone directly to voice mail. Just as well, I'm sure the guilt was going to be showing on my face the next time I saw him anyway. I hadn't seen hide nor hair of Kifirin since I'd seen him on Refizan and he'd been a big, tall, winged something or other.

Dragon said that the High Demons looked like that, only they were a bit shorter when they went to what he called Full Thifilathi. Kifirin had said that word to me once before, after he'd sunk his teeth into my neck. He'd said the Thifilathi must be satisfied, whatever that meant.

Honestly, he looked more like a demon to me in that shape than the ones that Dragon had called demons. Those guys were ugly, all right, but if you wanted demons, well, Kifirin would come to mind every time.

"What does Wlodek want?" I asked, coming downstairs later, dressed in nice slacks and a pretty blouse with low heels and a little jewelry. Thankfully, my hair now covered Kifirin's marks, otherwise I'd be explaining those, I'm sure.

"He'll tell us when we arrive," Merrill replied stiffly. I just shrugged as Merrill led the way to the Range Rover—it was raining again.

The drive usually takes half an hour, if the weather is good. That night it took an extra ten minutes. The rain was heavy at times, drumming on the roof of the Range Rover and the wipers had a tough time keeping up.

Merrill had an umbrella in the car and he held it over both of us as we dashed inside; Rolfe was there holding the door open. I gave him a smile as we raced through the door; he seemed a little more solemn than usual.

Charles was also there, offering a lop-sided grin as he led us upstairs to Wlodek's study. What surprised me was finding Gavin waiting inside—the schmuck hadn't returned my phone call yet here he was, standing against the wall next to the Monet. Wlodek sat behind his desk, being his usual, unreadable self. His gold pen was in his hands and he was already playing with the thing.

"Lissa has news for you, Honored One," Merrill said, first thing. One of Wlodek's eyebrows rose slightly. "Tell him about the misters," Merrill urged as I sat on one of the guest chairs.

Gavin hadn't said anything, so I didn't say anything to him. Did he know about Kifirin? Had somebody told him? I was worried, suddenly. Gavin, like Wlodek, had something in his hand that he was toying with but I couldn't see what it was.

"I learned from a vampire on Refizan that the misters and mindspeakers have Elemaiyan blood," I began, watching Wlodek's face. "He told me that the ones who go bad all have Dark Elemaiyan blood. The others have Bright Elemaiyan blood. Saxom's misters all had Dark Elemaiyan blood. I got a good scent off both and I can smell the Elemaiya, now, both Bright and Dark."

"You're sure about this?" Wlodek sounded only half-interested. I wondered then what else was occupying his mind.

"Yeah. After I got the scent, I knew right away that Henri and Gervais, as well as Robert and Albert, all have Bright Elemaiyan blood."

"So, if someone were to walk up to you—a human—you would be able to tell if they had this blood?" Uh-oh. I'd trapped myself and probably some poor, mostly-human schmucks out there.

"Ye-es," I'd gone cautious suddenly and Wlodek knew it.

"We will discuss this later," Wlodek sighed. "There are other, more important things that we must speak of tonight."

Someday, maybe I'd learn to read the signs—the ones that say the cliff with the big drop-off is only a step or two away and now's the time to turn tail and run just as fast as you can in the opposite direction. Nope—I have to fall over the cliff. Head right toward the bottom, in fact, because I never see it coming.

"Lissa, you are not a Queen," Wlodek said, first thing. "You are susceptible to compulsion, although your other talents are formidable." The creeping hand of fear was reaching toward my heart, ready to grasp it and squeeze. I wasn't frightened yet, however—far from it, in fact. So far, Wlodek was only repeating what I already knew. Or what they already knew, or thought they knew.

"We have learned that Xenides is actively searching for you, wishing to capture you and put those talents to use for his own twisted purposes."

Okay, as news went, that wasn't so good. But if I ever caught up with Xenides, it was going to be a battle royal, let me tell you. I wouldn't give up until one of us was dead.

"We cannot allow Xenides to get his hands on you, Lissa. The fate of the world could hang in the balance if he does. He could use you in terrible ways, moro mou. That I will not countenance. While you were away, the Council and I decided to move your marriage to Gavin forward and it was performed in absentia. Your marriage has been duly recorded in the Council's records."

Stunned might have been a good word. I couldn't move or breathe for a few moments; all I could do was stare at Wlodek, gasping like a fish, I'm sure.

"But what does marriage have to do with Xenides or anything else?" I almost couldn't get the words out, I was so shocked. They'd done this behind my back. Couldn't they have waited until I returned, at least, and let me argue my side before hauling off and doing this, without my knowledge or consent?

"The Council," Wlodek hesitated for a second or two, "will look the other way if a spouse lays compulsion on his mate or companion, if it is in the mate's or companion's best interests."

That was the bomb and as bombs go, it was quite effective, shattering everything around me. Splintering it, in fact. They were going to allow Gavin to hold me under his thumb. He was going to dictate everything I did from that point forward. There would never be freedom for me. Ever. Of any kind.

Gavin, and more than likely Wlodek, would decide if I went anywhere. Did anything. I'd be told where to eat, how to dress, when to blink. That last thought was the one that brought my anger to the fore, and it was blazing hot.

CHAPTER 13

I whirled on Gavin first. "What happened to that promise you made—that all my decisions would be my own where you were concerned?" I was nearly shouting at him.

"Lissa, the circumstances have changed!" Wlodek was getting in on this, now. Well, he was about to get it, too.

"You scheming old warlock!" I spun around and shouted at him. Yes, I called the Head of the Vampire Council a name and yelled at him; that had probably not happened in, well, forever. The evidence had been in front of him all along, he'd just been too stupid to ask the right questions.

"Do you think for even one minute that the fucking vampire who showed up at the hotel in New Mexico didn't try to place compulsion? Do you?" I was breathing with difficulty and shivering at the same time. "Because he most certainly did," I yelled. "And you know what? It didn't work. Merrill's compulsion before that didn't work, either. I could have misted right out of that holding cell where I was kept afterward at any time—only I didn't, because I just figured you guys would hunt me down and have me killed. Yeah, that's right, I was afraid. I figured that you'd just have your pet Assassin over there kill me while I slept if I stepped out of line, I was so afraid of you." I flung my arm toward Gavin. "Well, this time you've gone past that. I'm tired of being afraid. Take your best shot, Wlodek. Place compulsion. Feel free. Because I assure you it will not work and when I mist out of here, if you see me again you can kiss my ass!"

I got up out of the chair in a blur and headed straight for the door. "Lissa!" Wlodek shouted, the compulsion thundering in his voice, "Come back this instant!"

"That shit doesn't work on me anymore," I gritted, whirling to face him as I slowly turned to mist. "But keep trying—maybe you'll have a breakthrough." I turned completely to mist and shot out of there so fast it was blinding.

Gavin slid to the floor of Wlodek's study, his head buried in his hands. Merrill still sat in the same chair he'd chosen when he first came in. Wlodek was up and pacing, muttering profanity in Greek.

"Well, Wlodek, you had a little Queen all along," Merrill ventured to say. He'd understood the Greek, all right—Wlodek was cursing himself. Lissa had been right—if any of them had thought to ask—but they hadn't.

She'd told them she'd gotten away from the vampire in New Mexico. It only made sense he would try to place compulsion right away. Merrill hadn't realized that his hadn't worked. Griffin had said Lissa was special but Merrill had never questioned that statement. He should have. They'd all frightened her. Gavin had been right in that respect; they were all males and Lissa had grown up afraid of males in authority. Her stepfather had seen to that. They all knew now that he hadn't been Lissa's real father, just as he'd claimed. He'd gone to extremes as a result, punishing Lissa and her mother over that fact.

"We need her back. Now!" Wlodek started speaking English again. "This changes many things. We still need to protect her; she is still young as a vampire and her training is not complete. But a Queen," Wlodek's voice was almost reverent.

"How do you propose we get her back?" Merrill was as calm as he could be under the circumstances. He glanced at Gavin, who was still sitting on the floor, about to experience a meltdown.

"If you ask the proper person, it might be arranged," Griffin appeared in Wlodek's study, lifting a paperweight off the corner of Wlodek's desk. It was a huge gold coin, minted by the Royal Canadian Mint and valued at approximately a million dollars, U.S.

Gavin lifted his head and growled, although he hadn't moved; Wlodek and Merrill were accepting the sudden appearance with calm.

"Don't growl at me, you deserve what you're getting right now," Griffin chided.

"Don't threaten Griffin, you'll be sorry, I promise," Merrill added. "Will you bring back my little girl?" He asked the retired Saa Thalarr.

"I'll bring her back, but she's not your little girl," Griffin replied.

"He's her surrogate sire," Wlodek interrupted haughtily. Merrill, however, was looking strangely at Griffin.

"What is going on?" he demanded.

"My punishment is lifted," Griffin offered his friend a sunny smile. "Lissa isn't your little girl. Has never been your little girl and won't ever truly be your little girl. Go ahead; ask me how I know this."

"All right, I concede. How do you know this?" Merrill stared at Griffin. The light went on suddenly, however. "I should have known," Merrill almost laughed with relief. "You know who her real father is, don't you?"

"Oh, yes," Griffin nodded. "I went looking for her mother, you know. She was a quarter Bright Elemaiya. As was I, before I was turned. Lissa's mine. And if any of you mistreat her again, you'll answer to me."

I was back in my bedroom in a matter of minutes, gathering up my cell phone and what little cash I had in my underwear drawer. I couldn't take Merrill's credit card; they'd track me that way. I was shaking harder, now; reaction was setting in from what I'd done.

Wlodek would send his Enforcers and his Assassins after me, and since Sebastian was dead, that left only Gavin and Trevor. They'd do their best to kill me if they found me; no way could they force me with compulsion to come back for a sentencing by the Council.

Franklin and Greg didn't know I'd come back and that was for the best. I wouldn't be putting either one in jeopardy by letting them know what happened. I left Merrill's credit card on my bedside table, jerking Gavin's ring off my finger and leaving it there as well.

He'd stepped over the line and I was so angry and hurt over that, I didn't know what to do. He'd been prepared to treat me that way, placing compulsion over everything. I'd never be able to choose my friends or who I spoke to or laughed with. I'd be jailed and brought out once in a while like the good silver, only to be put away immediately after, once my service was complete. I couldn't live like that. It was a lie, after all. Oh, I could pretend, but there would come a day when I wouldn't be able to stand it any longer and they'd find out anyway.

Less than ten minutes it took to mist into London, but I had no idea where to go or what to do. Everything except pubs and bars was closed. I materialized outside a pub near Whitehall, pulled out my cell phone and scrolled through the numbers. There was only one person I knew who might be able to help me and I was still angry with him, too. That left either Weldon or Winkler. I hit Winkler's number on speed dial. He picked up on the second ring.

"Lissa?" He sounded surprised to hear from me. I suppose he should be.

"Winkler, I'm having a bit of a problem," I said. "I just pissed off Wlodek, Gavin and Merrill, and now I'm running away from home. If you don't want to get involved in this because it could become dangerous for you, then I'll understand."

"Lissa, whatever you need, it's yours," Winkler's voice was warm and caring and right then I might have given anything to have his arms to lean on. I was frightened out of my wits, to be honest.

"That's just it, I don't know what I need," I sniffed. I was about to cry and doing my best not to. "I have a little cash, but I had to leave my credit card behind; they'll track me. They may be able to do it anyway, if I have to show my ID or Passport."

"Hold on, let me get Weldon on the phone," Winkler said. I heard buttons being pushed. Weldon came on the line in seconds. Winkler explained what he knew so far.

"Lissa, Paul is in Paris with Tony Hancock's brother at the moment, otherwise I'd have him pick you up," Weldon sighed. "They still hold out hope that they can find who bombed Tony's hotel."

"Tony's hotel got bombed?" This was the first I'd heard of it.

"Lissa, Tony got killed—they say his body was destroyed, along with several others. That terrorist, Rahim Alif? He's taken responsibility."

My fingers had gone numb; I nearly dropped the phone and I felt so cold and so incredibly alone, right then, I wasn't sure I was still on the planet. "You didn't know?" Winkler figured it out after I'd gone silent. "Lissa, it happened six days ago, baby."

"Wh-where is Paul in Paris?" I definitely wanted to cry now and wiped tears off my face. Tony was dead? That couldn't be. It just couldn't.

"Lissa, I'll call him and have him call you, all right?" Weldon heard my sniffling, I'm sure.

"All right," I stifled a sob and hung up. I didn't have a thing with me to wipe away the tears, but a very nice woman who walked out of the pub gave me a handful of tissues and asked if I needed anything. I told her that I only needed the tissues, so she smiled and patted my shoulder before leaving with her date. There were still nice people in the world, after all; they all didn't want to blow up hotels that had people inside whom I cared about.

Paul called me a few minutes later. He had a beautiful accent. "Lissa? The Grand Master tells me you might need my help."

"Honey, I hope we can help each other," I wiped my cheeks again. "I just need to get to you; I hope I can track down the asshole that did this to Tony."

"Where are you, darlin'?" He knew I was crying.

"In front of a pub near Whitehall," I said, giving him the name.

"How about I have someone pick you up? I think I can get you to Paris tonight; I have friends at NSY. They can arrange something, I think."

Paul should have friends at New Scotland Yard; he'd helped crack the child murder case that was plaguing the U.K. recently. "Just hang tight," he added. "Someone will be there shortly. If not, I'll call you back."

"Okay," I said and ended the call. It took less than twenty minutes before a police car pulled up.

"Are you Lissa Huston?" The policeman got out of his car and came over to talk to me.

"Yes," I said. "Did Paul send you?"

"He did. I'm to take you to the airport; do you have your passport with you?"

"Yes," I pulled it from my purse and showed it to him.

"Good enough," he smiled. He had blond hair, green eyes and a nice smile, helping me into the car before climbing in and driving away. "This jet belongs to a business magnate who happens to be traveling to France this evening," the officer, who identified himself as Raymond Jeffries, informed me. He walked with me to the end of the jet's steps and I climbed up.

An attendant waited just inside the door, and she greeted me by name. "Mr. Harding is inside his office, conducting business," the woman said. "Please have a seat and buckle yourself in; we'll be leaving shortly."

"Thank you," I said. I figured my face still showed evidence of my tears so I pulled a small mirror from my purse and tried to set myself to rights as the attendant closed the door and let the pilot know that everything was ready. We took off fifteen minutes later.

The flight from London to Paris isn't a long one; little more than two hundred miles. It was no time before we were landing at Charles de Gaulle. Paul and another werewolf were there to meet me; I figured he had to be Tony's brother and that thought almost caused me to break down again. "Come on, let's get you to the hotel," Paul held me up as best he could as we walked toward their rental car.

Deryn Alford, Tony's half-brother, put me in the front seat while Paul drove. Deryn sat in the back.

"We'll take you out tomorrow night and see if we can find anything," Paul promised as we drove to the hotel. "We have a meeting with some of the local authorities tomorrow," he added.

"All right," I nodded. "I want to warn you, what I have on is all I have at the moment." I hadn't bothered to take any of my clothing with me.

"We'll work on that, too. Mr. Winkler said he would reimburse us for all your expenses." I just nodded my head so I wouldn't start crying again.

They put me in a hotel room; it was right across the hall from theirs and I learned that night that somehow the translation skills that I'd gotten while on Refizan were still working. I understood everything that was said in French around me. I wasn't about to try my skill at speaking the language in case I tripped over my own tongue. The French weren't forgiving if you butchered their language.

"We had a little help." Paul handed three bags of clothing to me; I was wrapped in a towel after my shower. At least I had a comb in my purse so my hair wasn't a tangled mess on my head.

"Thanks," I said. I'd gotten up and found a bag of blood in one of the hotel's ice buckets beside my bed. Paul had kept the extra key card to my room the night before and somehow he'd managed to get my dinner. The clothes were just a bonus.

"Who helped?" I asked, peeking inside the bags. Jeans and tops, plus a pair of athletic shoes were inside the first one, underwear and other necessities were inside the others.

"A female werewolf," Paul coughed. I could see he was both embarrassed and pleased by the help.

"Tell her thanks," I said, and started laying clothing out on the bed. She'd even laundered it for me, which meant I owed her big time.

After I dressed, we went out. Deryn hadn't said much to me yet, allowing Paul to do most of the talking. Deryn had brown hair to Tony's black, and that plus his nose were the biggest differences. I didn't know what to do with the other information I had—Tony was supposed to be Deryn's half-brother but I couldn't make the scent connection. Maybe it was because I was upset; I didn't know. We drove first to the site of the bombing, but much of it had been combed through already. Nevertheless, I found the spot where Tony had been.

"He was here," I said, pulling a bit of debris aside. Very little had been cleaned up as yet and I'd had to place compulsion to get where we were. The scent of Tony's blood was all over this one little space, which puzzled me. If he'd been blown to bits, the scent of it shouldn't have been as strong as it was and it would have been scattered.

It wasn't, though, and I explained that to Deryn and Paul. There was also another scent but it wasn't nearly enough to sort out; the blood and death smell all around took care of that. I moved a few feet away, catching more of Tony's scent, but once again, it was localized, like drops of blood or something.

Holy fuck.

"He was moved," I said. I kept going in the same direction, picking up more scent evidence as I went along until we were well away from the hotel property and into an alleyway behind. Actual drops of blood were there and they were Tony's, even if they were days old. His scent was unmistakable and I was picking it up easily.

Deryn and Paul followed me, puzzled looks on their faces until they detected Tony's blood scent as well. The scent and the blood drops stopped abruptly at the back wall of a nearby building.

"Did they just go through the wall?" I muttered to myself. As far as I knew, I was the only one who could do that. Deryn and Paul were now sniffing around the last drops of blood that I'd pointed out to them. Both werewolves were now looking at me expectantly. I shrugged.

"I don't know," I said, shaking my head uncertainly. "He was carried away, but it was right here that they just vanished or flew away or something." I walked around for a few seconds, making sure I hadn't missed anything—any turns or veering off to go in another direction. I went back and picked up the trail once more, following it again right to the edge of the building.

"Crap," I grumped. "It's as if they just jumped the building or something."

"Did they climb it?" Deryn came to stand beside me. That caused me to look up.

"Are you afraid of heights?" I asked.

"No. Why?"

"How about you, Paul?" I looked at him; he was walking over to us.

"Not afraid of heights, no," he said.

"Good," I said and turned all three of us to mist. We sailed right to the top of the six-story building and landed on the edge of it, corresponding to the spot where the blood spatters had ended. We found more drops there, and I also found something else.

"Oh, my God," I said. My legs wouldn't hold me up any longer and my butt hit the rooftop with a dusty thump.

"What is it?" Paul asked, holding his hand out to help me up.

"We need to stop looking for Tony right now and concentrate on Xenides and Rahim Alif," I said.

I knew Tony had been on top of this building and that he'd bled on the roof, not far from where I'd fallen. I also knew who else had been on that roof and it wasn't Rahim or Xenides. Tony might still be alive, at least in some sense of the word.

"Someone told us earlier today that Xenides and Rahim have been inside a room at a nearby hotel," Deryn offered. "Probably where they planned all this," he jerked his head toward the rubble below.

"Which hotel?" I asked.

"You can see it from here," Paul said, pointing off to our right. A tall building stood not far away, and it was one of the nicest hotels in Paris. Well, nothing but the best for fanged terrorists, I guess.

"Either of you uncomfortable with being mist earlier?" I asked.

"Was that what it was? I just felt weightless for a few," Paul smiled.

"Yeah, you were mist with me," I said. "Want to go again?"

"I'm game," he replied. Deryn nodded; he was ready, too. We sailed over rooftops, going right through the designated hotel. The man wandering around his room in the nude might have been quite surprised if he'd known we'd zipped right past him. He might have felt a slight breeze, but that's all.

Two werewolves and a female vampire stepping out of the ladies' powder room on the first floor might have caused a stir if anyone had actually seen us—who cared, anyway. The people there just turned their heads away and minded their own business. Maybe we would have raised more eyebrows if they'd known what we were. They didn't.

"The room is on the fourth floor and may still be cordoned off," Paul informed me quietly as we made our way toward the elevators.

The elevator dinged pleasantly as we got off on the fourth floor and walked silently down the hallway, the carpet deep and thick beneath our feet. Paul was correct; the room had notices hung on the door. I looked around carefully, making sure there were no witnesses or security cameras before turning all of us to mist again and going right through the locked door.

Paul and Deryn most likely thought I'd lost my mind as I rushed them out of the room, much faster than we'd gone in. They were dropped once more in the ladies' room on the first floor.

"There's a mister inside that room!" I hissed. "Go back to your hotel, now. I have to deal with this!" I turned to mist and left both of them gaping after me as I disappeared, flying right back to the suite on the fourth floor.

The mister was hovering near the ceiling, and I can only imagine he was waiting for me or perhaps Henri or Gervais; they were the only others who might be in danger from this one. Definitely one with Dark Elemaiyan blood; his mist was a purplish gray, just like others of his kind.

Henri or Gervais would be a greenish mist, if it were one of the Enforcers. Knowing that I would have to do this sooner or later, prepared or not, I materialized inside the room. Looking around and sniffing everything, I could barely detect Xenides' scent and even less of Rahim Alif.

Yes, I knew Rahim's scent—he'd been inside the house in Georgia that I'd searched with Tony. Yes, I was still angry with Tony, but I was terrified for him, too. Shoving those thoughts aside, I turned back to the scents inside the room. Rahim Alif and Xenides' scents notwithstanding, there was another scent there and it was likely my mister.

I was also doing my best to tick off seconds in my mind, knowing that the mister would take at least a couple of minutes to become solid. I was correct, but a couple of minutes, closer to three, to be exact, was what it did take.

Much to my surprise, however, the vampire wasn't male, and that was the greatest shock, perhaps, in my career as a vampire.

"You're not going after her now?" Merrill fidgeted and he never did that. He was usually the cool and collected vampire, even when Wlodek lost his temper.

Griffin sat at the kitchen island, eating spaghetti that Franklin reheated for him. Griffin loved Italian. "There's something she has to do, first, before we go," Griffin gave his friend a small smile.

Gavin stood in a corner of the kitchen, his arms folded over his chest while he glowered at the delay. He wanted to touch Lissa; he'd only seen her briefly inside Wlodek's office and now he had groveling to do. The sooner the better, too.

"Things will happen when they happen," Griffin turned to Gavin. "I am more than a hundred thousand years old and have learned this during my long life. You are not the only one with groveling to do, sir vampire. My little girl will not be happy in the least when I try to explain that as her father, I could not help her or her mother when she was young."

"Explain that to me," Merrill said.

"When Lissa's mother became pregnant, my direct supervisor, Thorsten, discovered it and declared that I had interfered. Of course, there was punishment and my punishment was that Lissa and her mother were hidden from me. I couldn't find them to check on them.

It was as if they didn't exist for me. I didn't know what was happening or I might have committed other infractions. As it was, she ended up in your care, my friend, and when you called out to me the first time she became ill, I knew immediately who it was. Therefore, it was easy for me to check on her after that, although I was still prevented from doing anything other than the smallest of things for her. I got around the punishment because of you, my friend, and the help you rendered long ago. I am allowed to reciprocate, as you know." Griffin took a moment to drink a bit of the red wine Franklin served.

"However," Griffin continued, "when I convinced Thorsten to allow her to help Dragon, things came to the attention of Thorsten's supervisor, Belen. And Belen, after hearing everything I had to say, has determined that having a child is not interfering. The punishment was lifted. I cannot go back and change Lissa's past; that he forbade. I am now free to act as her father from this point forward; to tell her who I am and why I was prevented from seeing her when she was younger. We will see whether she accepts me or not." Griffin sounded wistful. "Amara already wishes to meet her; she has always wanted a child and desires very much for Lissa to accept both of us. We will see how that turns out."

"Amara is your mate? And she has no trouble accepting that you produced a child with another woman?" Gavin couldn't believe what he was hearing.

"Our kind cannot experience jealousy, Gavin, and if you expect to keep my Lissa, you will have to set it aside as well." Merrill's head jerked around at Griffin's statement.

~

"So, it's Wlodek's little bitch." She was pretty—really pretty, with long, platinum blonde hair, had the stink of Saxom and the Dark Elemaiya about her and seemed nasty as hell—in temperament, anyway. Otherwise, she was dressed quite fashionably in designer clothing that had probably cost a fortune. I wondered who was footing the bill for her wardrobe.

"Well, Saxom's bitch, right back at ya," I snorted, squaring off across the hotel suite with her. It was as if we were sizing each other up. The fact that I'd known who made her surprised her greatly, although she hid it well.

"You think you can come against me?" She laughed. "I am a true Queen, not a little pretender." Well, she was taller than I was, by about eight inches. Certainly dressed better, if that meant anything, but she'd only heard what everyone else thought they knew about me. I just shrugged at her statement.

"Guess we'll have to find out, now, won't we?" I said. We were still circling carefully; I'm sure she'd seen me materialize in a blink and wanted to catch me before I could go to mist again so her opportunity to place compulsion wouldn't be lost. She cursed softly in German as she bumped into a chair. I understood her words, though, which made me smile.

"Why are you smiling?" she asked.

I couldn't resist. "Because I know something you don't," I said.

"And that is?"

I smiled wider, turned to mist in a blink right in front of her and in another blink I had her turned to mist with me, screaming out to anyone who could hear me for help.

"The first vampire rule is never kill your donor, or any human, unless they present a threat to you," René was teaching Tony, who was quite happy to be vampire and curious as hell about the rules. René realized that he would have to present his newest turn with an accelerated course; Tony wasn't slow or stupid and was learning everything quite rapidly, in addition to watching all the news programs concerning world events.

René knew Tony was used to getting his reports directly from the source and was now displaying mild impatience with what the news agencies were reporting. Tony was just about to ask questions when he received Lissa's mindspeech.

"René, I can hear Lissa." Tony was on his feet in an instant. "She's shouting for help."

"Our little rose is nearby?" René was on his feet as well. "Can you contact her? She will hear you?"

"She always has before," Tony nodded.

"Then ask what she requires," René's voice held urgency.

～

Lissy? René says to ask you what you need. I received unexpected mindspeech from Tony and could have wept with relief.

Tony, I have someone who needs to be kept in a secure room until the Council can decide what to do with her, I sent. *Where are you? Please tell me you're at René's chateau.*

We are, came the reply. *Why?*

Because René has an underground vault that would be perfect for this, I replied.

～

Tony swiftly informed René of Lissa's problem. "Tell her to come, does she remember the way?" René asked as he motioned for Tony to follow him. Tony relayed the message, receiving the affirmative from Lissa.

"She says she remembers," Tony assured his sire.

"Good. Tell her to come as quickly as possible. In the meantime, you and I have much moving to do." René unlocked the door to his basement, leading Tony down a flight of steps.

～

Tell René to leave the door locked, I instructed. I was getting close; I recognized the road leading to René's chateau. I no longer had to get inside using the kitchen vent; I could go straight through the walls and the Queen Vampire I had inside my mist was quite angry as I carried her along. She wasn't used to being manhandled, poor thing. She wanted to kill me, too; that vibe came in loud and clear.

We're ready, Tony's voice came back. I imagined that he and René had been doing some rapid transfers; I didn't think René wanted his priceless collection of stolen artifacts to be touched by a prisoner inside his vault.

The Queen Vampire gave a mental shriek as we misted right through the walls of René's home and then through the floor and into the basement. René and Tony were standing outside the locked door of René's vault; piled all around them were boxes and containers with jewelry, artifacts and other priceless treasures inside.

I went through the door of the vault—it was tighter than a drum when René close it off—dumped my prisoner on the floor and misted out again. I materialized away from all of René's objets d'art.

"Lissy!" Tony was weeping, he was so happy to see me. He grabbed me up and nearly cracked my ribs, he hugged me so hard.

"Hey, stop that!" I pounded on his back to get him to loosen his grip; I could barely breathe.

"Child, you are stronger than you were," René reminded him pleasantly. Tony set me down, held my face in his hands and kissed me. Gavin was going to hear about that. For sure.

"Lissy, I'm so sorry. So sorry, baby," Tony gave me another smack.

"Tony, René is Gavin's cousin," I mumbled dryly when he came up for air.

"Really? Does that mean I'm related to Gavin now?" Tony's eyebrows drew together in a frown as he pulled me against him again.

"Stop that, you schmuck," I swatted at him. "And that's for making me think you were dead."

"Merrill and Gavin did not inform you?" René asked.

"There may not have been time." I was only now recalling that I might be getting René in trouble, just by being in his home. Well, I was going to get into trouble anyway. Pulling my cell from a pocket of my jeans, I hit Merrill's number on speed dial.

~

Griffin had finished his meal and was placing his dishes inside the dishwasher when Merrill's cell phone rang. Merrill checked the ID. "It's Lissa," he said and answered the call. "Sweetheart, you're not in trouble," Merrill didn't bother with a greeting. He wanted Lissa to know the important information right away.

"Really?" She sounded so surprised. Griffin and Gavin both were listening in on the conversation.

"Of course not, sweetheart. I think Wlodek is quite upset, mostly with himself for not discovering this earlier, but that will smooth over with time. Where are you? We will come to get you and bring you home."

I was shocked by Merrill's words. "I'm really not in trouble? Are you telling me the truth or just trying to trap me?" They could be—how was I to know?

"I'm telling the truth. Where are you, sweetheart? We will be there right away."

"That might be a little hard to do," I replied. "I'm in France, right now. Merrill, listen carefully, I need your help with this. I went to a hotel room in Paris because that's where they said Xenides and Rahim had been before Tony's hotel got bombed. I wanted to check it over for scents, but I found another mister inside. Merrill, if I'm mist, I can see other misters who are mist. I knew this wasn't one of ours—Henri and Gervais are a greenish mist. The others, the ones with Dark Elemaiyan blood, are a purplish-gray color. I thought it was just another one of the usual, like the ones I've already killed. I was wrong. This was a female, and she calls herself a Queen."

I think Tony and René heard the gasps from Merrill and Gavin; I now knew that Gavin was there with Merrill. I wasn't sure how I felt about that. I wanted to beat on him with my fists, to be honest.

"Lissa, that one is very dangerous. Where is she now? You didn't try to fight her, did you?" Merrill sounded worried.

"There wasn't time for her to fight me," I said. "I turned her to mist before she could blink and now she's inside the airtight vault at René's chateau."

"You captured her?" Merrill sounded surprised. Honestly, his and Wlodek's opinion of my abilities underwhelmed me, most of the time.

"Yes, I captured her," I had to hold myself back from mimicking him. "That's why I need your help. You're the only one who might be able to take care of this situation, I think."

"Lissa, my compulsion won't work on her any better than anyone else's." Merrill warned.

"Mine will." Kifirin was there beside me, causing René and Tony to have fangs and claws out in a blink. I truly wasn't prepared to see Tony with fangs and claws. "There is nothing to fear," Kifirin informed both vampires. The claws and fangs disappeared immediately.

"Who is there with you?" Merrill demanded.

"René, Tony and Kifirin," I replied.

"Tell your sire and the others to come. We will deal with this. That one inside the vault is threatening my little Queen," Kifirin said. I guess he had good hearing, just like the rest of us.

"Now we can go," Griffin stood, smiling at the turn of events.

"Who is Kifirin?" Gavin demanded. He'd heard the *my little Queen* statement, just like everyone else.

"The one you have to lose your jealousy over," Griffin replied. "I warn you, do not threaten or anger him in any way. He knows you care for Lissa and that will keep you alive unless you attack him." Merrill listened to the exchange in alarm. He also was wondering who —and what—Kifirin was. Griffin folded the three of them to René's basement in France.

"Quite the collection, René," Merrill remarked dryly, glancing around at the contents that had previously graced René's vault. "Mr. Hancock." Merrill nodded at Tony. Tony was seeing Gavin up close for the first time and now saw two rivals for Lissa's affection. Both would be something to contend with.

"Saa Thalarr," Kifirin nodded to Griffin.

"High Lord," Griffin nodded back.

"Will someone be so kind as to introduce all of us," René demanded.

"I am Griffin, now retired from the Saa Thalarr," Griffin held out his hand and René took it. "This is Kifirin, High Lord of the Dark Realm," Griffin introduced Kifirin. Kifirin smiled while a bit of smoke escaped his nostrils.

CHAPTER 14

Well, now I was hearing Kifirin's title and it didn't reassure me at all. High Lord of the Dark Realm? That sounded like a god of some sort. Griffin smiled. Was he reading my thoughts again?

"Let us deal with the dark Queen first." Kifirin may have been reading my thoughts too. "Lissa, would you like to go in and bring her out or would you prefer that I do this for you? I will be pleased to do so."

"If you wouldn't mind." I felt like I needed a bath to get clean after carrying her around.

Kifirin reached inside the vault, his arm going right through the door, and pulled the Queen Vampire out by the throat. She stared up at him, scared witless, I think. "You will do as I say and will not escape or turn to mist or send mindspeech," Kifirin commanded. She could barely nod—Kifirin held her too tightly.

"I don't think she's used to obeying anyone," Griffin chuckled.

"We will transport her to your Blood King," Kifirin announced. "Do you all wish to go, or would some of you prefer to stay?"

"I wish to see this," René declared. Tony was also nodding, his eyes wide with surprise. He was seeing things that he never suspected he might see—even as Director of the Joint NSA and Homeland Security Department. There really were more things in Heaven and Earth, just as Shakespeare claimed.

"Very well." Kifirin must have been the one to take us; we all went, landing right inside Wlodek's study just as Charles was handing him papers. Wlodek was startled, I could tell, but he covered it very well. Charles, who is eternally curious, looked all of us over, gathering information, I'm sure.

"Who is this that has captured Jovana?" Wlodek's voice held amazement.

"Lissa captured her, I merely transported her here, after placing my own compulsion of course; she threatened my little Queen." Kifirin let Jovana go. Wlodek had known of her, obviously. I wondered how long he'd known about her.

"Charles, will you bring in chairs for our guests?" Wlodek said smoothly. Honestly, the man never turned a hair and his usual, non-expression slid right into place.

We were all seated after a bit; Griffin helped Charles bring in extra chairs. Jovana remained standing before Wlodek's desk while waves of hate and anger boiled off her. She was well and truly pissed. She got what she had coming, though, if she was in that hotel room waiting for me, Henri or Gervais.

"Where did you find her, Lissa?" Wlodek asked, first thing.

I barely held back a growl as I answered. "In a hotel room in Paris. Paul and Deryn told me the local authorities searched the room—Xenides and Rahim had been there before the bombing. I thought at the time that Tony was dead, and well, I was a little upset." Tony grinned at my words. I ignored him. "I was searching for information on Rahim and Xenides," I continued, "but I found bitch Queen there instead."

"Jovana was mist, Wlodek," Merrill interrupted. "Lissa can see other misters, if she is mist herself."

"A rare talent, but then my Lissa has many of them," Kifirin jumped into the conversation before Wlodek had time to deliver a lecture.

"And you are?" Wlodek went back to playing with his gold pen, his eyes hooded and a slight frown tugging at his mouth.

"I am Kifirin," he replied. "Often referred to as High Lord of the Dark Realm. I am also known by many other titles, but my true name none may speak."

He was sitting in the chair to my right; Gavin made sure to get the chair on my left. I had no idea what to do with either of them at the moment. We were all sitting in a semi-circle around Wlodek's desk; Griffin was sitting beside Kifirin, with Merrill next to him. René and Tony came after that.

Kifirin leaned over and said something to Griffin, but he must have muted his words; I didn't hear them. Griffin nodded, said "Excuse me," and disappeared, returning a few minutes later with Paul and Deryn. Wlodek's proceedings were halted for a few minutes as Deryn and Tony held a tearful reunion, with Deryn learning that René had saved Tony's life by turning him. Deryn wasn't completely opposed to the act, I could tell. His brother was alive and intact, thanks to René.

"Now, may we get back to the business at hand?" Wlodek straightened his tie and lifted the gold pen, glaring imperiously at the rest of us. Jovana had remained where she was; Kifirin hadn't allowed her to move. Paul and Deryn slid to the floor beside Tony's chair so our discussion could resume.

Wlodek questioned Jovana that night, making a thorough job of it. She'd killed Lucius, her vampire companion, at Saxom's urging—he'd recognized her Dark Elemaiyan roots, although she wasn't aware of them herself. Kifirin admonished her to tell the truth and that was what we got from her. She'd been oblivious of the reasons Saxom wanted her turned. Paul and Deryn were getting a lesson, too, on things the vamps had only recently discovered.

"What is Xenides' ultimate purpose?" Wlodek asked Jovana finally. She laughed.

"To kill you all," she replied. "Vampires and humans. Saxom's orders were very clear—if he died, then all of you must pay. Of course, I didn't hold with that; his ability to control me died with him. I like this world too much; it is amusing to me. Besides, if we kill the humans, who will feed us? Xenides has not thought past the destruction, I do not think."

"He is under Saxom's compulsion, still. He did not have the ability you were born with, little dark Queen," Kifirin made the reply. "He will most likely be unable to link the destruction of the planet to his own death." Kifirin snorted, a curl of smoke floating from his nostrils. I wondered yet again how he did that. He turned a beautiful smile on me. Yeah, he's not connected to my head or anything. Too bad Flavio wasn't here; he could be the second most beautiful male in the room for a change. Kifirin's smile became wider at that point.

Charles, in his usual efficient manner, set up a temporary workstation near the door and dutifully tapped away on his computer. He was recording notes from Wlodek's interrogation. Jovana wouldn't leave the room alive; she'd already admitted to killing Lucius and several others. Most of the names I didn't recognize, but several of them made Wlodek growl. Displaying that much emotion was truly out of character for him.

Lucius' death had been first on that list. Jovana's status as a Queen would warrant the immediate execution, I knew; it would be too dangerous to attempt to keep her in a cell until the Council might be convened.

"Very well," Wlodek sighed eventually. "Does anyone else have questions?"

"Have you had dealings with Rahim Alif?" Tony was standing now, still acting in his former capacity. Jovana snorted.

"That plaything?" Contempt was in her voice. "Xenides plucked him from the streets in Afghanistan after Rahim managed to bomb a few U.S. installations. Xenides has him under his thumb and they are two halves of a whole, I think. I do not speak with that *drecksau*," she muttered.

"Do you have any idea where he might be?" Tony continued his questioning.

"Find Xenides and find Rahim," she replied.

Tony was disappointed, I could tell. "Where is Xenides, then?" I asked.

"He was in France, the last I saw of him. He said you would come to investigate the hotel room after his target was killed. He promised me a large sum of money if I would go and wait for you." Jovana turned and gave me a nasty smile.

Well, that smile, along with her head, was going to be removed shortly. Xenides had targeted Tony, because not only was Tony a major irritant to him, but also because he'd somehow learned that I wouldn't let Tony's murder go without an investigation. I schooled my face into the vampire non-expression.

"Where in France?" Tony demanded.

"He was leaving Paris when I spoke with him; he has plans to take Rahim back to the U.S." Jovana replied.

"Flying or driving?" Tony asked.

"Driving out of France and possibly other transportation past that. He does not make me privy to his many secrets and I do not wish to know them anyway."

"When did you see him last?"

"Two hours before I was captured." Jovana wasn't happy about that fact; she'd been led to believe she was the top of the dung heap, after all.

"Plenty of time to get out of the country," Tony grumbled. We'd been at this for more than three hours, from capture to questioning. Xenides could be anywhere.

Wlodek asked again if there were other questions. This time there were none. "Gavin," Wlodek nodded to his Assassin.

"No," René said, holding out a hand. "I ask that you allow me or my newest child to perform this service, in partial retribution for my Aubrey."

"That is acceptable," Wlodek nodded. Gavin, who'd risen, seemed content to sit down again.

"Child, release your claws," René was instructing Tony, who slid his claws out easily. They were quite large and long, as nearly all the males' were. "Do not make your target suffer, one quick swipe across the neck here," Rene indicated the best spot on Jovana's neck.

She was hissing, now, although she still couldn't move. Tony nodded his understanding, so René stepped aside to allow him room. Tony was fast, exceptionally so. Jovana was decapitated swiftly, in mid-hiss. Her head and body dropped to the floor and began to flake away on Wlodek's priceless, antique Persian rug.

Tony was now staring at his claws. This was his first kill—as a vampire, anyway. Wlodek was eyeing Tony speculatively and I could almost see the little wheels turning. Wlodek was down an Assassin. Tony might be a quick study. I wasn't sure how I felt about that.

"Get ready," Griffin stood suddenly. I was bewildered at this swift turn of events.

"They are coming," Kifirin agreed, rising as well.

"Who?" Merrill was used to Griffin and didn't question, really, he just wanted to know who they were.

"Xenides has sent an army, little Queen," Kifirin turned to me. "They can only come so close, however. The Saa Thalarr and I have the home shielded. We will go out to them instead."

"Prepare for a fight," Merrill announced and went to follow Griffin, who was already walking toward the door. Wlodek didn't ask questions either; he merely removed his suit coat and tie, preparing to go with Merrill, Griffin and Kifirin. Well, they weren't leaving me behind, and Gavin was right behind me, followed by René, Tony, Deryn, Paul, and then Charles.

Rolfe stood at the open door to Wlodek's mansion, looking out over the hundred vampires lined up outside, a hundred and fifty feet away from the walls of the manor. Kifirin and Griffin had used power to keep them at that distance and I could tell the rogue vampires were well and truly pissed about it.

They'd planned to swarm over Wlodek's manor, killing everybody inside. The plan might have worked, too, if we hadn't had so much firepower at our disposal. Even so, we still had a fight brewing and one we could still lose. I had no idea how much assistance Griffin and Kifirin were prepared to give, once we engaged the enemy.

Deryn and Paul were already shucking their clothes to turn to wolf. Charles, who'd tossed aside his own jacket and tie, was rolling up his sleeves. Kifirin took the lead and we all followed him toward the line of vampires when Dragon appeared, both blades in his hands, prepared to join us. Dragon was in full battle gear, dressed in leathers, head to foot. Only the tattoos on his arms were visible—his vest was sleeveless, his hair braided tightly and swinging at his back as he joined our ranks.

"I owe Lissa," he said, when Griffin raised an eyebrow. Griffin nodded silently.

"Hi, honey," I said to Dragon. He gave me a grin. There were now thirteen of us, to fight the horde.

"We come at Xenides' bidding," one of the vampires spoke. "We are Saxom's children and follow his first child, now that our sire is no longer among us." He didn't need to tell me they were Saxom's get; I could smell them from where I stood. A number of them—a good number of them, had Dark Elemaiyan blood.

"You threaten me and you threaten my Queen and the ones she cares for," Kifirin spoke for us. I wondered whether that irked Wlodek, to be forced to take a back seat to Kifirin. "If you choose to leave now, I will not pursue. Stay to fight and I will not leash my wrath."

"Who the bloody hell are you?" One of the rogue vampires, Irish in origin I could tell, spoke now.

"I am Kifirin, the one chosen to create the balance, maker of the Dark Worlds and High Lord therein. Once all vampires knew me and knew to bow before me. Now you know nothing, as your sire failed to train you properly. If you attack me, I will not allow you to live."

The first one who'd spoken burst out in harsh laughter. "You expect us to believe your bluster?" he shouted. A bit of smoke curled from Kifirin's nostrils. I don't know if the vampire saw that or not. He didn't step back, I know that much.

"What is he going to do?" Gavin leaned down and whispered in my ear.

I blew out a breath. How could I describe what I'd seen Kifirin become on Refizan? "Gavin, have you ever seen a demon?" I asked.

"My sire described them to me once; he said they were humans that had been bitten by the same kind of creatures, turning them to demon as well," Gavin spoke quietly.

"Those aren't really demons," I whispered. "Those are Ra'Ak spawn. If Kifirin turns, you'll see what a demon looks like. He told me once that the High Demons were made in his image. I understand they're slightly smaller, though. If Dragon turns, just get the hell out of his way," I warned.

"Does he become demon as well?"

"No. He becomes a dragon," I replied with a shrug.

"Enough of this!" Wlodek was now taking charge and shouting at Xenides' army. "Are you leaving or staying to fight?"

"We were instructed to kill you, old man," the vampire sneered. "We will not leave until that has been accomplished."

"Very well," Wlodek nodded. I don't think the lead vampire ever saw Wlodek attack, he was so swift. Wlodek kept his seat as Head of the Council, Blood King or whatever his title was, because he was able to keep it. Saxom's vampire child dropped to the ground, headless, as did the two that flanked him before Wlodek became anything other than a blur.

I wasn't about to let him fight alone—I went to mist and had six heads lopped off before that line of vampires ever knew I was among them. The battle was joined, then; I saw Dragon off to the side, fighting with both blades and shouting in his native language while he did it. Merrill was also in hurricane force; any vampire that came against him died. Gavin? Nobody wanted to mess with him. He had to chase some of his opponents; they were running away from him.

Deryn and Paul teamed up with Charles, forming a triangle; the wolves were attacking and tossing vampires onto the ground and Charles, efficient as ever, relived them of their heads. Rolfe was wading into the knot of Saxom's get, René and Tony with him, and they were doing fierce battle.

Kifirin was in his smaller Thifilathi form and if any of the vampires touched him, they burned. Screams went up around him—the screams of dying vampires. Kifirin was a great surprise but the biggest surprise, I think, was seeing Griffin fight. Now I knew what he'd been before.

Dragon told me that he was once Warlord on Falchan. Griffin—I didn't know what his homeworld had been but he had been vampire before becoming Saa Thalarr. He had fangs and claws out and he was something to see. Eventually, he was fighting alongside Wlodek; nothing lived if they attacked and nothing got past them, either.

My job was easy, that night. If a rogue tried to get away, I misted after him. Finally, I went to help Charles and the werewolves. Deryn and Paul had taken a few hits and were bleeding sluggishly. They were glad of the help I think, as we did away with the very last of Xenides' army. I only wished that Xenides and Rahim Alif had been there; I would have taken a great deal of pleasure from removing their heads.

"A very productive evening," Wlodek examined the slice in one of his sleeves; the silk shirt was hanging in two tattered pieces off his right arm. Otherwise, he looked as if he hadn't been touched. Rolfe had a wide slash across his chest but he was holding Charles away from him with one hand.

"It will heal with the sleep," he kept telling Wlodek's assistant. "I always said you were a Queen," Rolfe grinned at me as I came to pull Charles away from him.

"And you were right," I gave him a hug. Rolfe put one large arm around my shoulders and squeezed before letting go.

Charles put both arms around me and hugged me tightly, kissing my forehead before he released me. "I don't get to fight often," he said.

Griffin and Dragon were tending to the two werewolves, Tony standing beside them, watching his brother get patched up. The Saa Thalarr have healing abilities of their own; I learned that. Merrill spoke with René while Gavin and Kifirin came to find me. Well, more fur might fly, I suppose.

"You will feel no jealousy toward me," Kifirin informed Gavin. Gavin blinked for a second and then seemed all right with that. Well, la de da. Is that all it took? Kifirin had become his usual self the minute the battle ended, and now leaned down to give me a warm kiss.

A bit of smoke escaped his nostrils as he pulled away and offered me an angel's smile. Piles of vampire ash lay all around us as I stood on tiptoe and gave Kifirin a second kiss before smiling back. Somebody had a mess to clean up on Wlodek's lawn and I wasn't about to volunteer.

"Does vampire ash have good fertilizing properties?" I asked Kifirin. He burst out laughing and then hauled me into his arms, giving me another huge kiss. A cell phone rang somewhere nearby.

I expected it to be Charles's phone. Or Merrill's, or one of the others. It wasn't. It was a phone lying amid a pile of ash. Wlodek went to pick it up. "Wlodek here," he answered the call himself.

"I will kill you if I must do it myself," a voice growled on the other end. Xenides—I recognized that voice.

"We've eliminated your army and did away with Jovana tonight," Wlodek said congenially. "We have met, you and I, only Saxom introduced you as Catulus. You truly are Saxom's whelp, aren't you?"

"In every sense of the word," Xenides agreed. "I still intend to take your little princess and force her to my bidding. She must have caught Jovana unawares to escape her compulsion. Yes, I know her weakness, Sanguis Rex. You can't hide her from me forever." Xenides terminated the call.

"Fucker," I grumbled. I was still in Kifirin's arms and he kissed me again.

~

Griffin took us home. It was nearly dawn, after all, and I barely had time to get a shower before sunup. Kifirin wasn't the one who ended up in my bed, however; it was Gavin. I frowned at him and pouted when he stalked in, scooted me over and climbed into bed beside me.

"Wlodek will tell you later, but I am telling you now, cara mia, that he would never ask nor would I ever do what you said before." He nuzzled my neck gently, placing light kisses, here and there. "Kill my love while she slept?" He huffed against my skin, his breath cool and pleasant. "My little love, my perfect rose," he murmured in French. I wasn't sure whether it was a good thing or not that I could understand his words, now. I might have still been considering that dilemma when my eyes closed with the rising of the sun.

"Mom, I have news." Deryn was exhausted but wanted to place the call before he passed out in the huge bed that Merrill found for him. Paul's bedroom was next door on the third floor and the Welsh policeman was already asleep.

"What is it, baby?" Deryn would always be Corinne Alford's baby boy, no matter how old he was. Since Tony's disappearance and probable death, she couldn't help herself.

"Mom, when the hotel got bombed, Tony was hit by flying metal."

"They found his body?" Corinne started to cry again.

"In a manner of speaking," Deryn replied. "Mom, something cut his femoral artery and he was bleeding to death. Someone found him. Somebody who knew he was dying and that the emergency crews wouldn't be able to save him, even with a doctor standing over him. The one who found him was a vampire. Tony asked the vampire to keep him alive, so he did. In the only way he could. Mom, Tony's a vampire now." Deryn heard the phone clatter to the floor and the thump as his mother's unconscious body hit immediately afterward.

"What the hell are you saying, son?" His father lifted the phone and shouted into the receiver.

The End